James Frothingham Hunnewell

Bibliography of Charlestown

James Frothingham Hunnewell

Bibliography of Charlestown

ISBN/EAN: 9783337327255

Printed in Europe, USA, Canada, Australia, Japan

Cover: Foto ©Raphael Reischuk / pixelio.de

More available books at **www.hansebooks.com**

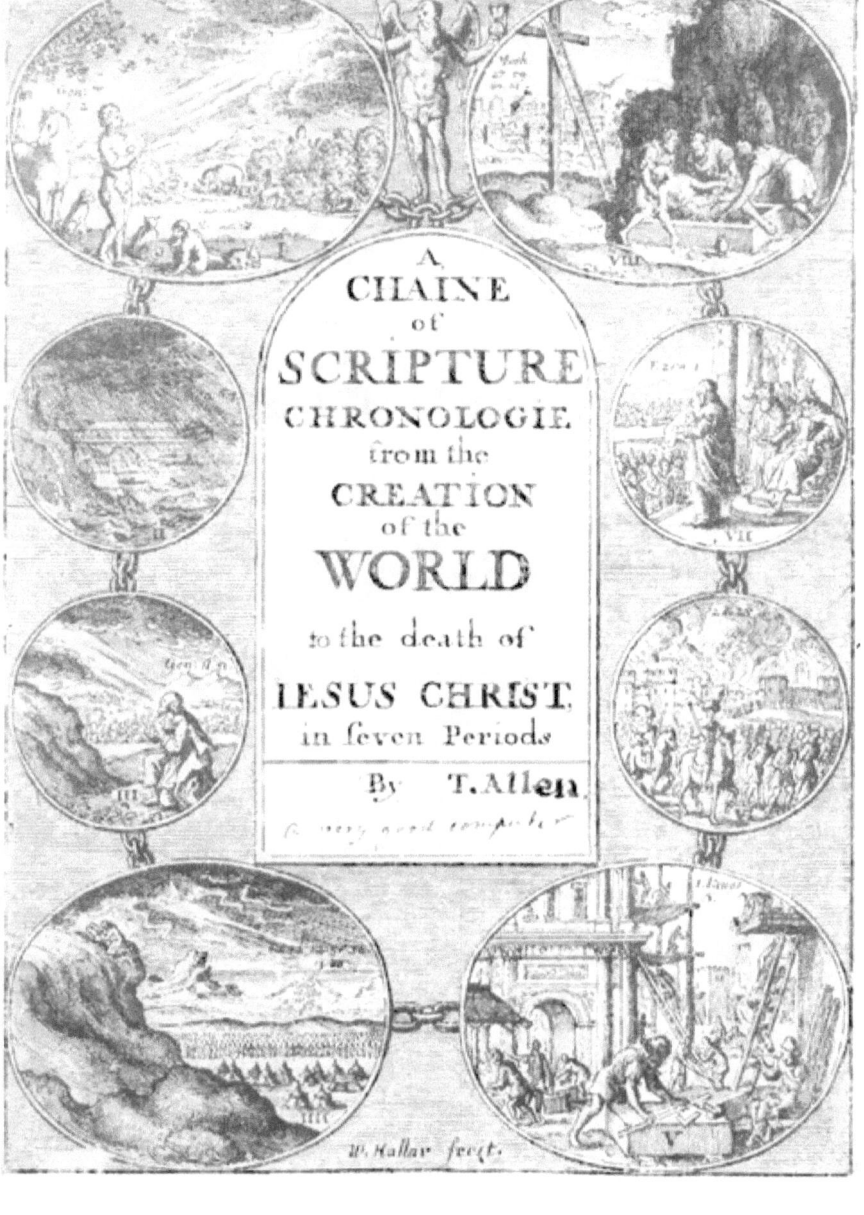

A
CHAINE
of
SCRIPTURE
CHRONOLOGIE.
from the
CREATION
of the
WORLD
to the death of
IESUS CHRIST,
in seven Periods

By   T. Allen.

W. Hollar fecit.

BIBLIOGRAPHY

OF

CHARLESTOWN,

MASSACHUSETTS,

AND

BUNKER HILL.

"Wherever pamphlets abound, there is freedom; and therefore have we been a
nation of pamphleteers." — Rt. Hon. B. Disraeli.

"Μεγά βιβλίον μεγά Κακὸν." — Rev. Charles Morton.

By JAMES F. HUNNEWELL.

BOSTON:
JAMES R. OSGOOD AND COMPANY.
1880.

University Press:
John Wilson & Son, Cambridge.

INTRODUCTION.

THE following pages show results of an effort made by the writer to ascertain the nature of what might be called the literature of his native town, — how the thoughts or affairs of those who have been born or resident in it have found an expression on printed pages. These results have been a surprise, a pleasure, and a satisfaction to him, and he trusts that they will be to others, — a surprise from the number and often the rarity of the works, which it is a pleasure to enumerate; and a satisfaction, joined with this pleasure, that their almost unexceptional characteristic is that of religious faithfulness, of patriotism, of help to charity, to education, or to good citizenship, and that there is so little that the authors would wish to efface. This general estimate, after a review, seems fairly and sufficiently to annote the collection.

And this material does not make a merely local story, for it touches wider than local subjects, and also shows to some extent, representatively, what an old New England town — neither obscure nor preeminent — thought, did, witnessed, or produced, and through two and a half centuries has had put on many printed pages. It is not a mere dull list of things nearly passed away and forgotten, but an interesting story of growth from small beginnings to all we now enjoy; and one that illustrates how, on wider sphere and scale, far more widely spread populations have also been growing. It becomes, indeed, to a considerable extent an outline history of the intellectual and material life of the times and of the people. It shows how through much of the Colonial period the chief expression of thought was by the ministry, and religious, with little of the amusing, but something of the imaginative, and more of the historical; how the Revolution associated much writing with a place; how in the earlier period of the nation a wider variety of thought and of addresses was developed; how, for fifty years, the fervid emotions of the Fourth of July Oration were proclaimed, as in many of the greater and minor towns; how changing theological opinions grew; how political and educational and benevolent affairs became more prominent; how the press flourished; how general business enterprise expanded; and how literature increased in scope, and often in value.

We find, thus, early religious works by divines eminent in their time, printed in the old home they had left, or by the rude presses of their new country. We find early American poetry by Johnson, by Oakes, by Anne Bradstreet, — not the sweetest, but what we had. We find that the once engrossing subject of witchcraft was treated by a minister, a Charlestown boy, in a book that now brings more than its weight in gold. We find some of the marked events celebrated as they passed, some of the well-known inhabitants commemorated when they died. Then comes the long Bunker Hill story, productive of a paper almost to every patriot engaged, and the battle not yet ended in print. Then the town resettled after war, and the printing-press established, — the first newspaper, first pamphlet, first volume, first copper-plate, first octavo, first American map of Bunker Hill, — all firsts, until the earlier first that bibliographers sometimes discover. Meanwhile, and afterwards, appear continuous legislative acts on various affairs, and, in time, municipal publications, — at first small, but finally growing to bulk, to multiplicity, and to nearly utter extinction. Then follows a wider and wider range of subjects, as the record shows.

One reason, and not a minor one, for the production of this work is a renewal of what the writer has advocated for certain libraries with which he has been associated, the claim of the importance of placing and preserving on their shelves all proper aids and illustrations to Local History pertinent to the position or purposes of the collection. And he offers this work as a suggestion — not a model — of something that seems still to be needed for many towns. The acquisition of what such lists may contain need not be, even now, excessively difficult; for although when attempted by a single person it may be one of those efforts nearly enough impossible to be exciting and interesting, when undertaken by a hundred persons, each of whom supplies even a single book or pamphlet, a large aggregate can be formed by small individual sacrifice or contribution. Pamphlets that, scattered separately may be of moderate interest or value, often become, when put together, like the signatures of a complete and important book. And signatures like these are every year becoming more scarce. Through the country the omnivorous junk-dealer has drawn his net, and the waste-basket received its victims. And yet the old closets, drawers, or boxes may still yield things desired.

If some one in each town forms a List of Publications related to it, a great index of thought, biography, and history would be made.

Nearly all the works mentioned on these pages are to be found in public or corporate libraries; no one of which, however, contains more than a portion. A great deal is thus accessible to those who search for information. To such collections the writer is much indebted.

This book was begun early in 1879, and a considerable portion written in that year, but articles to be mentioned were so continually found that the writer hesitated to print. The type was, however, set in the spring of 1880, and then a European tour caused a suspension of the work. Meanwhile the Memorial History of Boston, including Charlestown, was announced, and the writer curtailed the notes for the latter part of his book. Its divisions explain its plan: first, compositions by founders of the town who did not remain long in it; then monographs by natives or longer residents while colonial relations remained with Great Britain, chronologically arranged, and passages in various books. Then the Bunker Hill material, with references to over four hundred publications, besides newspapers, some important articles only in which it was practicable to mention. Finally, the more copious matter related to the town, after the Revolution, chronologically arranged to show what appeared year by year. A note on the thirtieth page explains this portion, that altogether contains about a thousand titles, besides a large number mentioned in previously printed lists to which reference is made. In addition is a list of publications printed in the town during fifty years from the establishment of the press there in 1786, and, in the Personal Index, reference to about four hundred and fifty memorial or biographical articles.

The collection of titles proved no easy affair. They belong to publications often so rare that only a single copy could be found; accounts of some must be taken from descriptions not always full; and some are so rare that, as far as the writer has learned, no copies have been for many a year owned in the town to which they are related. Records of not a few were scattered, and only to be obtained by search, and not a few also were unrecorded. No public or corporate library, as already stated, appears to possess more than a fraction of them. Even the town itself does not possess a complete collection of its own municipal publications, and such a one of the personal memorials described hereafter has probably never been formed. All the publications described that appeared during the lives of their authors have been, perhaps without exception, made public by their act or consent, and the writer trusts that he has not passed the line that should protect private affairs. The titles of many minor works, chiefly later, are abridged, but sufficiently given. Some very long titles are thus treated. The full matter would be unnecessary, and be impracticably bulky. All, it is believed, are directly related to the town or to an inhabitant.

Notwithstanding the number of names and titles and much labor, omissions will, very likely, be found. If the last title for such a list was awaited, it could hardly ever be printed. Accuracy, also, has been sought, but evidence has been met that it is not attained in all cases, and that reference to the word is to be made with modesty. Statements will occur, as, for example, on a title-page (p. 89), that mentions an Address by Mr. Webster, at Bunker Hill, June 17, 1775, but does not tell us how he managed the performance on that interesting occasion. Or, two notes (pp. 25, 32) show how a couple of ardent Frenchmen had a desperate grapple with some of our proper names. There are also some other statements, not quoted on these pages, that appear more to need alteration.

With a desire to help in preserving the names and the words of many good people who have gone, the present book appears as a guide; a help to its own enlargement; a memorial of life, of thought, and of history in Charlestown; and a contribution to the commemoration of its two hundred and fiftieth birthday.

J. F. H.

Nov. 10, 1880.

THE BEGINNING.

A PENINSULA a mile long, nearly surrounded by broad, still waters, varied by five low hills, and overgrown by forests of oaks, except where clearings had recently been made towards the outer and larger end, and inland some square miles of wild lands; a few poor, cheerless cottages and a Governor's house in the clearings; a few small settlements hardly within hail; north and west and south a vast wilderness, more mysterious than are now the recesses of the Dark Continent, and eastward three thousand miles of rough and stormy sea, only to be crossed in cramped and comfortless vessels; dear old homes, much of kindred, and almost all of civilization and Christian fellowship beyond that sea; a few hundred people, worn, sick, or sorely tried, endeavoring to call and make this place home and country.

That is where the works of these Charlestown people began.

Small indeed were the opportunities of literature, and yet on pages not few — plain, or even rude perhaps, like nature there — the founders impressed what they have stamped on more than them and that peninsula. For they were no illiterate emigrants and frontier adventurers. With human infirmities, perhaps, but with grand purpose and strong religious principle, certainly, they showed their quality from the start, whether on the roughly printed leaf, or on the stern land they and their associates conquered for God and for freedom.

Thirty years later the view grew better.

The little village was covering more of the peninsula, and farms were scattered inland; some look of the snug comfort and the quaintness of Lincolnshire and Yorkshire country appeared; neighborly settlements were growing along the coast and among the thick forests around. Yet there was plain fare and plenty of hard work for almost every one, and the old home was scarcely easier to reach; the number of the people was a little greater, health better, material wealth very moderate; but just as resolute purpose, a sturdy support of a pious and learned ministry, and a College and a printing-press in the next town, — a Charlestown boy graduated at the one, and his little book printed at the other, while two of the ministers were publishing in London.

Slow growth, perhaps, followed, and no overcrowding of the press by the townspeople. But let us look at their work in a literary way, and learn what came of it when the town they planted had fairly taken root. Crops are not apt to grow fast in New England soils, but they are apt to prove worth harvesting.

ILLUSTRATIONS.

NOTE. — For fac-similes of title-pages of Anne Bradstreet's Poems (1650 and 1678) and of "Sion's Saviour" (1654), see works described on p. 1. See also "Bunker Hill," pp. 13-19, 23, 26-29, for references to engravings and fac-similes. For Portraits, see pp. 49 and 80 for Dr. Morse ; p. 50, Rev. W. Fay ; p. 54, Rev. H. Jackson ; p. 64, Rev. J. Wilson ; p. 65, J. Evarts ; p. 72, M. Whiting; p. 75, Thos. Dowse ; p. 87, Dr. J. Walker, James Hunnewell, and T. B. Wyman ; p. 86, Prof. S. F. B. Morse.

A portrait of Dr. Budington has also been engraved, and one of Hon. R. Frothingham is in the B. H. M. Ass'n Proceedings, 1880. D. Devens is in "Biographical Sketches of Eminent Americans;" Hon. M. Dow, in "Boston, Past and Present." There are also portraits of Rev. E. H. Chapin, Hon. E. Everett, Rev. T. S. King, Gov. J. Winthrop, and probably of others.

AN ELEGIE
UPON
The Death of the Reverend
Mr. THOMAS SHEPARD,
Late Teacher of the Church at
Charlstown in New--England:

By a great Admirer of his Worth, and true Mourner for his Death.

Isai. 57. 1. *The righteous perisheth, and no man layeth it to heart, and merciful men are taken away, none considering that the righteous is taken away from the evil to come.*

Zech. 1.5,6. *Your Fathers where are they? And the Prophets do they live for ever? but my words and my statutes, which I commanded my servants the Prophets, did they not take hold of your Fathers?*

Heb. 13. 7. *Remember them which had the rule over you, who have spoken unto you the word of God, whose Faith follow, considering the end of their conversation.*

CAMBRIDGE,
Printed by Samuel Green. 1677.

CHARLESTOWN, MASSACHUSETTS.

COLONIAL PERIOD, 1630–1775, MONOGRAPHS.

WORKS BY FOUNDERS OF THE TOWN WHOSE RESIDENCE IN IT WAS NOT LONG.

"THE | TENTH MUSE | Lately fprung up in AMERICA | OR | Severall
Poems, compiled | with great variety of Wit | and Learning, full of
delight," | etc. "Alfo a Dialogue between Old *England* and |
| New, concerning the late troubles, | with divers other pleafant
and ferious Poems. | By a gentlewoman in thofe parts. | " Sm.
8° pp. 222. Stephen Bowtell.   *London*, 1650
———— "*The fecond Edition, Corrected by the Author,* | *and enlarged
by an Addition of feveral other* | *Poems found amongft her Papers
| after her Death.* | " 16°. pp. 14, 255, 1.
                          John Foster, *Boston* (N. E.), 1678
———— The Same, 3d ed. Cr. 8°. pp. xiv + 233.   *Boston*, 1758
———— "The Works of Anne Bradstreet in Profe and Verfe, edited
by John Harvard, Ellis," with an Introduction, Life of A. B., etc.
Imp. 8°. pp. lxxvi. + 434, 2 pl., 2 *fac. fim.* Printed by J. Wilson
& Son, Cambridge, published by A. E. Cutter. 250 copies printed.
                                       Charlestown, 1867

<small>1630, dau. Gov. T. Dudley, wife Gov. S. B., earliest poetess in Am. Sales; 1st ed.
Fraser (1852) £2. 3s., Rice (N. Y. 1870) $157.50, Menzies (N. Y. 1875) $77.50.
Mr. Ellis and Mr. Cutter were both residents of C. This admirable edition was at
this date probably the hand-omest book ever published in the town.</small>

DUDLEY, Gov. Tho. (1630). "Letter to the Counters of Lincoln,
March, 1631. With Explanatory Notes by Dr. John Farmer." 8°.
pp. 19.   *Washington*, 1838

<small>No. IV. of Vol. 2, of Peter Force's Tracts. A very early and interesting Account of
Massachusetts. Lowndes mentions a 4°, n. d., by George Dudley. Also rep. in Chronicles of Mass. Bay, by Dr. A. Young, pp. 303–44. *Boston*, 1846.</small>

JOHNSON, Capt. Edward (1630, 1636–42, in Bow. St.).
"A | HISTORY | of | New-England. | From the Englifh planting in
the Yeere | 1628, untill the Yeere 1652. | " etc. or, "Wonder-
working PROVIDENCE | OF | SION'S SAVIOUR IN N. ENGLAND. | "
Sm. 4°. pp. 4 + 236 + 103*–120*. Nath: Brooke. *London*, 1654

<small>Written abt. 1649–51 (Poole xv.). Nearly all reissued, London, 1659, in "America
| Painted to the Life, | " etc., by Ferd. Gorges. See also Mass. Hist. Soc. Colls.,
Vols. 12–14, 17, 18. Original extremely rare; Brinley (N. Y. 1879) 2 copies, $150
and $80.</small>

JOHNSON, Capt. Edward. The same, with an Hist. Introduction, Life, Index, etc., by W^m. F. Poole. 4°. 200 copies, and 10 on dr. paper, and 50 L. P. Printed by J. Wilson & Son.

W. F. Draper, *Andover*, 1867

WILSON, Rev. John (1630). "A Seasonable Watch-Word unto Christians against the Dreams and Dreamers of this Generation: Delivered in a Sermon November 16th, 1665," (his last). Sm. 4°. pp. 4 + 19. *Cambridge*, 1677

His only published work, "excessively rare." Brinley, red mor. (Bedford) $57.50 (bought for the library of Congress).

WINTHROP, Gov. John. " A | JOURNAL | of the | Transactions and Occurrences in the Settlement of | Massachusetts and the Other New England | Colonies, from the Year 1630 to 1644." 1st ed. from the M. S. 8°. pp. 6 + 364. *Hartford*, 1790

———— The same, with the 3d vol., 1630–49, with Notes by J. Savage. 2 vols. 8°. *Boston*, 1825–26

———— Third ed. with additions, etc. to the 2d, by J. Savage. 2 vols. 8°. *Boston*, 1853

———— See Life and Letters of, by Hon. R. C. Winthrop. 2 vols. 8°. *Boston*, 1863, and 2d edition, enlarged; plates, do. 1869

PRINTED WORKS AND MEMORIALS OF INHABITANTS, WORKS RELATING TO THE TOWN, AND ADDRESSES AND SERMONS DELIVERED IN IT.

Charlestown is often, hereafter, abbreviated C. Placed within brackets after a name, and before a date, it shows that a person was born in the town, preceded by a dash, — C., shows, died in the town.

1659.

ALLEN, Rev. Thos. " A | CHAINE | of | SCRIPTURE | CHRONOLOGIE | from the | CREATION | of the | WORLD | to the | Death of | JESUS CHRIST, | in seven Periods. | " 4°. *London*, 1659

"The most esteemed of this celebrated Non-conformist's works, with a frontispiece by Hollar, reprinted 1668." — *Lowndes*. The author, it is said, began this work while he was in C.

———— Also, An Invitation to Thirsty Sinners to come to their Saviour. (Printed at Cambridge, (N. E.?) The Glory of Christ set forth, with the Necessity of Faith; in several Sermons on John 3d and 5th. 8°. 1683. The Way of the Spirit in bringing Souls to Christ, in Ten Sermons. 16°. *London*, 1676

Letter in "Strength out of Weaknesse." Lond. 1652 (in Mass. H. S. Colls. III., iv, 194). Also edited, with prefaces, two works by Rev. John Cotton, viz., 2d ed. of "A Treatise of the Covenant of Grace." Sm. 8°. *London*, 1659; and "An Exposition upon the 13th chapter of the Revelation." 4°. *London*, 1655. ("To the Reader," has Mr. Allen's statement of "of having lived in that American wilderness about 13. or 14. years in the Towne next adjoyning to Boston").

BRIGDEN, Zechariah. An Almanac of the Celestial Motions for this present Year of the Christian Æra 1659. By *Zech: Brigden,* Astrophil. Samuel Green, *Cambridge,* 1659
This is probably the *earliest American book* by a C. author.

SHEPARD, Rev. Thos. (of Cambridge, N. E.) "THE | PARABLE | OF THE | Ten Virgins | Opened and Applied | Being the Substance of divers | SERMONS | ." *Published by " Jonathan Mitchell,* Minifter at Cambridge," and " *Tho. Shepard,* Son to the Reverend Author, now Minifter at *Charles-Town* in NEW ENGLAND." Folio, 2 pts. in 1 vol., pp. 8 + 240 + 203 + 5. *London,* 1660
——— The same. pp. 6 + 232 + 190 + 5. *London,* 1695
Also in folio Lond. 1659, 1695; in 8° 2 vols. 1797; in 12° Aberdeen, 1838.

Authorship, or publication, by natives, or those for years residents, of the town, seems to have begun in 1659. Mr. Allen, minister of C. 1639–51, had returned to England and was settled in Norwich, d. 1673. Mr. Brigden (C. 1639), who was one of the earliest graduates of Harvard Col. (1657), and probably was the author of the Almanac, died 1662. Mr. Shepard was minister of C. 1659–77.

1665.

NOWELL, Alexander. An Almanack of Celestial Motions for the year of the Christian Epoch 1665. By Alex. Nowell φιλόπονιρος. Sm. 8°. Samuel Green, *Cambridge,* 1665
The author was a son of Elder Increase Nowell, born in C.? died in 1672, and is said to have published several almanacs. The only copy of this one seen by the writer is now in the National Library, Washington.

1672.

SHEPARD, Rev. Thos. " EYE-SALVE, OF A WATCH-WORD *From our Lord Iefas Chrift unto his Churches:* Especially those within the Colony of MASSACHUSETS IN NEW ENGLAND, *To take heed of Apoftacy:*" etc. The Election Sermon, by the "Teacher of the Church of Chrift in *Charlftown, who was appointed by the Magiftrates to Preach on the day of* ELECTION *at Bofton, May* 15, 1672." Sm. 4°. pp. 4 + 52. Samuel Green, *Cambridge,* 1673
Two long texts, etc., also, on the title. Rev. T. S. born 1634, was min. at C. 1659 to death in 1677. *Sales,* Rice, $50, Brinley, $20.

1677.

OAKES, Rev. Urian. " AN ELEGIE | UPON | *The Death of the Reverend* | MR. THOMAS SHEPARD, | *Late Teacher of the Church at* | *Charlestown in New England:* | By a great Admirer of his Worth, and true Mourner for | his Death. | " Sm 4°. pp. 16. Broad black border around the title. Samuel Green, *Cambridge,* 1677
One of the earliest poems printed in British America, and now extremely rare. Twenty-three of the fifty-two stanzas are reprinted in Budington's Hist., 1st ch., pp. 215–18. *Sales,* Brinley, (2 copies, mor.) $45, — and $41.
Dr. A. Holmes (Mass. H. S. Colls. vii, 53) says this work "rises, in my judgment, far above the poetry of his day, and it is plaintive, pathetic, and replete with imagery."

1678.

NOWELL, Rev. Sam¹ "Abraham in *Arms ;* | or | The firſt Religious | GENERAL | WITH ITS | ARMY | *Engaging in* | A WAR | *For which he had wisely prepared,* and by | which, not only an eminent | VICTORY | Was obtained, but | A BLESSING | gained alſo. | Delivered in an Artillery Election Sermon June 3, 1678. By S. N." Sm 4°. pp. 4 + 19. John Foster, *Boston*, 1678

The Preface is printed in Budington's Hist. 1st ch., 191.
The "excellent " and " never to be forgotten " "fighting chaplain " of Mass. troops in Philip's War, Son of Elder Increase Nowell, born C. 1644, died in London 1688. The invitation to his funeral was:— "You are desired to accompany the Corps of M! Samuell Nowell, minister of the Gospell, of Eminent Note in New England, deceased, from M! Quick's meating place in Bartholomew Close, on Thursday next at two of the clock in the afternoon precisely, to the new burying place by the Artillery ground." Drake's Fields (1874), p. 278. See Magnalia, VII., 50.

CHURCH AFFAIRS, See Mass. Hist. Soc. Coll's, Ser. III. vol. 1, 1825.

1681.

WILLARD. Rev. Sam¹ *The Fiery Tryal no ſtrange* thing; | DE-LIVERED IN A | SERMON | Preached at | CHARLSTOWN. | February 15. 1681. | Being a Day of | Humiliation : | etc. Sm. 4°. pp. 4 + 20. For Sam! Sewall, *Boston*, 1682

1686.

MATHER, Rev. Cotton. MILITARY DUTIES, | RECOMMENDED | to an | ARTILLERY | COMPANY; | *At their* ELECTION *of* OFFICERS, | In CHARLS-TOWN, | 13, d. 7, m. 1686. | etc. Sm. 8°. pp. 8 + 78 + 2. Richard Pierce, *Boston*, 1687

1689.

BULKELEY. Gershom. "The PEOPLE'S | RIGHT TO ELECTION | ," etc. " To which is added, the *Writing* delivered to *James Russell* | of Charlestown Esq; warning him and others concerned, | not to meet to Hold a Court at *Cambridge,* within the | County of *Middle-ses.* | By *Thomas Greaves,* Esq." Sm. 4°. pp. 18.
Assignes of William Bradford, *Philadelphia*, 1689

Extremely rare. *Sale,* Brinley (mor.) $235; Reprinted in Conn. Hist. Soc. Coll's, Vol. I., pp. 57-81, 1860. T. G. (C. 1639 — C. 1697), H. C. 1656.

THE Humble Address of Sundry Your Majesty's Subjects inhabitants in Charlestown. See Frothingham's Hist., p. 230, and Andros Papers, vol. 2, Prince Soc., Boston, 1869, pp. 79-81.

1691.

"THE Humble Address, [to the King] of divers of the Gentry, Merchants, and others, * * * inhabiting in *Boston, Charls-Town* and places adjacent, within Your Majeſtic's Territory and Dominion of NEW-ENGLAND in *America*, with a Letter. dated *Charles-Town, New-England*, Novemb. 22, 1690, giving an Account of the unfortunate Expedition to *Quebec* in *Canada*, the Inducements to it," etc. Sign'd L. H. Licenſed *Apr.* 28th. 1691. 4°. pp. 8.
[*London*], 1691

"The | Humble Addrefs | of the | Publicans | of | *New England* | to which King you pleafe. | With some | Remarks | Upon it." 4°. pp. 35. *London*, printed in the Year, 1691

A reply to, or abuse of, the above. It states that "this Famous *Publican* Address, has not only been Signed by all the Trash they could Rake together, but also with a **Cum multis aliis.**" Of the 31 signers named to the first above, 11 may have been of C., viz.: Cap't Laur. Hammond (abusively mentioned p. 29 of Reply), Nath. Dows, Nath Rand, John Cutler, Jr., Tim. Cutler, Cap't Rich? Sprague, Fr. Littlefield, Sam! Phillips, Sam! Walker, Dr. Thos. Greaves, and Edw. Palmes (Palmer ?).

1692.

Lawson, Rev. Deodat. *The Duty & Property* | of A | Religious Houfe-holder | Opened | In A | Sermon | Delivered at **Charles-town**, on | Lord's Day December, 25, 1692. | etc. Sm. 8°. pp. 8 + 64. *Boston*, 1693

1693.

Morton, Rev. Chas. The | SPIRIT | of | MAN: | or | Some Meditations (by way of *Effay*) on | the Senfe of that Scripture. | 1 Thef. 5, 23, etc. Sm. 8°. pp. 8 + 100 + 2.

Printed by B. Harris. for Duncan Campbell, *Boston*, 1693

Recommended by Increase Mather, James Allen, Samuel Willard, John Baily, Cotton Mather, as "the Worthy Labours of a Learned, Pious, and now Aged Servant of the Lord Jesus Christ in the Ministry of the Gospel. He is a person too considerable in his Generation, to want any of our Commendation."

"The Worthily Famous, Mr. Morton," with "Sense enough for a Privy Counsellour, and Soul great Enough for a King." See Douton's Letters, Prince Soc. IV, 296-7, with a high estimate of his abilities and accomplishments.

Born 1626, d. C. 1698, minister of C. 1686-98. Ordination Friday, Nov. 5, see Sewall, Mass. Hist. Soc. Coll's, V. v., 155. He preached in Eng. until 1686, then kept an Academy at Newington Green. De Foe, author of Robinson Crusoe, was one of his scholars. His other books, all small, are : —

The Little Peace-maker; Discovering Foolish Pride the *Make-bate*; from *Prov:* 13, 10. 16°. pp. 86 + 2. *London*, 1674

The Way *of Good Men*, for Wise Men to Walk in; or Animadversions upon Prov. 2, 20. 16°. pp. 95. *London*, 1681

Debt's Discharge, or Some Considerations on *Romans* 13, 8. 16°. pp. 4 + 60 + 4. with some Meditations on the History recorded in the first fourteen chapters of Exodus in Meeter. (16°. pp. 16.) *London*, 1684

The *Gaming Humour* Considered and Reproved, or the Passion-Pleasure, and Exposing Money to hazard, by Play, Lot, or Wager, Examined. 12°. pp. 2 + 52 *London*, 1684

Also, "Two little things in English Meeter. The one, Meditations," (above). "The other, The Ark, its *Loss* and Recovery; being like Meditations on the beginning of 1 Sam."

A Discourse on Improving the County of Cornwall (portion in Phil. Trans. Royal Soc. vol. 10, 1675 (April); "Considerations on the New River"; "Letter to a Friend, to prove money not so necessary as imagined"; "Season Birds"; an "Inquiry into the sense of Jeremiah viii. 7.³"; "Of Common Places"; or "Memorial Books"; "Compendium Physicæ"; "System of Logic."

1702.

Hale, Rev. John. A Modest Enquiry | Into the Nature of | Witch-craft, | and | How Persons Guilty of that Crime | may be *Convicted*; And the means | used for their Discovery Discussed, | both *Negatively* and *Affirmatively*. | according to Scripture and Experience. | Sm. 8°. pp. 2 + 176. *Boston*, 1702

(C. 1636, d. 1700, 1st min. Beverley, Mass.) The rarest of books on N. E. Witchcraft. *Soles*, Menzies (bro. mor.) $32. Brinley, 2 copies. (sheep) $105, (red mor.) $120. "Mr. Brinley was, perhaps, the only collector, in the present century, who has had the good fortune to secure *two* fine copies of this *Extraordinarily rare* book." (Cat. p. 181.)

1708.

[MATHER. Rev. C.] Corderius Americanus. An Essay upon the
Good Education of Children. In A Funeral Sermon upon Mr.
EZEKIEL CHEEVER, etc. Sm. 8°. pp. 6 + 34. *Boston*, 1708

E. C. (1615-1708) Schoolmaster in C. 1661-70. *Sales*, Wiggin (1876) (poor copy)
$6.25. Brinley (time) $25. Reprinted, with "a selection from the poems of Cheever's
manuscript never before published." 8°. pp. 24. *Boston*, 1828. Also, do. 1774.

1709.

[CHEEVER, E. Latin Accidence]. A Short Introduction to the
Latin Tongue. For the Use of the Lower Forms in the Latin
School, etc. 8°. pp. 2 + 46 + 15 + 1. *Boston*, 1709

The earliest ed. seen by the writer. This very popular text-book, composed 1638-50,
reached the 20th ed. (1785), 17 of wh. were pr. in Boston before the Revolution — the
15th, in 1771. See 1757, 1856, and 1879. Also, an ed., *Boston*, 1838.

1715.

ELEAZAR PHILLIPS "removed to Charlestown, near Boston. He
was the only bookseller who had settled in that town prior to the
revolution." He was also a binder. Died 1763.

He was a small dealer in books printed in N. E. See Arch. Amer. VI, 216, 232. His
son Eleazar (b. in Bost.) was first printer in the Carolinas, at Charleston, 1730. See do.
V. 340.

1717.

CUTLER, Rev. Timothy, D. D. (C. 1684-1765; Pres. Yale 1719-
22, then rector Christ Ch. Boston, which was gathered for him;
lived in C. 1684-1709 ?) Connecticut Election Sermon 1717, *New
London*, 1717; Ser. before Gen. Assembly Conn., Oct. 18, 1719,
N. L., 1720; Ser. Deaths John and Elizabeth Nelson, *Boston*,
1735; Ser. see 1747; Memorial on, see 1765.

1719.

GOOSE, or VERGOOSE, Elizabeth (Foster). " Songs for the Nursery,
or Mother Goose's Melodies for Children. Printed by T. Fleet, at
his printing-house, Pudding Lane, 1719. Price two coppers."
[*Boston*], 1719

"Something probably intended to represent a goose with a very long neck and a
mouth wide open, covered a large part of the page." (Ed. 1879, p. xiv.) The *Editio
Princeps* of " Mother Goose." There have been doubts of this excessively rare ed.
See W. H. Whitmore, N. E. Hist. Gen. Register, April, 1873, p. 144. The poetess was
born in C. 1665, and died in Bost. abt. 1758; m. Isaac V. 1692.

——— New Edition. " Mother Goose's Melodies, with Illustrations
[8] in color by Alfred Kappes." 4°. pp. 21 + 186.
Houghton, Osgood & Co., Riverside Press, *Boston*, 1879
The *Edition de luxe* of " Mother Goose."

1720.

SYMMES, Rev. Thomas. Good Soldiers Described and Animated. Artillery Election Sermon, Boston, June 6, 1720. Preface by Benj. Colman. Sm. 4°. pp. 37 + 1. *Boston*, 1720

1678-1725, grandson Rev. Z., early life in C. See Budington's Hist. p. 240. Mr. Symmes also was author of The Reasonableness of Regular Singing, etc. 16°. pp. 24, *Boston*, 1720; Monitor for delaying Sinners, 1720 ?: Dis. concerning Prejudice in Matters of Religion, pp. 22, and Ser. at Ordination of Joseph Emerson, 12°, both, *Boston*, 1722; Utile Dulci; or a Joco-Serious Dialogue concerning Regular Singing, etc. 16°. pp. 59; *Boston*, 1723; The People's Interest in One Article, etc. 12°. pp. 43. *Boston*, 1724; Lovewell Lamented, or a Sermon occasion'd by the Fall of the Brave Capt. John Lovewell, etc., Bradford, May 16, 1725, pp. 32. With an Historical Preface, or Memoirs of the Battle at Piggwacket, pp. 4, 12, (32). *Boston*, 1725. 1st ed. (Uncut), thought to be unique, richly bound by Bedford, at Brinley Sale (for Chicago) $215. The same, 2d ed. Sm. 8°, do. 1725 (Excessively rare, Brinley sale, $55). Sundry reprints, a very fine one, with additional matter, by F. Kidder (245 copies 4°), pp. 138. *Boston*, 1865.

1723.

STEVENS, Rev. Joseph. Another and Better Country | even an Heavenly : | In Reserve | For all true Believers. | Being the last | SERMONS | of that Memorable Servant of | Christ, the Reverend | Mr. Joseph Stevens | Late Pastor of the Church in | C. With a Discourse on the Death of Rev. Wm. Brattle. In 1 vol. 12°. pp. 2 + xii. + 116. (Figures 69, 70, repeated.) *Boston*, 1723

Mr. S. was minister at C. 1713-21. His son, Rev. Benj. D. D. (C. 1721, d. 1791), was minister at Kittery. The following were by him : —
—— Rev. Benj. Sermon on the Death of Andrew Pepperell, Esq., only Son of Sir Wm. Pepperell, Bart., who died March 1, 1751. 8°. pp. 31. *Boston*, 1752
—— Sermon on the Death of Sir Wm. Pepperell, Bart.; who died July 6, 1759. 4°. pp. 24. *Boston*, 1759. Mass. Election Sermon, 1761. 8°. pp. 72. *Boston*, 1761. The Gospel Ministry vindicated from Contempt. Convention Sermon Portsmouth, Sep. 26, 1764. Large 8°. pp. 42. *Portsmouth*, 1765
The last, printed by Thomas Furber, apprentice of Daniel Fowle (C. 1715), 1st printer in N. H.

—— —— The Pastor's Office and Business while among his people while living, and the People's Duty toward a Faithful Pastor when deceased. Funeral Sermon on Rev. Wm. Brattle. *Cambridge*, March 24, 1716-17. " Now Publish'd as a Special Monitor for *Charlestown*, under their Sorrowful *Bereavement* of the Worthy *Author*." 16°. pp. 46. *Boston*, 1723

1725.

BROWN, Rev. John. Divine Help Implored. Funeral Sermon at Bradford, Oct. 31, 1725, on Rev. Thomas Symmes, with " A Particular, Plain, and Brief Memorative Account " of him. 8°. pp. 70. *Boston*, 1726. The Ser., Memoirs, etc., pp. 168. *Newburyport*, 1816.

1726.

PENHALLOW, Judge Sam¹ The History of the Wars of New England with the Eastern Indians, from Aug. 10th, 1703, to Aug. 5th, 1726. 8°. pp. 2 + iv + 2 + 134 + 1. *Boston*, 1726
Extremely rare. *Sales*, Brinley (orig. bind.) $130, do. (fair) $30. Reprinted 4° (150 copies), Cincinnati, 1859, with Memoir by N. Adams.
Born 1665, d. 1724, came to C. 1686, memb. Ch. C. till 1717.

1730.

BROWN. Rev. John (Haverhill). Ordination Sermon preached at Arundale (M^e) Nov. 4, 1730, at Ordination of Rev. *Thomas Prentice.* 16°. pp. 30. *Boston,* 1731

<small>The church at A. was dispersed by Indians, and Rev. T. S. became (1739) min. at C.</small>

1735.

ABBOT, Rev. Hull. Jehovah's Character as a Man of War, illustrated and applied. Artillery Election Sermon, 1735. 8°. pp. 35. *Boston,* 1735

<small>1702 — C. 1774, minister at C. 1724–74. See 1746, 47, 53.</small>

RAND, Rev. Wm. (C. 1699. Min. Sunderland, 1724–45 ; do Kingston, 1746–79). Sermon at Sunderland, (Mass.) Nov. 2, 1735, pp. 21. *Boston,* 1736 ; Ser. at Hadley, (Mass.), Ord. Rev. D. Parsons Nov. 7. 12°. *Boston,* 1739 ; Ser. at Ord. Rev. J. Ballantine, (Westfield), June 17. 8°. *Boston,* 1741 ; Ser. at Road-Town (Shutesbury, Mass.) Ord. Rev. A. Hill, Oct. 27. 12°. *Boston,* 1742 ; The Late Religious Commotions in N. E. considered ; An Answer to the Rev. Mr. Jonathan Edward's Ser., etc. 8°. pp. 64. *Boston,* 1743 ; Ser. at Ord. Rev. A. Williams, Sandwich, (Mass.), June 14. 4°. *Boston,* 1749 ; Ser. at Ord. Rev. C. Turner, Duxbury, July 23, 1755. 8°. pp. 23. *Boston,* 1756 ; Convention Ser. 1757. 8°. pp. 23. *Boston,* 1757 ; Charge at Ord. Rev. C. Gannett, Cumberland, N. S., Oct. 12. *Boston,* 1768 ; Charge at Ord. Rev. Z. Sanger, Duxbury, July 3. *Boston,* 1776.

1742.

THE DECLARATION of the Associated Pastors of Boston and Charlestown, relating to the Rev. James Davenport. 16°. pp. 7. *Boston,* 1742

CROSWELL, Rev. Andrew. Reply to same. 8°. pp. 18. *Boston,* 1742

1743.

PRENTICE. Rev. Thos. Preface to Wm. Thompson's Funeral Sermon on Rev. Saml Willard, (Biddeford), and S. W.'s Ser. at Ord. Rev. John Hovey. 12°. pp. 60. *Boston,* 1743

<small>1702–1782, minister at C. 1739–82. See 1730, 45, 48, 55, 56.</small>

1745.

PRENTICE, Rev. Thomas. When the *People* and the *Rulers* among them willingly offer themselves, etc., the LORD is to be Praised. Thanksgiving Sermon in C. July 18, 1745, for the Reduction of Cape Breton. 8°. pp. 39. *Boston,* 1745

WHITEFIELD, Rev. G. Letter from two Associations of Ministers to the Associated Ministers of Boston and C. relating to the Admission of Mr. W. into their pulpits. 4°. *Boston,* 1745

1746.

ABBOT, Rev. Hull. The Duty of GOD's People to pray for the Peace of *Jerusalem*, etc. Sermon on the Rebellion in Scotland, 1745, preached at C. Jan. 12, 1745–46. 8°. pp. 26. *Boston*, 1746

The titles of the three above, entire, would occupy about the whole of this page.
The two important historical events were duly commemorated in C. by these sermons.
The one by Mr. Prentice, especially, contains admirable passages.

1747.

ABBOT, Rev. Hull. A Disswasive against the impious Practice of Profane Swearing and Cursing in Common Conversation. Sermon at C. 8°. pp. 30. *Boston*, 1747
————— Early Piety. a Sermon at C. (1739 ?) *Boston*, n. d.
CUTLER, Rev. Dr. Tim° The Good and Faithful Servant. and the Joy awarded to him. Sermon at Boston, June 28, 1747, on the Death (June 19) *Hon. Thos. Greaves*, of Charlestown. 8°. pp. 21. *Boston*, 1747

1748.

PRENTICE, Rev, Thos. The Vanity of Zeal for Fasts, without Judgment. Mercy. and Compassions. Ser. at C. Jan. 28, 1747–48. Public Fast after Burning of the Province Court House. 8°. pp. 27. *Boston*, 1748

LORD. Rev. Joseph. The Great Privilege of the Children of God, etc. Ser. at Eastham, Feb. 24, 1730–1. 16°. pp. 29, *Boston*, 1731. Two 12° vols on Baptism, *Boston*, 1719 ? Letter to General Convention of Ministers, Mass., 1728. 8°. pp. 16. *Boston*, 1734

C. about 1671. H. C. 1691. Min. Dorchester, S. C., 1st communion in Carolina Feb. 2, 1696, min. at Chatham, Mass., d. 1748, aged abt. 77.

1753.

ABBOT, Rev. Hull. R. H. Fellowship at Ord. Rev. Stephen Badger (see 1774). March 27. (Ser. by N. Appleton ; ch. Rev. Jos. Sewall). 8°. pp. 34. *Boston*, 1753

1755.

BRADSTREET, Rev. Simon. Sermon at Marblehead, Jan. 12, 1755, on the death of *Samuel Bradstreet*. 4°. pp. 28. *Boston*, 1755

Rev. S. B., (C. 1709), and Sam'. (C. 1711), sons of Rev. S. B. of 1st. ch. C., the latter resident of C., died Jan. 4, 1755. Also, by Rev. S. B., Rt. Hand at Ord? of Rev. Wm. Whitewell, Marblehead, Aug. 25, 1762, with sermon by Rev. T. Barnard. *Boston*, 1762

FOWLE, Daniel (C. 1715). "A Total Eclipse of Liberty; An Account of the Arraignment and Imprisonment of Daniel Fowle on Suspicion of his being concerned in Printing and Publishing a Pamphlet entitled ' The Monster of Monsters.' Written by himself." [Also, 12°. Boston, 1775]. 12°. pp. 24. *Boston*, 1755

FOWLE, Daniel. "An Appendix" to the same, "Being some Thoughts on the End and Design of Civil Government; also, the inherent Power of the People asserted and maintained." 8°. pp. 24.
[D. Fowle]. *Boston*, 1756

The "Monster," a severe satire on the debate on the Excise Bill in Mass. (Boston, 8°. pp. 24, 1751), was suppressed by order of the Gen. Court, and is now very rare. $22. Brinley sale. See Arch. Amer. V. 129–32. Mr. Fowle removed to Portsmouth, N. H., and printed the first newspaper in N. H., *The Gazette*, No. 1, Oct. 7, 1756. For Hist. and *Facsimile*, see N. E. H. G. Reg. xxvi., 132–40.

PRENTICE, Rev. Thos. The Believers Triumph over Death and the Grave. Ser. on death of *Mrs. Anna*, late Consort of *Mr. Richard Cary*, of C., Mch. 2. 8°. pp. 28. *Boston*, 1755

Dr. Badington (Hist. p. 234) mentions as seen (1842) a copy of "some of Mrs. Cary's sayings a few days before her death," once well known. The writer has not seen a copy.

1756.

PRENTICE, Rev. Thos. Observations, Moral and Religious, on the late terrible Night of the Earthquake. Ser. at the Boston Lecture Jan. 1. 8°. *Boston*, 1756

1757.

CHEEVER, Ezekiel. Scripture Prophecies Explained. In Three short Essays. 8°. pp. 36. *Boston*, 1757

1762.

SKINNER, Rev. Thos. Sermon on the Death of Mrs. Mary, his wife, Dec. 8, 1745, Colchester, Conn. 8°. pp. 43. *Boston*, 1746. The Faithful Minister's Trials. Ser. at Ord. Rev. Grindall Rawson, May 9, 1751. 4°. pp. 49. *New London*, 1751

Mr. S. and his family lived in C. (Dr. Bartlett.) He grad. H. C. 1732, was min. of Westchester Society in Colchester, and died 1762.

1765.

CANER, Rev. Henry, D. D. The Firm Belief of a Future Reward a Powerful Motive to Obedience and a Good Life. Sermon at Funeral of *Rev. Timo* Cutler, D. D., Aug. 20, 1765. 4°. pp. 24. (See 1717.) *Boston*, 1765

1768.

CARY, Rev. Thomas (C. 1745). Ordination 1st Ch. Newburyport, May 11, 1768. Ser., E. Barnard; Ch., Rev. Mr. Wingate; *R. H., Rev. T. Prentice, of Charlestown*. (pp. 5.) 8°. pp. 47. Printed by Edes and Gill, *Boston*, 1768. Rev. T. P. was minister, and Rev. T. C. and Benj. Edes were natives of Charlestown. By T. C. The Importance of Salvation considered, etc. 8°. pp. 76. *Boston*, 1773. See also 1797, and 1808.

Prentice, Rev. Thos., Ad. to C. ch., Sept. 25, 1768, "a student of Holliston," 1770 — min. at Medfield; 1785, and other years, pub'd 12 (or more) Discourses.

1774.

BADGER, Rev. Stephen (C. 1726–1803). The Nature and Effects of Drunkenness Considered, in Two Discourses at Natick, Oct. 1773. 8°. pp. 56. *Boston*, 1774. Substance of do. 16°. pp. 24. *Do.* 1811.
———— Letter concerning the Natick and other Indians, see Mass. Hist. Soc. Coll's, I. vol. v., 32–45. Rev. S. B. was a missionary who preached to the Indians at Natick. See 1753.

PASSAGES IN THE WORKS OF VARIOUS AUTHORS.

DESCRIPTIONS OF THE TOWN OR ITS AFFAIRS.

BRADFORD, Gov. Wm. Hist. Plymouth Plantation, 1646. Mass. Hist. Soc. Coll's, IV. iii. (1856). See p. 96, pp. 277–9.

BYFIELD, Nath. Account of the late Revolution in N. E., London, 1689. Rep. in Force IV. 10, and Sabin, 4°. No. 1. N. York, 1865. See p. 4.

CLAP, Capt. Roger. Memoirs, 1630. Boston, 1731 (rep. 1766, 1774, 1807, 1824), and Colls. Dorchester Antiq. and Hist. Soc., *Boston*, 1844. Settlement, see pp. 41, 42.

DRAKE, S. G. History of Boston, *Boston*, 1857. Settle! 57–9, 92–4, and various items.

DUNTON, J. Letters from N. E., Prince Soc. No. 4, description C., 1686, p. 149.

DUDLEY, Gov. See "Founders."

GORGES, F. Tracts, *London*, 1659, see p. 35, curious error about *Harverd* Colledge in C., and *Harnes* at Cambridge.

GORTON, Sam! Simplicities Defence, *London*, 1646. Rep. Force IV. 6, see p. 73 *et seq.*

HIGGINSON, Rev. F. N. E.'s Plantation. *London*. 1630. Rep. in M. H. Soc. Coll's, I. i.; Force's Tracts, I. 12, p. 13 (1630) : —

"There are in all of vs both old and new Planters about three hundred, whereof two hundred of them are settled at *Nehum-Kek*, now called *Salem*: and the rest haue Planted themselues at *Mayabalets* Bay, beginning to build a Towne there which we doe call *Cherton*, or *Charles Towne.*"

HUTCHINSON, Gov. T. Collections. Boston, 1769. Rep. Prince Society, Nos. 1, 2. See pp. 51, 55.

GOOKIN, D. Hist. Acc't 1675–7 in Arch. Amer. II. See pp. 466, 474, 509–10. Also in M. H. S. Coll's, I. (1792).

JOHNSON, Ed. See "Founders." — Account of C. (1631) Ed. 1867, p. 40; Settlement, 37–42; items, 53, 70, 121, 133, 176, 190, 192, 208, 211; great fire (1650), 221.

JOSSELYN, J. Two Voyages to N. E., London, 1675; Rep. Boston, 1865. Account of town 1st ed. 163–4 (1865), 126. Do. Chronological Obs. to 1673, p. 201 (1660), "a damnable cheat * * printed *June*, pretending that 18 *Turks-men* of War the 24 of January

1653 landed at a Town called Kingsword (alluding to *Charles-town*) three miles from Boston, kill'd 10, took Mr. *Sims* minister prisoner, wounded him, kill'd his wife," etc.. "burnt the Town." etc.; loss £12,000; "£8,000 ransom for prisoners demanded." Early but not latest "history" manufactured about Charlestown people.

LECHFORD, T.   Plain Dealing, *Lond.*, 1642.   Rep. Boston, 1867. He visited C.   General information.

MASSACHUSETTS RECORDS, 1628–86, 5 vols.   4°.   Boston, 1853–4. A large number of references too numerous or too brief, to be enumerated here.

———— Histories of, by Barber (pp. 364–74), Barry, Bradford, Hutchinson, Minot, and Palfrey (in N. E.) contain various references.

———— Historical Soc. Coll's or Proceedings, contain many items; Example, List of Fires in C. to 1800, see vols. iii. and xi. ; History of C., vol. xii. 163–84; vols. xvii., xviii.

MORTON, N.   N. E.'s Memorial, *Cambridge*, 1669.   Rep. 1721, 1772, 1826 (two ed's), and *Boston*, 1855.   Chiefly church affairs. But see p. 108, settlement of C.

OGILBY, J.   America, Description.   London, 1671, description of C., p. 159, and "Harnes" college. 160.

PRINCE, Rev. T.   Annals of N. E.   *Boston*. 1736, many items to 1633.

SEWALL, Judge Samuel.   Diary 1674–1729 printed in Mass. Hist. Soc. Coll's. V. v., vi.   This very interesting work contains many references to C. and its inhabitants.

SMITH, Capt. J.   Des⁰ of N. E.   *Lond.* 1616, brief notices of Bay, islands, etc., pp. 44. 46.

———— Advertisements, or Pathway, etc., *London*, 1631.   (1630) p. 24.   Rep⁴ *Boston*. 1865, p. 13.

WINTHROP, Gov. J.   Hist. N. E.   (See "Founders"), *Boston*, 1853. *Vol. I.*, settlement, pp. 34–40; Ambrose new masted at, 55; John Sagamore, 59, 67, 69, 71, 143; items, 72, 92, 148, 166, 184; Conference on grievances (1632), 98–105.   *Vol. II.*   Ship Mary Rose blown up (1640), 13, 87, 89; Knore's death, 52, Turner's do. (1641), 73; items, 109, 129, 336, 391, 422, 424; fortifying, 187, 298; Painter's case. 213; La Tour business (1644), 245, etc.; fishing New'd, 291; T. Coytmore wrecked, 292, ship seized, 302; tide mill, etc. (13 (11) 1646), 373; F. Willoughby, 392 (and I. 274); Margaret Jones, witchcraft (1648), 397; Wood's case, 425; Tuttle (1657), 426; Ed. Converse to keep ferry 3 yrs., 427; Winthrop's will, 439.   Names " of such as desire to be made freemen," (Mass. Oct. 1630–48), 411–57.   Coytemore property, etc., 458; deaths of T. Allen, Harvard, T. James, Symmes, 472–3; Morton, 476; others, 480–2.

WOOD, Wm.   N. E.'s Prospect, *London*, 1634.   Rep. *Boston*, 1865 (Prince Soc. 3), Description of C. Pt. I. ch. 10, p. 43.

CHURCH OR RELIGIOUS AFFAIRS.

FIRST CHURCH. See Budington, 1845, and Records, 1880.
HUTCHINSON, Gov. T. Hist. Mass. (1630–2) I. p. 22.
MASS. HIST. SOC. PUBLICATIONS. Some acc't Early hist. in Ecc.
Hist. Mass. churches, I. ix, 19; Prince's Annals (1630–3 inc.) II.
vii., 99; Dr. A. Holmes order of founding, I. vii., 15; " C. Church
Affairs," " relating to a cause of Ecclesiastical jurisdiction," III. i.,
248–64, 1st, to Council at C. Nov. 5, 1678, 2d, Reasons of dissent in
calling Mr. Daniel Russell, 3d, Brief Narrative Passages of this ch.
etc., since death Mr. Thos. Shepard, Dec. 22, 1677 (these articles
not in ch. record); Result of this Council, IV. viii., 91–2; Inc.
and Cotton Mather's letter (not in hand of either) to ch. in C., Boston, July 2, 1678, IV. viii., 119–21.
See also Biographical List at end of this work, etc.
MATHER, C. Magnalia, London, 1702, (1630) I. 22–3, also see Biog.
Notes at end of this vol.
——— I. Prevalency of Prayer, Boston, 1677, p. 8; Rep. do. 1861,
p. 26, for Fast. 1676.
PRINCE, Rev. T. Annals, Boston, 1736, for 1630–33.
MORTON, N. N. E.'s Memorial (above), 1630, and Boston, ed., 1855,
p. 442. founding and covenant, 461. Etc. Boston ch. 109.
WINTHROP, Gov. J. Hist. N. E. Vol. I., founding ch. (1630)
112–13; fast (1634) 182: building meet. ho. (1636) 225; Mr.
James (1633) 151; do. (1636) 217.

BATTLE OF BUNKER HILL.

HISTORY AND LITERATURE: MONOGRAPHS.

N. B. The name is hereafter often abbreviated B. H.

ALLEN, James (died 1808). Epic. poem, "Bunker Hill."
See Swett's Hist. 3d ed. for a portion. The writer has not found a complete copy.

AMERICA Invincible. An Heroic Poem; In Two Books: A Battle
at B— H—. The Americans gain the day, etc. By an Officer of
Rank in the Continental Army. Sm. 8°. pp. 40. *Danvers*, 1779
(ANONYMOUS.) A Sketch of the B. H. Battle. Also a Sketch of
Boston Tea Party. 8°. pp. 24. no p. or d. [1843?]
[BRACKENRIDGE, H. H.] The Battle of Bunkers-Hill; a Dramatic
Piece in five Acts, in heroic measure. By a Gentleman of Mary-
land. Frontispiece, by Norman, "The Death of Warren." 8°.
2 l. pp. 49. *Philadelphia*, 1776
The plate is said to be the earliest known specimen of engraving in Br. Am. by a
native artist. *Sabin*. Sales at auction: London, 1860, £1 15s. Brinley, 1879, red mor.
$23.

[Bradford, A.] A Particular Account of the Battle of Bunker, or Breed's Hill on the 17th of June, 1775. By a Citizen of Boston, 2d ed. 8°. pp. 27. *Boston*, 1825

B. R. H. The Battle of Bunker Hill, a Poem. 18° size, pp. 34. *Norwich*, 1874

Brown, Mrs. J. B. See Warren, Gen. J. (Stories.)

Burk, J. B. H.; | or the | Death of Gen. Warren; | an | Historic Tragedy | In | Five Acts. | Sm. 8°. pp. 55. Printed by T. Greenleaf, *New York*, 1797. Also Sm. 8°. pp. 44. *New York*, 1817

Carter, Lieut. Wm. A | Genuine Detail | etc. | with an | Accurate Account of the Blockade of Boston; | and a | Plan of the Works on Bunker's Hill, | at the time it was | Abandoned by his Majesty's Forces | on the 17th of March, 1776. | In a series of Letters to a Friend. | Engraved plan, 4°. 2 leaves, pp. 50. Printed for the Author and sold by him. Price 2s. 6d. *London*, 1784

Very rare. Rice sale (1870) cf. $23. Menzies (1875) cf. $27. Brinley (1879) 18 scarce extra plates $45. See p. 224 for a description and a Note. Aspinwall (1879) hf. mor. $54.

[Child, David L.] An Inquiry into the Conduct of Maj. Gen. Putnam at B— H—, and Remarks on S. Swett's Sketch. (Reprinted from the Boston Patriot, Nov. 1818.) 8°. pp. 58. *Boston*, 1819

A claim that Gen. Putnam was not in the battle.

Clarke, J. An Impartial and Authentic Narrative of the Battle. etc., (long title). 8°. pp. 36, [1st and] 2d. ed. *London*, 1775

A ? might be inserted after the word "Authentic." Rare. Rice, fine cf. $17. Menzies, do. (uncut) $44. Brinley $43.

———— Reprint of same (99 copies), Roy. 8°. [*New York*, 1868]
Also rep. in Drake's B— H—, pp. 42-59.

[Cockings, George.] The American War, a Poem, in which the names of the officers who have distinguished themselves during the war are introduced. In Six Books. Curious view of the Battle of B— H—. 8°. pp. 181. *London*, 1781

Scarce. Rice (uncut) $10. Menzies hf. mor. (port. ins.) $8. Brinley, cf. $7. Portion rep. in Drake's B— H—, pp. 62-74.

Coffin, Charles. History of the Battle of Breed's Hill, by Generals Heath, H. Lee, Wilkinson and Dearborn. 8° pp. 38. *Saco*, 1831
———— Second edition. 8°. pp. 36. *Portland*, 1835

Dawson, H. B. Maj.-Gen. Israel Putnam. A Correspondence of this Subject, with the Editor of the "Hartford Daily Post" By "Selah," of that city, and H. B. D. *Morrisania, N. Y.*, 1860
Edition 250 copies, Imp. 8°, 117 of which were burned.

Dearborn, Maj.-Gen. H. An Account of the Battle of B— H—, written for The Portfolio. With H. De Berniere's map, corrected by Gen. D. 8°. pp. 16. *Philadelphia*, 1818
Rep. in Hist. Mag. July, 1868, pp. 402-6; also VIII. (1864), 257-72.

———— The same. 8°. pp. 8. *Boston*, 1818

DEARBORN, Maj. Gen. H. Vindication — Reply to D. Putnam.
See Boston Patriot, No. 321, Boston, June 13, 1818. Reprinted
in Hist. Mag. July, 1868, pp. 414–23. See also do. pp. 423–37,
reprint from Columbian Centinel, Boston, July 4–15, 1818, of Hon.
John Lowell's Review of the same.
——— See Magazine Articles.
DRAKE, S. A. Bunker Hill; the Story told in Letters from the
Battlefield by British Officers engaged. Plate. 8°. pp. 76.
Boston, 1875
——— Gen. Israel Putnam, the Commander at B. H. 8°. pp. 24.
Boston, 1875
EMMONS, R. The Battle of B— H—, or the Temple of Liberty; an
Historic Poem in Four Cantos. 6th ed. Port. 12°. pp. 144.
Boston, 1842
[ELLIS, Geo. E.] Sketches of B— H— Battle and Monument; with
illustrative documents. Map, plate, 12°. pp. 172.
Charlestown, 1843
——— History of the Battle of Bunker's [Breed's] Hill, etc. Map.
16°. pp. 144. *Boston*, 1875
——— The same, recast with changes, Map and Note. 8°. pp. 69.
See also New York *Herald*, June 8, 1875. *Boston*, 1875
FARNHAM, Ralph, (Soldier at B— H—). Life of. 12°. pp. 48.
Boston, 1860

Additional particulars, N. E. H. G. Reg. XVI. 183; Hist. Mag. 312. In 1860 last
survivor of the battle, and aged 105.

FROTHINGHAM, Richard. History | of the | Siege of Boston, | and of
the | Battles of Lexington, Concord, | and | Bunker Hill. | Also, an
Account of the | Bunker Hill Monument. | With Illustrative Docu-
ments. | 3 plates, 3 maps. 8°. pp. x., 420. *Boston*, 1849
For *List of Authorities* B— H— Battle see pp. 372–81. 2d ed.
1851; 3d Dec., 1872; 4th, 1873. *The Magnum Opus of this whole
subject.*
——— The Command in the Battle of B— H—, with Reply to S.
Swett. 2 pl. pp. 57. 8°. *Boston*, 1850. The Battle Field of
B— H—, with a relation of the Action by Wm. Prescott, etc. 3 pl.
8°. pp. 46. *Boston*, 1876. Illustrations of the Siege of Boston.
8°. pp. 40. Plates, privately printed. *Boston*, 1876
——— The Centennial; Battle of B— H—. *Fac-similes* of Page's
plan and Romane's view, etc. 16°. pp. 136. *Boston*, 1875
——— See also Life of *Warren*; Mass. Hist. Soc. Proceedings 1876.
HALE, Rev. E. E. One Hundred Years Ago. See ch. 4. 8°. pp. 40.
Boston, 1875
GOODRICH, J. W. The Battle of B— H— and other poems. 16°.
pp. 48 + 2. [*Worcester*], 1855
HUDSON, Chas. Doubts concerning the Battle of B— H—. Ad-
dressed to the Christian Public. 16°. pp. 41 + 2. *Boston*, 1857
HOWE, Lord Viscount. Three Letters to (originally in London
Chronicle, 1779). 8°. pp. 47. A portion in Frothingham's Hist.
Siege, p. 398. *London*, 1780

LUNT, Paul. Diary, May — Dec. 1775. Privately printed by Dr. S. A. Green. 8°. pp. 19. *Boston*, 1872

MAGAZINE and REVIEW Articles. *Centennial*, July, 1875. Atlantic Monthly by H. E. Scudder; The Galaxy by Launce Poyntz; Harper's Monthly by Rev. Sam! Osgood. See Annual Register, pp. 133*–37*, (E. Burke?) London, 1775; Gentleman's Magazine, xlv., do. p. 397, *et seq.*, (with a plan of the redoubt, woodcut, p. 416, plan of Boston, p. 41, plan of the country around, p. 293; plan of the Town of Boston, p. 493:) Pennsylvania Magazine, Sept. 1775 (with eng. of battle); Analectic Mag., Feb. and March, 1818 (the former no. with eng. of H. DeBerniere's plan of battle, "the first American engraving of a full plan of the battle"?); The Portfolio (Philadelphia), March, 1818 (see Dearborn); do. July, 1818 (see Putnam, and Rep. Hist. Mag., June, 1868, p. 407; North American Review, July, 1818, by D. Webster; Dawson's Historical Magazine (N. Y.), Aug. 1864 (Dearborn's Account reprinted), and July, 1868); Potter's American Monthly (Phil?), July, 1875.

MOORE, F. Ballad Hist. Am. Rev., 1765–83, B. H. Number (Part II.). 4°. pp. 64. *New York*, 1875

MORSMAN, Oliver, (Revolutionary Soldier). A History of Breed's (commonly called) Bunker's Hill Battle. 8°. pp. 17.
                               Sacket's Harbor, 1830

PARKER, F. J. Col. W!ᵐ Prescott, the Commander in the Battle of B— H—. 8°. pp. 21. *Boston*, 1875

POTTER, I. E., (a soldier at B— H—). Life, etc. 1st ed. 18°. pp. 108. *Providence*, 1824

PULSIFER, D. An Account of the Battle of B— H—, compiled from authentic sources. Map. 12°. pp. 75. *Boston*, 1875

PUTNAM, Daniel. A Letter to Maj.-Gen. Dearborn on Maj.-Gen. Putnam. 8°. pp. 17. *Philadelphia*, 1818

———— Another Edition. 8°. pp. 12. And Account of battle by Dearborn, pp. 8. *Boston*, 1818

SUMNER, Gen. Wm. H. Reminiscences of Gen. Warren and Bunker Hill, pp. 16. Reprinted from N. E. Hist. Gen. Reg. Apr. and July, 1858. See also Hist. Mag. July, 1868, pp. 407-14.

SWETT, S. Historical and Topographical Sketch of the Battle of B— H—. 16°. pp. 104. [*Boston*], 1818

———— History of the Battle of B— H—, with a Plan (large) 3d. ed. with notes. 8°. pp. 58 + 4. *Boston*, 1827; (2d. ed. was 1826). Who was the Commander at B— H—. 8°. pp. 39. *Boston*, 1850

VOYAGE to Boston (The). A Poem. By the Author of American Liberty, a Poem. General Gage's Soliloquy, etc. 8°. pp. 24.
                    Editions, *Philadelphia* and *New York*, 1775

WARREN, Maj.-Gen. Joseph. An Oration April 8, 1776, King's Chapel, Boston, on the Re-Interment of his Remains, by *Perez Morton*. 2d ed. 4°. pp 13. *Boston*, 1776

———— Biographical Sketch, with his Orations, 1772 and 1775. "By a Bostonian." 16°. pp. 85. *Boston*, 1857

———— An Eulogium on, by a Columbian. 8°. pp. 22. *Boston*, 1781

Pl. 1

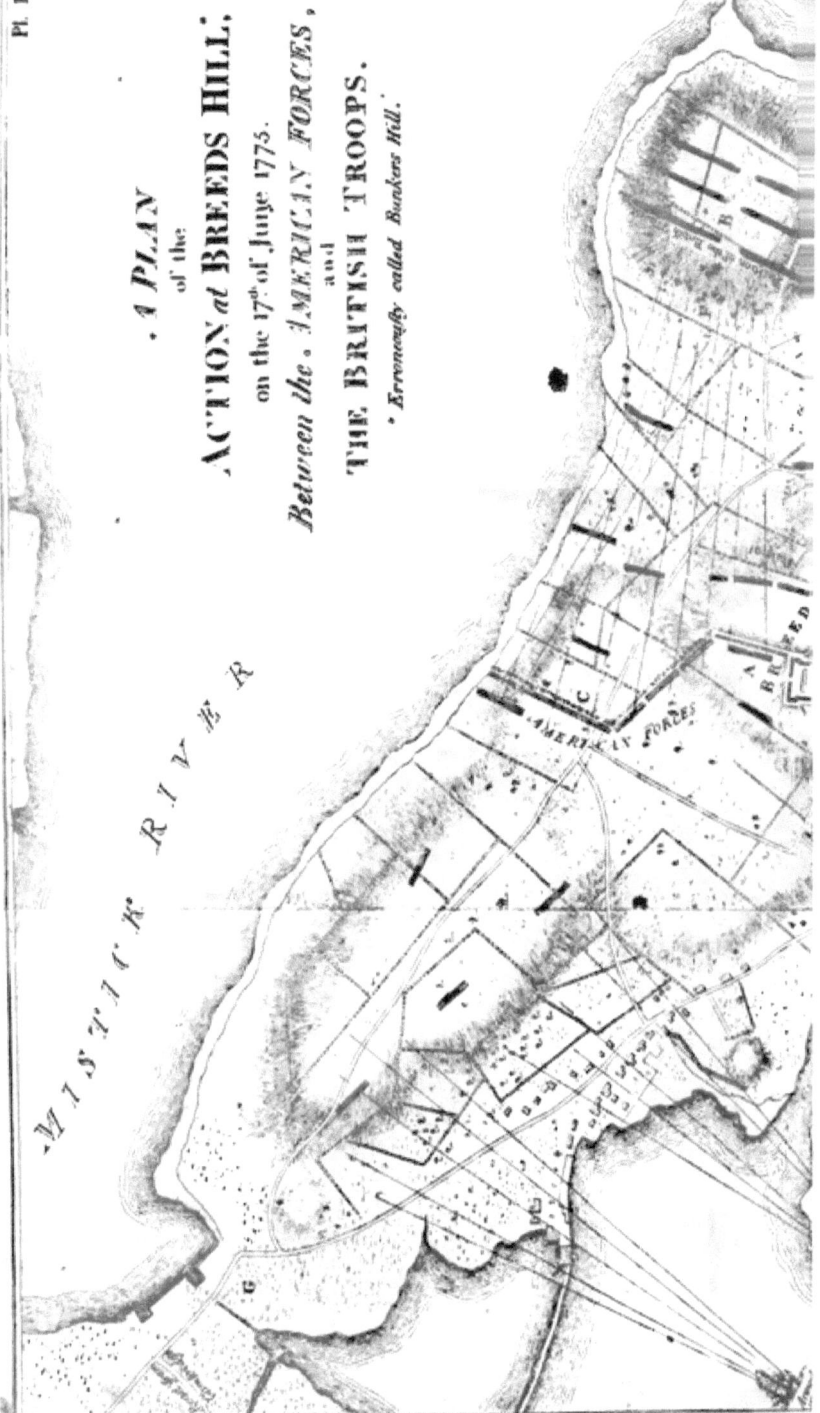

A PLAN
of the
ACTION at BREEDS HILL,
on the 17th of June 1775.
Between the AMERICAN FORCES,
and
THE BRITISH TROOPS.

* Erroneously called Bunkers Hill.

MISTICK RIVER

AMERICAN FORCES

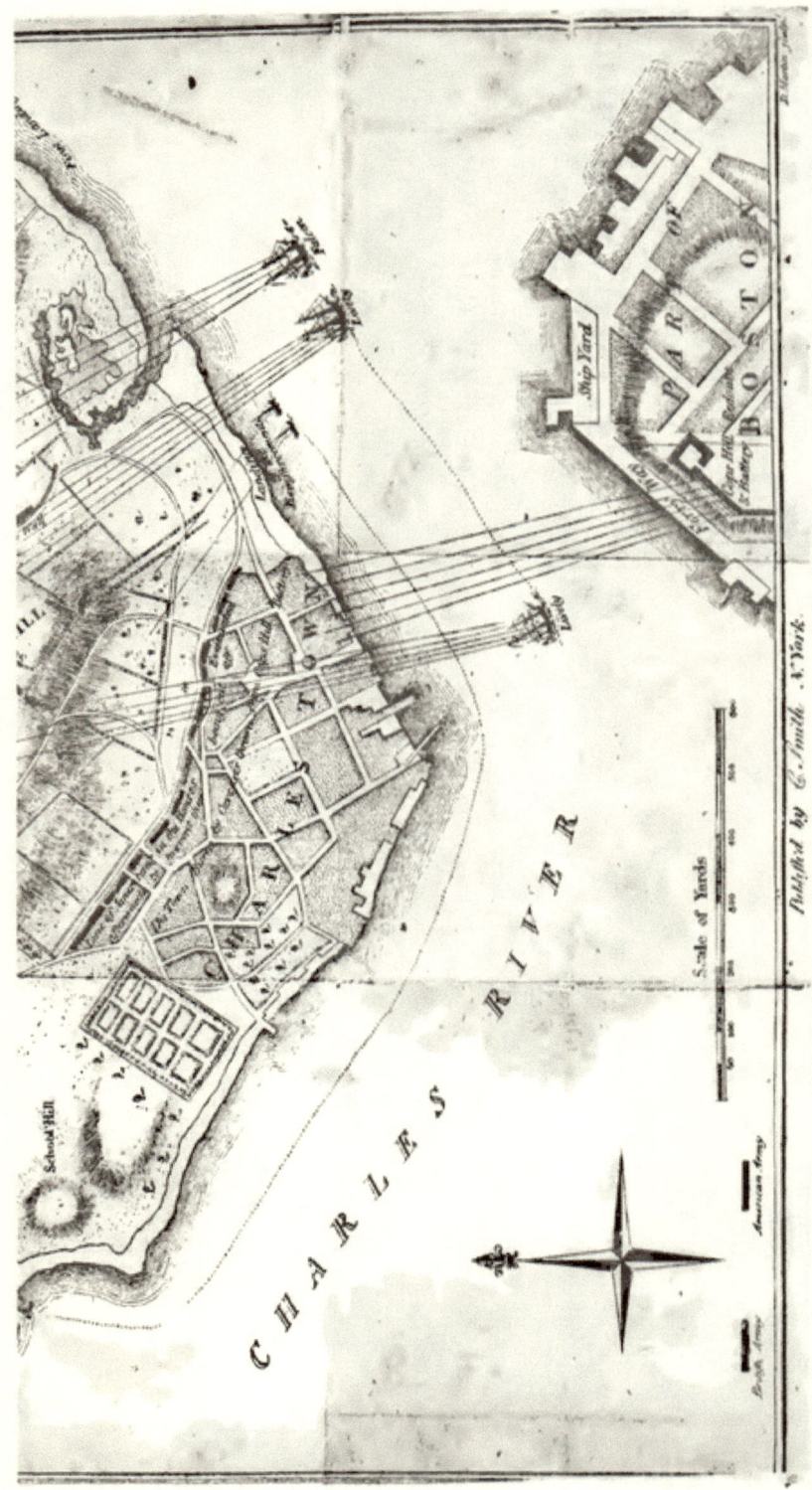

CHARLES RIVER

Scale of Yards

Published by C. Smith N. York.

PART OF BOSTON

Ship Yard

School Hill

British Army

American Army

WARREN, Maj.-Gen. Joseph. Stories of, in relation to the 5th of March Massacre, and the battle of B— H—. 12°. pp. 112. *Boston*, 1855
Said to be by Mrs. J. B. Brown, his granddaughter.

——— Life and Times of, by *Richard Frothingham*. 8°. pp. 558.
Boston, 1865
See pp. 535-42 for an account of Eulogies on Gen. Warren.

——— Life of, by *A. H. Everett*. In Sparks's Series Am. Biography.

——— See Essex *Gazette*, July 21; and June 29, 1775, and Mass. *Spy* (Worcester), No. 228, July 5, 1775 for Epitaphs. See Sumner, above. See Hist. Mag., I., 20, and 45, 243, 365-7, account of Relics of Gen. W. See French Accounts (below), Chas et Lebrun. See Dr. J. Jeffries, in Boston Medical and Surgical Journal, June 17, 1875; Mass. Hist. Soc. Proc., Sept. 1866, on W.'s sword. Loring's Boston Orators, etc.

WHEILDON, W. W. A New History of the Battle of B. H. Map. 2d ed. 8°. pp. 56. *Boston*, 1875. Siege and Evacuation of Boston and Charlestown. Map. 8°. pp. 64. *Boston*, 1875-6

WINSOR, Justin. The Literature of Bunker Hill, with its Antecedents and Results. See City of Boston "Centennial," pp. 151-74.
Boston, 1875

——— The Reader's Handbook of the American Revolution, 1761-83. 16°. pp. v. + 328. *Boston*, 1880
Both works, that contain a vast amount of information admirably condensed, were not seen by the writer until much of this B. H. List was formed, but have helped to its completion.

MAPS AND PLANS.

1. CARTER, Wm. Plan of the (British) Works on B. H., 1775-6. *London*, 1784. See Carter above, and *rep*. F.'s Siege, 330.
2. DAVIS, Thos. W. Plan showing the Redoubt, Breastwork, and Rail Fence and Grass Protection of the Americans on the 17th of June, 1775. See Proceedings of the B. H. Monument Ass'n, June 17, 1876; also pp. 23-31. *Boston*, 1876
3. DEARBORN, H. Map (based on 4, with corrections in red), 19½ × 12½ inches, published in the Portfolio, March, 1818, and in 8° pamphlet, both *Philadelphia*, 1818. See his remarks in both; Dawson, Hist. Mag. July, 1868, p. 406; the Analectic Mag. March, 1818, rep. H. M., 438: Sumner (above).
4. DE BERNIERE, H. (14th Roy. Inf.) "Sketch of the Action on the Heights of Charlestown June 17th, 1775," etc. Engraved by Kneass, Young & Co., and published in the Analectic Magazine, *Phil*. [Feb. 1818]. See Dearborn (above); Hist. Mag. July, 1868, p. 406. F.'s Battle Field, 6 and 7.
5. FELTON and Parker's Survey of Charlestown, 1848, a large map serving this subject in several particulars.

6. GENTLEMAN'S Magazine, xlv., 4 plans, etc. See Magazine
   (above), *London*, 1775. Plan of (Am.) redoubt (erroneous) in
   F.'s Siege, 198, "as a curious memorial of the battle."
7. MAP. A New and Correct Plan of the Town of Boston, and
   Provincial Camp. See Centennials, Coolidge, and Rand and
   Avery's; also, Wheildon's Siege, Moore's Ballad Hist.
8. MAP. The Seat of War in N. E. by an American Volunteer,
   with the Marches of the several Corps sent by the Colonies
   towards Boston, with the Attack on B. H. R. Sayer and J.
   Bennett, London, Sept. 2, 1775. " It is more curious than valuable." — R. F. See Boston Public Library, Cent'l Graphic.
9. MAP. " Plan of the Battle on B.'s H. Fought on the 17th of
   June, 1775. By an Officer on the spot. London, Printed for
   R. Sayer and J. Bennett, No. 53, in Fleet St., as the Act di-
   rects, 27 Nov., 1775." Sheet with text, Burgoyne's Letter to
   L'd Stanley. Reduced in Moore's Ballad Hist.
10. MONTRESOR, see Page No. 11.
11. PAGE. " A Plan of the Action at Bunker's Hill," etc., by " Lieu,
    Page of the Engineers, who acted as Aide-de-Camp to General
    Howe in that Action. N. B. The Ground Plan is from an
    Actual Survey by Captain Montresor." *London*, 1776 or 7.
    Also, on copper for Frothingham's Siege, 1849,* and Centennial,
    1875. See Stedman (below), F.'s Battle Field, 1876, pp. 5–6,
    13. *This is " much the best " plan.* See 15 (below). Reduced
    in several publications. * See also Page's Plan of Boston.
12. PLAN of the Town of Boston, with the Attack on Bunker's Hill in
    the Peninsula of Charlestown. For T. Robson, Newcastle upon
    Tyne. With a curious map of C. See *fac-similes* in Pulsifer,
    Osgood (C. only), and Wheildon (above).
13. PENNSYLVANIA Magazine, June, 1775, " A New Plan of Boston
    Harbour from an Actual Survey." Engraved for Penn. Mag.
    C. Lownes, sc.
14. RIVINGTON'S Gazetteer, New York, Aug. 3, 1775. A rude plan
    shown by printer's rules, reproduced in Frothingham's " Siege,"
    397, and Hist. Mag., 390.
15. SMITH, C. " A Plan of the Action at Breed's Hill * on the 17th
    of June, 1775 Between the American Forces and the British
    Troops. * Erroneously called Bunker's Hill." " D. Martin,
    Sculp!" Plate I. in " The American War from 1775 to 1783."
    Published by C. Smith, New York, 1797.

    This rare plan is finely engraved, and a reduced but careful copy of 11 (Page), substi-
    tuting " American " for ' Rebel," (where the latter occurs in 11.) and making a few
    other changes in lettering. This work contains six other fine maps of Revolutionary
    battles, and when complete is excessively rare.

16. SMITH, Geo. G. " Sketch of the Battle of B. H. by a British
    Officer," Boston, June 17, 1843. 12 × 19 in. Based on 4,
    but with alterations.
17. STEDMAN, C. Hist. Am. War, London, 1794. No. 11 (Page's)
    map reprinted with altered title.

18. STILES, Rev. E., (Newport). A rude sketch in his Diary (1st plan made of the Action ?), engraved in Hist. Mag. 393.
19. STONE, Jas. E. Map (16⅜ × 14 in.) of Charlestown, and plan of Battle combined. Published by L. Prang & Co., Boston, 1875.
20. SWETT, S. Sketch of B. H. Battle (18½ × 12¼ in.), based on 4. See his Hist. 1827, and Ellis, 1841 (Celebrations B. H.); reduced in several Centennial Publications.

Map of Boston and vicinity (chiefly harbor), in Botta's Hist. (Paris, 1812), also map in Ridpath's U. S. See Note (below) for *Views*.

COTEMPORARY NEWSPAPER ACCOUNTS OF THE BATTLE.

Originals of these are rare; sets are generally defective, and lack the numbers mentioned below. References to the Historical Magazine (Dawson's), abbreviated H. M., are to the number for June, 1865.

Boston Gazette, June 19, 1775, *Watertown; reprinted*, H. M., 370.
Connecticut Journal, June 21, 1775. *New Haven; reprinted*, H. M., 373.
Essex Gazette, June 22, 1775, *Cambridge;* see in part. H. M., 375; 29th, do., do. 381; also. July 6, 13, 21, 1775; Gen. Burgoyne's Account of Battle, Nov. 23, 1775; Col. Scamman's trial, Feb. 29, 1776, see H. M. 400.
London Gazette, July 25, 1775, *London*, see Frothingham's "Siege," 386.
——— *Chronicle*, see Aug. 1775, *London.*
Massachusetts Spy, Boston, June 21, 1775 (no. 226) short accounts, rep. H. M. 372. Frothingham's Centennial, 135, and *fac-simile* in Centennial Graphic.
New Hampshire Gazette and Historical Chronicle, *Portsmouth*, Tuesday, June 20, 1775, and no. 977, July 11th.
New York Gazette and Weekly Mercury, by Hugh Gaine, *N. Y.*, no. 1237, Monday, June 26, 1775, two accounts. H. M., 372.
New York Gazetteer, N. Y., June 21, 1775, *rep.* H. M. 373; do. 29th, 373, 75; do. July 13th, do. 378 and 384; do. Aug. 3, do. 389 (with plan); Frothingham's Siege, 397 (with plan).
Pennsylvania Gazette, Phil, Wed., June 28, 1775 (no. 2427).
——— *Journal, Phil*, Wed., June 28, 1775 (no. 1699); a little, July 5th.
——— *Evening Post, Phil*, Tues., June 27, 1775 (no. 67).
Providence Gazette, Prov. R. I, July 1, 1775, rep. H. M. 384.

The following may also be consulted: *Boston News Letter; Connecticut Courant*, (Hartford); do. *Gazette*, (New London); *Georgia Gazette*, (Savannah); *London Evening Post*; do. *Morning; Maryland Gazette*, (Annapolis); do. *Journal*, (Baltimore); *Newport Mercury*, (R. I.); *Pennsylvania Ledger*; do. *Packet*, (both Phila.); *S. Carolina Gazette*, (Charleston); *Virginia Gazette*, (Williamsburg).

AMERICAN LETTERS, STATEMENTS, ETC., 1775-1817.

N. B. Much is mentioned that relates to the *command* in the battle, but some of the later articles on the extended controversy are not mentioned.

ADAMS, John. Letters to his wife Abigail, published by Hon. C. F. Adams, 1876.

Ashford (Conn.). Resolves, etc. Hist. Mag. I. 273.

Baldwin, Loammi. Letter to Mary B., June 18, 1775. See Frothingham's Battlefield, 43.

Bancroft, Col. E. Personal Narrative of Bat. B. H. in John B. Hill, Bi-Centennial of Old Dunstable, 57-66, Nashua, 1878.

Belknap, Dr. Extracts from his Note-books, etc., 1775-89, M. H. S. Pro., June, 1875, pp. 91-8.

Bradford, J. Letter to Col. Lincoln, see Rivington's N. Y. Gaz', June 29, 1775; rep. in Hist. Mag. July, 1868, p. 370.

Boynton, Thos. Journal, see Mass. Hist. Soc. Proc., March, 1877.

Breastwork on B. H. See H. M., p. 439, and B. H. M. Ass. Proceedings, 1876, pp. 26-31.

Bromfield, J. See "Letters" below, Mass. H. Soc. Pro., Feb. 1870.

Brown, Peter (private in battle). Letter June 25 to his mother. Frothingham's Siege, 392; Potter's Am. Monthly, July, 1875, p. 514 (from original).

Chester, Capt. John, Letter July 22, 1775, see F.'s Siege, 389; do. Battle Field, 12; H. M., 386. See Orderly (below).

Columbian Centinel Account, see Dec. 1824, and Jan. 1825.

Command in the Battle, Controversy on, see Winsor's Handbook, 48-53, for articles, also many herein.

Committee of Safety. See N. H. Hist. Soc. Coll's II. 143. Ellis (1843), 129.

———— Account Mass. to Cont'l Congress, see do. 140.

———— Do. to England, see do. 131; Force's American Archives IV., 1373; Journal 3d Prov. Cong. 1775; F.'s Siege, 382; H. M. 387.

Craft, Benj. (L't), 19th Reg. Journal, June 15, 1775, et seq., with notes by S. P. Fowler, Essex Ins. Hist. Coll's, Apr. 1861.

Dwight, Tim⁰ Travels in N. E. and N. Y. 4 v. N. Haven, 1821, see I. 468-76.

Elliott, Rev. And. (Boston). Letter to Rev. I. Smith (of B.) in London. See Ellis (1843), 151; H. Mag. 369.

Folsom, Gen. N. Letter to Committee of Safety in N. H. See Coll's N. H. Hist. Soc., II. 146; H. M., 373.

Gray, Samuel. Letter to Mr. Dyer, July 12, 1775. See Frothingham's Siege, 393; H. M., 385.

George's Cambridge Almanack for 1776.

Hall, Major. Hist. of the Civil War in America, (1775-7.)
London, 1780

Heath, W. Memoirs of Maj.-Gen. Heath. Boston, 1798

Henshaw, Wm. Orderly Book, Apr.-Sep., 1775, with notes by C. C. Smith, in Mass. Hist. Soc. Proc., Oct. 1876.

Hide, Captain Elijah. Account of battle, see N. Y. Gazette, June 26, 1775; Ellis (1843), 142; H. Mag. 378.

Holmes, Rev. A. American Annals. II., 331-34. Cambridge, 1805

———— Dr. O. W. Poem, " Grandmother's Story," see Centennials (Osgood's) and Mass. H. Soc. Proc., 1875, p. 33.

Hubley, B. Hist. of the American Revolution (Vol. I. only).
Northumberland, Penn., 1805

HUMPHREYS, Col. D. An Essay on the Life of the Hon. Maj.-Gen. Israel Putnam. 12°. *Hartford*, 1788, see pp. 107–12.

AN Impartial Hist. of the War in America between Great Britain and her Colonies to end of 1779 (long title). 8°. pp. 608, and App. 41. Map, 13 Portraits. *London*, 1780. Do. to end of the War, with "beautiful Copper Plates," 3 vols. 8°. *Boston*, 1781–4

"These Plates are exceedingly rude productions without the slightest resemblance to the men they are intended to represent." — J. R. B.

LATHROP, L. to T. Burr (Conn.), June 22, 1775. See Rivington's Gazetteer, June 29, 1775 ; Ellis (1843), 148 ; H. Mag., 374.

LEE, L⁰-Col. Henry. Memoirs of the War in the Southern Department of the U. S. 2 v. 8°. *Philadelphia* and *New York*, 1812

LETTER from John Bromfield (Newburyport, June 21, 1775 to ?). See Mass. H. S. Pro., Feb. 1870, p. 226. Do. from a Gentleman in Providence, June 20, 1775, see N. Y. *Gazette*, June 26, and H. M., 372. Do., do. in Philadelphia, June 22d, see Force's Arch. IV., and Hist. Mag., 375. Do., do. in the Army, June 27, 1775, see do. IV., and do. 379. Do. from the Camp at Cambridge. see H. M., 384. Do. from an Officer of Rank to Gentleman, N. Y., June 27, 1775, see Rivington's Gazetteer, July 6, and H. M., 380.

MISCELLANEA. Few for a long time cared to claim share in the battle, H. M. XII., 309. Burning of C., see H. M. I., 145.

MARSHALL, J. Life of Washington, Vol. II., 237–43, ed. 5 v., 4°. *London*, 1804–7

MARTIN, Rev. John. See Stiles, below.

MAYNARD, Needham (survivor, B. H.). Recollections, Boston paper (?), 1843.

MASSACHUSETTS Provincial Congress. To Committee of Safety, Albany, N. Y., see H. M., 380 ; Journal 3d Prov. Cong., June 20, 1775 ; To Continental Congress, H. M., 371 ; to Great Britain, H. M., 387, and Force's Am. Arch. IV., F's Siege, 381.

MAXWELL, Maj. Thompson. Statement on command at B. H. See N. E. H. Gen. Reg. xxii., 57, and H. Mag. xviii., 369.

NEW Hampshire troops engaged, see Rep. (vol. 2) for 1866, of Adj. Gen. of N. H., also C. C. Coffin in Boston Globe, June 23, 1875, N. H. Provincial Papers, vol. 7.

ORDERLY Book ; Chester, see F.'s Battle Field, 37–41 ; Fenno, see Mass. H. S. Proc., Oct. 1876, p. 108.

PAINE, Sam! Acc't of battle, June 22, 1775, printed from M. S. in H. M., 440–2.

PARKER, Abel. Letter, Jaffrey, N. H., May 27, 1818, in H. M. 420.

PRESCOTT, Col. Wm. Letter to John Adams, Aug. 25, 1775, see F's Siege, 395 ; H. M., 390. Command in Battle, see Winsor's Handbook, 48–53.

——— Manuscript, see Butler's Hist. Groton, 337 ; H. M., 437 ; Judge P. (below).

——— Judge Wm. Acc't of Battle of B. H., "quite different from what is called The Prescott Manuscript" (above). Printed for the first time in full in Frothingham's "Battle-Field," 18–29.

PRICE, Ezekiel. Diary May 23, 1775 to Aug. 18, 1776, in Mass. Hist. Soc. Proc., Nov. 1863, pp. 185–262. From MS. presented by Mr. Quincy.

PRISONERS (Amⁿ) taken at B. H. See N. E. H. Gen. Register, xix., 263.

PUTNAM, Gen. I. Command in Battle, see Winsor's Handbook, 48–53.

RAMSAY, Dr. D. The Hist. of the Am. Rev., 2 v. 8°. Philᵃ, 1789, see I., 201–6, acc't battle.

REGIMENTS in B. H. Battle, List of, see F.'s Siege, 401–4.

SCAMMAN, Col. J. Comments, etc., Gen¹ Court Martial, July 13, 1775, see Essex *Gazette*, Feb. 29, 1776, same in H. M., 400–2.

SMITH, Chas. "The American War from 1775 to 1783, with (7) Plans." 8°. *New York*, 1797, see 5–10. Also Monthly Military Repository, N. Y., 1796–7, " descriptions said to have been supplied by Baron Steuben and Gen. Gates," *Allibone*.

STARK, Col. John. Letter to Cont¹ Cong. June 20, 1775; do. N. H. Cong. June 19, see Coll's N. H. Hist. Soc. II., 144, Ellis (1843), 145, and H. Mag., 370.

STILES, Rev. E. Diary, cited in F.'s Siege ; *rep. from original MS.* (Yale Col.) H. M., 391–400 with plan.

STORRS, Col. Eph. Diary, printed in F.'s Battle Field, 34–7.

THACHER, J. Military Journal Am. Rev., 1775–83, *Boston*, 1823.

———— Rev. P. Narration printed from original MS. (Am. Antiq. Soc.), H. M., 381–4.

THAXTER, Joseph. Letter Nov. 30, 1824, in H. Mag. xv., 206.

TRUMBULL, Gov. J. Letter Aug. 31, 1779, see Coll's Mass. H. Soc. vi., 159. Life of J. T. by Stuart.

———— Col. J. Narrative as witness from Roxbury, see Autobiography, 1841.

TUDOR, Wm. Letter to Stephen Collins, June 23, 1775, from original MS., see H. M., 376.

VIEWS of the Battle B. H., Boston, etc., (chiefly American). The writer omits a considerable list, and refers to Winsor's Handbook. As a class the early plates are curious or ugly, and now rare and expensive. The art of drawing and engraving in the country was little developed.

WARREN, Dr. J. Diary, 1775, see F.'s Siege ; Life of Dr. W.

———— Mrs. Mercy, of Plymouth, Mass. Hist. of the Rise, Progress, etc., of the Am. War, 3 vols. 8°. *Boston*, 1805. See I., 217–24.

WEBB, Lieut. Sam¹ B. See Chester (above) ; F.'s Battle Field, 12, and letter to Silas Deane, do. 31. Conclusion of battle.

WHITNEY, Rev. J. Sermon occasioned by death of Gen. Putnam, 12°. *Windham*, 1790]

WILKINSON, Gen. Jas. Memoirs ; (1816). Ch. 19, sketch from observations on field, March, 1776.

WILLIAMS, Wm. Letter to Conn¹ del. in Cong. June 20, 1775. See F.'s Battle Field. pp. 41–3.

WINTHROP, Prof. J. Acc't to John Adams, Philᵃ, June 21, 1775. Mass. H. S. Coll. V., iv., 292.

AFTER 1818, Accounts or illustrations besides those above appear in General Histories and other works. See *Barry*, J. S., Hist. Mass. (1857), Vol. III.; *Bancroft*, G., Hist. of U. S., VII., ch. 38–40; *Bradford*, A., Hist. Mass. 1764–75 (1822), pp. 385–88; *Carrington*, H. B. (1876), Battles of Am. Rev., ch. 15; *Dawson*, H. B., Battles of the U. S. (1858); *Drake*, S. A., Hist. Fields of Middlesex (1874); *Elliott*, C. W., Hist. of N. E. (1857), II., 316–25; *Finch Silliman's* Journal (1822), traces of the works; *Female Review*, 1797 (Vinton's ed. 1866); *Grahame*, J., Hist. of the U. S. (1837, 52, etc.), book xi., ch. iv.; *Hinman* R. R., Conn't in Rev'n (1842); *Hollister*, G. H., His't of Conn't (1857); *Holmes*. A., Am. Annals (1805), II., 331–4 (1829), II., 209–11; *Lossing*, B. J., Field Book of the Am. Rev'n (1851), I.; *Morse*, J., Annals of the Am. Rev. (1824), 231–3; *Irving*, W., Life of Washington (1856), I., 418–41; *Shaw*, Sam!, Journal (1847); *Tudor*, W., Life of Jas. Otis (1823).

BRITISH ACCOUNTS.

[ALMON, J.] The Remembrancer, London, vol. for 1775, pp. 132–5.
ANDREWS, J. Hist. of the War with Am?, France, Spain, and Holland, 1775–83. 4 vols. 8°. *London*, 1785. See I., 301–5.
ANNUAL Register, *London*, 1775. account (E. Burke?). 133.*
BURGOYNE, Gen. J. Letter to Lord Stanley, June 25, 1775, with Observations on same letter, Ellis 106–14. Account of battle B. H. N. E. H. G. Reg. xi., 125.
DUNCAN, Capt. E. History of the Royal Regiment of Artillery. 8°. *London*, 1872, see I. 302–3.
EVELYN, Cap't W. G. (4th Reg. King's Own). Memorial Letters from North America, 1774–6. Edited and annoted by G. D. Scull, 250 copies privately printed. 8°. pp. 140. *Oxford*, 1879
GAGE, Gen. T. *Despatch* to Home Government, see Almon, 1775; Hist. Mag. 361; F.'s Siege, 386; Ellis (1843), 94. Observations on same, Ellis, 98–106. See Moore's Ballad History, p. 86. *Letter* to Earl of *Dartmouth*, see Force Am. Arch. IV.; Hist. Mag., 363; London *Gazette*, July 25, 1775. *Letter* to Earl of *Dunmore*, June 26, 1775, see Force Am. Arch. IV.; Hist. Mag., 366. Also Moore, Sundry extracts.
GENTLEMAN's Magazine, vol. xlv. See Magazines (above).
London, 1775
GORDON, Wm. (D. D.) The History of the Rise, Progress, and Establishment of the Independence of the U. S. A. 4 vols. 8°. *London*, 1788. See II. 39–53. Map of Boston, Harbor (chiefly) and Environs similar to that in Botta's Hist., Paris, 1812.
GRANT, Dr. Letter June 23, 1775, to friend, see Ellis (1843), 114; H. M., 361.
HARRIS, Captain. See Lushington, Life of Lord Harris, 54–6; H. M. 366; Drake, 37.
HISTORICAL RECORDS 4th Foot (p. 64), 5th (42), 10th (38), 18th (48), etc. 8°. R. Cannon. *London* (1837).

HISTORY of the War in America between Great Britain and her Colonies, to end, 1783. 3 vols. 8°. *Dublin*, 1779–85. See I., 82–6.

HOWE, Gen. See Monographs (above); entries in Orderly Book, Ellis (1843), 88–92.

HULTON, H. Letter June 20, 1775, see Ellis (1843), 123; H. M., 359.

JONES. Brig.-Gen. Letter to friend, England, June 19, 1775, see Frothingham's Battle Field, 45.

Jones's New York in the Revolutionary War, I. 52, has an account of Howe's mode of attack.

LAMB, Serg.. (Welch Fusileers). Journal of Occurrences during the late Am. War.

LETTER. Officer in the Army to friend in England, see Force Am. Arch., IV.; H. M., 365. Do. do. Boston, to? see Detail Am. War; F.'s Siege, 373; H. M., 367. Do. do. of Rank, Boston, June 18, 1775, to Gent'n in London, see Ellis (1843), 115; Force IV.; H. M., 357; Do. do. in ship, Boston, June 23, to friend in London, see Force; H. M., 360; Ellis (1843), 117. Do. Merchant, Boston, June 24, 1775, to brother in Scotland, see Ellis (1843), 119; B. to Scotland, 25th, see Force; H. M., 361.

LEVINGE, Sir R. G. A. Historical Record of the 43d Regiment Monmouthshire Lt. Infantry. Roy. 8°. *London*, 1868. See 61–1.

MAHON, Lord. Hist. of England, (Boston, 1853) VI., 55–60, and note, p. xxviii.

MAUDIT, I. Review of Battle in London Chronicle. See Howe.

MISCELLANEA. Ballad of B. H. by Br. Officer after the engage't, see H. Mag. II. 58; Do. on B. H., see do. V. 251. "Cerberus" frigate, etc., do. X. 346. Flags, B. H. on Reg'l Colors, do. I. 3d Ser., 285; do. of Cheshire Reg't at Chester Cathedral, do. III. 279. (They have been repeatedly shown the writer on visits there during the last twenty years.) Queries about battle, do. X. 291.

MOORSOM. Hist Record of the 52d Reg. (Oxfordshire) Light Infantry, 1755–58. Roy. 8°. 1860. With plates of uniforms at B. H.

MURRAY, Rev. J. Impartial Hist. of the War in Am. *London*, 1778, and *Newcastle*, n. d. (1782), see I., 467 (in Am. Hist'l Record II., 559), appearance of C., 1775.

NICHOLAS, P. H. Hist'l Record of the Royal Marine Forces, 2 vols. 8°. *London*, 1845, see I. 84–9.

PROCLAMATION by Gen. Gage, June 12, 1775, see H. Mag. Jan. 1868, pp. 1–10.

RANDON, John, (soldier R. A.). Letter June 18, 1775, to wife in England, see H. M., 358.

RIVINGTON, Jas. See Newspapers (above), N. Y. Gazetteer.

SIMCOE, Lieut. J. G. Case of Ed. Drewe (35th Sussex). *Exeter*, 1782; H. M. 368.

STEDMAN, C. Hist. of the Am. War, etc., 2 vols., 4°. Maps and plans. *London*, 1794. (Compiled by Wm. Thompson, LL. D.), see I. 125–9.

The Detail and Conduct of the Am. War, under Generals Gage, Howe, Burgoyne, and V. Ad. Lord Howe, (long title). 8°. pp. 190.
London, 1780

WALLER, Adj't J., (Roy. Marines). Acc't June 22, see Drake's B. H., 28.

FRENCH ACCOUNTS.

The following show, at least to some extent, French views on the subject.

AUBERTEUIL, M. Hilliard d'. Essais Historiques et Politiques sur les Anglo-Américains. 2 vols. (4 pts.) Sm. 8°. *Bruxelles*, 1782. See I. pt. 2, pp. 224–40.

This work contains a map of New England.

[BOUCHER.] Histoire de la Dernière Guerre entre Le G. B. et Les États-Unis de l'Am., la France, etc. 4°. *Paris*, 1787. See brief ref. p. 25.

CHAS (J) et Lebrun. Histoire Politique et Philosophique de la Révolution de l'Am. Sept. 8°. *Paris*, An IX. (1801), see 129–31.

This account begins: "Putnam partit de Cambridge avec deux mille hommes, et vint occuper le poste de Bunkerhil, situé auprès de Charles-Town, dont Gage vouloit s'emparer. Les Anglais firent entrer dans la rivière de *Mistich*, des batteries flottantes qui tiraient sur les revers des retranchemens, tandis que plusieurs vaisseaux de guerre et la batterie de Copshil les foudroyoient de tous côtés," etc. It closes with a eulogy "du ministre américain" "Nelson" (quoted also in Aubertuil, above), on Gen. Warren.

SOULES, F. Histoire des Troubles de l'Amérique Anglaise, etc. 4 vols. 16°. *Paris*, 1787. See I., 152–61.

CELEBRATIONS AND ORATIONS, ANNIVERSARY OF THE BATTLE.

First, see 1786 below. See Charles River Bridge, (the opening of).
Second, 1794. See Bartlett, Hon. J., Oration. (Also Siege Boston, p. 338.)
Third, 1801. See Austin, Wm., Oration. (Also Siege Boston, p. 339.)
1801–25, "there appears to have been no general celebration of the day." — R. F.

1825.

COLONNE de Bunker Hill, Monument élevé à la Mémoire des Patriotes Américains, morts sur le champ de Bataille où fut remportée la première victoire de l'Independance. 8°. pp. 40. *Paris*, 1825

Contains Discourses by D. Webster, and by M. Keratry, *Rich*.

EMMONS, Wm. An Address, Ev'g June 16th, in commemoration of the Battle of B. H. 8°. pp. 16. *Boston*, 1825

"SERVICES on Bunker Hill for 17 June, 1825," (hymns, ode, etc.), 8°. pp. 4.

LEVASSEUR, A. Lafayette en Amérique, en 1824 et 1825, ou Journal d'un Voyage aux États-Unis. 2 vols. 16°. *Paris*, 1829

This work contains Webster's Oration (28 pages), translated (not always closely) into French, and the most complete account of this celebration that the writer has met in a book. See II., 468–505. Also I., 65–9, acc't L.'s first visit to C., Aug. 1824.

MELLEN, G.   Ode for the Celebration of the Battle, at the laying of
the Monumental Stone, June 17, 1825.   8°.   pp. 16.   *Boston*, 1825
WEBSTER, D.   An Address delivered at the Laying of the *Corner
Stone* of the B. H. Monument.   8°.   pp. 40.   *Boston*, 1825
Five editions published, and a reprint. 8°. pp. 16. *Boston*, 1843. See Analectic
Magazine, Vol. XI.

———— Discurso pronunciado al Poner la Piedra Angular, etc., tra-
ducido por José Maria Heredia.   8°.   pp. 34.   *Nueva-York*, 1825

1827.

EMMONS, Wm.   Oration (and Poem) on B. H. Battle, delivered on
the Battle Ground in C., 18th June, 1827, (and Cauens Speech
May 9th, Faneuil Hall).   8°.   pp. 16.
                        Printed for the Author, *Boston*, 1827

1836.

EVERETT, Alex. H.   An Address at C. 17th June, 1836, "at the request of the Young Men, without distinction of party, in Commemoration of the Battle of" B. H.   Notes. 8°.   pp. 72.   *Boston*, 1836

1841.

ELLIS, Rev. G. E.   Oration at C. 17th June, 1841, in Commemoration of the Battle of B. H.   Reprint of Swett's Map.   8°.   pp. 72.
Delivered at the request of the Warren Phalaux.   *Boston*, 1841

1843.

WEBSTER, D.   Address at B. H. June 17, 1843, on the completion
of the Monument.   8°.   pp. 39.   T. R. Marvin, *Boston*, 1843
———— Another edition.   8°.   pp. 20.
                        Tappan and Dennet, *Boston*, 1843
———— Another edition.   4°.   pp. 8.   "Price 6 1-4 cts."
                        John Sly, *Boston*, [1843]

1850.

SEVENTY-FIFTH ANNIVERSARY.   Oration of Edward Everett (in
Ship House, Navy Yard) pp. 49, and a Brief Account of the Celebration, June 17, 1850.   In all, Roy. 8°.   pp. 80.   *Boston*, 1850

1857.

INAUGURATION of the Statue of Warren, by the B. H. Monument
Association, June 17, 1857.   Address (and portrait) E. Everett,
etc.   With an account of the Celebration, etc. 8°.   pp. 224.   Plate
of Statue.   By Authority of the Committee, *Boston*, 1858

1858–1874.

CELEBRATIONS, etc., described in Warren's History, and Proceedings
B. H. M. Association.   (See below.)

1875.

CELEBRATION of the Centennial Anniversary of the Battle of B. H. With an Appendix containing a survey of the literature of the battle, its antecedents and results. Imp. 8°. pp. 174.
Printed by Order of the City Council, *Boston*, 1875
PROCEEDINGS of the B. H. Mon. Ass'n. An. Meeting, June 23, 1875, with the Oration of Hon. Chas. Devens, Jr., and an Account of the Centennial Celebration. Roy. 8°. pp. 217.
B. H. M. Ass'n, *Boston*, 1875
"BUNKER HILL CENTENNIAL," (100,000 copies), many cuts, folio, pp. 8, *Rand and Avery*, Bo-ton; "Bunker Hill," *fac-similes*, sm. folio, pp. 4, *Geo. A. Coolidge*, Boston; Centennial *Graphic*, many cuts, large folio, pp. 16, New York; *Harper's Weekly* (June 26), many cuts, folio, pp. 20, New York; *Frank Leslie's* B. H. Centennial (June 26), do. do. pp. 32, New York; "One Hundred Years Ago," cuts, folio, pp. 16, *W. W. Marple*, Boston; Centennial Map, large sheet, *L. Prang & Co.*, Boston; A Song, *fac-simile* sheet, *Lockwood, Brooks & Co.*, Boston; Pocket Souvenir, map, etc., *W. F. Gill & Co.*, Boston; "Charlestown, Something of its History." 8°. pp. 12. *B. H. Times*, City Sq. C.; Memorial of B. H., cuts. 4°. pp. 16 + 4 (printed covers), *J. R. Osgood & Co.* An elegant and valuable work, with Dr. O. W. Holmes's poem, "Grandmother's Story," and Hist. Acc't by J. M. Bugbee. See also Magazines (above), and files of chief local newspapers. Several works produced at this period are mentioned above under Authors' names. See Drake, Ellis, Frothingham, Hale, Magazines, Pulsifer.

BUNKER HILL MONUMENT ASSOCIATION.

Acts of Incorporation, see 1823.
Publications. Address of the B. H. M. Ass'n to the Selectmen of the several Towns in Mass. (16° size) pp. 12, 1824. Circular 8°. pp. 8. Boston, Sept. 20, 1824. B. H. M. Ass'n An. Meeting, 1830, Com. Rep. Aug. 13, Account, Aug. 18, Address. 8°. pp. 17. Act of Inc., By-Laws, and a List of the Original Members of the B. H. M. Ass'n, Statement of progress, and Original Estimates; also List of Subscribers, and two plans. 8°. pp. 74. *Boston*, 1830. Address on the Concerns of the B. H. M. Ass'n, to the Citizens of Mass. 8°. pp. 8. *Boston*, 1831. Report of the President, Vice-Presidents, and several Directors, June 1831 to June 1832. 8°. pp. 15. *Boston*, 1832. Also, Petition to Leg. of Mass. Dec. 2, 1829, Broadside, to raise $50,000 by a Lottery. [See 1839, Sale of House Lots, and Plan.]
Proceedings. Ceremonies by the Ass'n on the Displaying of the National Flag from the Monument, June 17, 1861, with the Annual Proceedings of the Ass'n, pp. 44. Proceedings at An. Meeting 1862, pp. 20. Do. 1863, pp. 23. Do. 1864, pp. 31. Do. 1865, and Visit of Congregational Council, pp. 82. Do. 1866, pp. 31. Do. 1867, pp. 64. Do. 1868, pp. 40. Petition Laying out a Street,

with plan, pp. 12. 1868.   Arguments in favor of The New
Avenue, pp. 95, C. 1869.   Proceedings 1869, pp. 44.   Do. 1870,
pp. 53.   Do. 1871, pp. 56.   Do. 1872, pp. 48.   Do. 1873 (50th
Anniversary) pp. 52.   Do. 1874, pp. 71.   Do. 1876 (plan of
Breastwork) pp. 54.   Do. 1877, pp. 42.   Do. 1878 (*fac-simile* of
ins'n on plate under Corner Stone, pp. 39.   Do. 1879, pp. 48.
———— See Celebrations, 1857, 1875.
The History of the B. H. M. Association during the First Century of
the U. S. of A. by George Washington Warren (President 1847–
75), 11 engravings, 22 heliotypes (*fac-simile* letters, etc.).   Roy.
8°.   pp. xx + 427.   *Boston*, 1877
Bunker Hill Association, Constitution, pp. 8.   B. True, Printer, n. p.
or d.   Oration in commemoration of the Anniversary of Am. Independence. Boston. July 4, 1809, at the request of the B. H. A., by
Wm. Chas. White, and Introductory Ad. by David Everett, pp. 17
+ 2.   *Boston*, 1809.   Do. July 4, 1810, by Daniel Waldo Lincoln,
pp. 20.   *Boston*, 1810.   Do. July 4, 1811, by Henry A. S. Dearborn,
pp. 15.   *Boston*, 1811.   In 1809 and 1810 this Soc. met July 4th
with the "Washington Society," Boston.

BUNKER HILL MONUMENT. — HISTORY AND DESCRIPTION.

ELLIS, Rev. Geo. E.   Sketch of the Monument on Breed's Hill (1843).
See Ellis, above.
FROTHINGHAM, R.   History of the Monument, pp. 23, with Siege of
Boston.   See 1849.
PACKARD, Prof. A. S.   History of the B. H. Mon't, pp. 33.   *Port-
land*, 1853.   Also in Collections of the Maine Hist. Soc. vol. 3,
pp. 243–70.
SWETT, S.   Original Planning and Construction of the B. H. Mon't.
1 plate, pp. 12.   *Albany*, 1863.   Horatio Greenough, claimed as
designer.   See N. E. H. Gen. Reg. xviii., 61–5.
WILLARD, Solomon, Plans and Sections of the Obelisk on Bunker's
Hill.   With the details of Experiments made in quarrying the gran-
ite, 14 plates.   Roy. 4°.   pp. 31.   Chas. Cook, lithographer.
                                                       Boston, 1843
———— Architect and Superintendent of the B. H. Mon't, Memoir of,
by Wm. W. Wheildon.   Prepared and printed by Direction of the
Monument Association.   7 plates, pp. 272.   [*Boston*,] 1865
See also 1796, 1823, Acts, 1st Mon't, and Inc. B. H. M. Ass'n ; B. H.
M. Ass'n, above, especially Judge Warren's History.
FAIR, Sep. 1840.   Plan, 10 × 17 in., of Quincy Hall, Boston used
(382½ feet long) ; "The Monument," daily paper, edited by Mrs. S.
J. Hale, printed in the Hall by S. N. Dickinson (7 nos.?).   Broadside Circulars, Reports, etc., printed by David Francis.   Original
Charades, prepared for the Fair.   Sq. 12°.   (n. d.)   "Remarks"
on the B. H. Mon't "addressed to the Ladies getting up the Fair,
by Elliot," pp. 12.   *Portsmouth*, N. H., 1840.   A "peace" objection to a monument on a battle-ground.

(HORSFORD, E. N.) Effect of heat on perpendicularity of Mon't;
Pendulum at do. Proceedings Amer. Ass'n, v. 6, 1852.
PANORAMIC View from Mon't, from Drawings by R. P. Mallory. 4°.
Boston, 1848
STRANGER's Guide at Mon't. (3½ × 5 in.), pp. 15. C., Printed for
J. B. Goodnow, 1856, etc.

TOWN PERIOD.

1776-1847.

THE History of the town, previous to this period, has been fully
written by Mr. Frothingham (see 1845-49), and Dr. Budington (see
1842-45). Its Church Records (see 1880) have been reproduced in
print. Its experiences during June 1775, and immediately afterwards,
have been described fully by Mr. Frothingham (1849), and by Dr.
Ellis (1843). Dr. Bartlett gave, with ample and interesting notes, an
account of its affairs to 1814. Some of these notes, with others from
rare published works or hitherto unprinted records, that appear along
the following dates, present a concise yet rather minute review of the
leading incidents of the history of the town to the present time, and
various works mentioned show a great deal already in print about its
thoughts, doings, societies and individual inhabitants — a mass of material that if reproduced would make a single work impracticably large,
and treating too much, perhaps, of subjects of moderate importance.

The events of June 1775 terminated the Colonial period, and
within a year, an action by the people began a new period in the history of the place, when, May 28, 1776, in Town Meeting they
" *Voted Unanimously*, That it is the mind of the Inhabitants, that
our Representatives be advised, — That if the Continental Congress
should, (for the safety of the Colonies,) declare them Independent of
the Kingdom of Great Britain, they will in that case, solemnly engage
with their lives and fortunes, to support them in that measure." Also,
" Voted Unanimously, that the town clerk serve our Representatives
with a copy of this vote for their direction." And thus Charlestown
ratified the great Declaration thirty-seven days before it was proclaimed " and published to the world."

After the destruction of the town within the peninsula, " many of
the former inhabitants returned " from the exile into which they had
been forced, and (continued Dr. Bartlett), " commenced according to
their respective means, to repair their waste places. A few of the
number were able to erect convenient dwellings, whilst others, like
their hardy predecessors, were only covered with temporary shelters."
The Parish Records state that in " 1777 * * the returning inhabitants
in their then distressed situations, did make it one of their first objects
to provide a house to re-establish the public worship of God in this

town." They "found no other or better place in which to worship than an old block-house left by the British troops * * in 1776." This stood upon "Town Hill," and "was appropriated as a school-room, a meeting-house, and for other necessary purposes." "The first administration of the Lord's Supper [said the venerable pastor, Thomas Prentice] in Charlestown since the destruction by the cruelest British Enemies, was Nov. 8. 1778, with great solemnity and fulness of members beyond expectation," (Church Record). In the block-house, wrote Dr. Bartlett, "Sept. 4, 1780, * * uninfluenced by political dissentions, we gave our first suffrages for a chief magistrate and legislators, under the Constitution of this Commonwealth." There were 48 votes.

Through discouragement and trial, through suffering and earnest effort, the town once more arose, along its " main street," and lesser ways around the parts of the peninsula towards Boston, around its old market square, then so suggestive of the market places in pleasant English country villages from which not a few ancestors of its people came, and on and around the old Town Hill, that from its history and its associations, well deserves a title sometime given it, truly describing it an " American Shrine."

Little help had the people from Congress, lottery, or other public sources then feeble in means, but much, it seems, from their own good arms, and hearts, and heads. They had to work out their loss, £156,960, 18s. 8d., — a large sum at that period. And out they worked. In 1785 five hundred and fifty persons had one hundred and fifty-one buildings, wrote Dr. Bartlett. In 1783 a handsome meeting house had been built on " Town Hill." It was 72 feet long, 52 wide, had " an elegant steeple," " a bell of 1300 weight presented by Messrs. Champion, Dickason and Burgis, merchants of London," (three times recast, now in the tower), and a clock by Hon. Thomas Russell, (Dr. B.). Various manufactures that had flourished before 1775, were revived, " particularly * * of pot and pearl ashes," vessels, " rum, leather in all its branches, silver, tin, brass, and pewter," and still later, other kinds, and general trade were added. (Morse, 1797.)

Meanwhile the town's affairs were getting into print, and the account of publications about them, is continued. There does not appear to have been much to record before 1785, when the Printing Press was set up in Charlestown. More than one hundred and seventy books or pamphlets, some large, some small, all now rare, that came from it within fifty years, are hereafter mentioned. There seems little evidence that any considerable amount of literary treasure had been destroyed in the great conflagration. Ways of the world and the modern paper-mill have made more havoc among publications related to the town than did the " cruelest British."

MONOGRAPHS, AND LEGISLATIVE ACTS AND RESOLVES.

Works by residents, published before their stay in the town, are given under the first mentioned; published after, under the last, or under memorials at their deaths. Works published before or after a brief residence, and magazine or other articles not separately published, are, generally, not enumerated. Later editions, or Acts, are mentioned under the first described; serial publications at years of their commencement. The titles of many minor works are too long for insertion and are abbreviated. The size of all the following works is octavo unless otherwise specified.

Abbreviations. C. = Charlestown; ch. = chapter; Leg. = Legislature; Rep. Report; rep. = reprinted; sec. = section.

1781.

" AN ACT [Massachusetts Legislature, May 16] for the better Government and Regulation of the *Ferry between Boston and C.*; and for repealing the laws heretofore made for that Purpose."

" ———— [Do. Oct. 30] for widening and *amending the Streets, Lanes, and Squares,* in that Part of the Town of C., which was lately laid waste by Fire." Under this Act "the principal streets were widened, straightened and improved." See 1790.

[Orders to Capt. Parson's Co. on duty at C. 1781, see N. E. H. Gen. Reg. xxii., 454.]

1783.

WELSH, Dr. Thos. Oration at Boston, March 5, 1783, commemorative of the Boston Massacre. 4°. pp. 18.   *Boston,* 1783

Author b. C. 1751 ?; oration reprinted with others, sm. 8°. *Boston,* 1785. This year the Meeting house was built (see above), and King Solomon's Lodge was chartered (see 1785, 83, 93, 94, 96, 97).

1785.

" AN ACT [Mass. Leg. March 9] for incorporating certain Persons for the Purpose of building a *Bridge* over *Charles River* between *Boston and C.,* and supporting the same during the Term of forty Years." (See 1792).

The Corporators were John Hancock, Thos. Russell, Nath'l Gorham, Jas. Swan, and Eben Parsons. The bridge, a great work in its time. — "considered as the greatest" yet undertaken in the country. — was 1503 ft. long, 43 ft. wide; had 75 piers, 40 lamps, and a draw 30 ft wide. (B.) Its opening, June 17th, 1786, was "the first celebration of this anniversary" (Warren's B. H., 1877), conducted "with the greatest splendor and festivity" (B). It was the beginning of communication by bridge with the peninsula. A programme, now very rare, relates to the occasion. See Financial results, *Report,* 1827.

" AN ACT [Do. Nov. 29] in addition to an Act made in the Year 1772, entitled An Act to prevent the Destruction of *Oysters* in *Charles* and *Mistick Rivers.*" Repealed Feb. 26, 1795.

" THE *American Recorder,* AND THE CHARLESTOWN ADVERTISER. Published every Tuesday and Friday, by [John W.] ALLEN and [Thomas C.] CUSHING, at their Office, near the FERRY, in CHARLESTOWN." No. 1, Friday, Dec. 9, 1785, to No. 110, May 25, 1787, the last No. " A neat, small paper," [13½ × 8¼] in. pp. 4] * * * " the only newspaper issued from a press in the County of Middlesex." (Thomas Hist. Print., 1810). Nos. 1 and 2 contain " A Geographical Account of the Town of Charlestown, August 1, 1785."

Mr. Cushing, a native of Hingham, removed to Salem. See Streeter, (1856,) Pro. Essex Institute.

STILLMAN, Rev. Sam¹ Charity Considered, in a Sermon before the Society of Freemasons in C. June 24, 1785, pp. 19. *Boston,* [1785]

1786.

BARTLETT, Josiah, (P. M.) Oration at C. March 14, 1786, at the Dedication of Warren Hall, before the Hon. Soc. of Free and Accepted Masons. 12° (?) pp. 12. Printed by Allen and Cushing, *Charlestown*, 1786.

The first work in book or pamphlet form printed in the town [?]

1787.

" AN ACT [Mass. Leg. ch. 69, March 1] for incorporating certain persons, (Thos. Russell, Richard Devens, Sam¹ Swan, Jonathan Simpson, jr., and Wm. Tudor.) for the purpose of building a Bridge, where Penny-Ferry has been usually kept, and for supporting the same." (*Malden Bridge*).

Additional Acts, 1801, and chapter 218, Apr. 19, 1837. To make a new Draw, ch. 121, Apr. 1, 1851. Made free (Apr. 1, 1860), ch. 99, 1859. Support of, ch. 265, 1869. Malden Bridge was finished in six months, and cost £5,000. The property is vested in 120 shares. It is 2,400 feet long, including the abutments, 32 feet wide, has a convenient draw, and 8 lamps. (Dr. B.)

1788.

THACHER, Rev. Peter, (Brattle St., Boston). Sermon at the Funeral of *Joshua Paine, Jun.*, C., Feb. 29, 1788, pp. 21. *Boston*, 1788

Mr. Paine, eldest son of Rev. Joshua, Sturbridge, Worcester Co., in Nov. 1786, was unanimously called to C ch., was settled Jan. 10, 1787, first min. after rebuilding of the town, and died in the ministry Feb. 27, 1788, æ 25. " His sermons exhibited the Piety and Christianity of his Heart, and the exalted and social virtues of his mind, secured the Esteem and Friendship of all his acquaintance, and presented an agreeable prospect of his usefulness in the Ministry. He was sincerely lamented by all who knew him, and especially by the flock committed to his charge. His remains were decently and respectfully entomb'd at yᵉ expense of the Parish March 1, 1788." — *Church Records*.

1789.

"AN ACT [Mass. Leg., June 17] to enable the Town of C. to exchange a Part of the *Ministerial Lot* in said Town for an equal Quantity of other Land."

BELKNAP, Rev. Jeremy, (Federal St., Boston). " A Sermon, preached at the *Installation* of the *Rev. Jedidiah Morse*, A. M., to the Pastoral Care of the Church and Congregation in Charlestown, on the 30th of April, 1789," pp. 32. *Boston*, 1789

" Les citoyens J. Chas et Lebrun," in praise of eminent Americans (Hist. Politique, etc., Paris, An IX. (1801), express the following foreign estimate of the two above:— "M. M. Jedidiah, Morse, Belknev, Ramsay, sont des historiens savans et instruits; ils réunissent les talens et les graces du littérateur au goût, au sentiment et à l'amour de la vérité."

CARY, Richard. Letter to the Members of the Soc. for Propagating the Gospel among the Indians and others in N. A. 4°. pp. 9.
Boston, [1789]

1790.

" AN ACT [Mass. Leg. June 24] for the *Relief of the Town of C.*" (To extend the time for raising money by Lottery to pay for Streets, etc., Act 1781).

Morse, Rev. J.   A Sermon, Feb. 28, 1790, upon the Death of *Richard Cary*, Esq., of C., who died Feb. 7, Æ 73.   Pub. by particular desire.   4°.   pp. 27.   *Boston*, 1790

———— 1784, Geography made easy. With maps. 12°. pp. 214. *New Haven*, 1784.   A 2d ed., *Boston*, 1790 ; 5th ed., 12°., *Boston*, 1796 ; 10th, *Boston*, March, 1806 ; 15th, *Boston*, Aug., 1812.   12° from 16th Boston ed., *Troy*, 1814 ; another (by S. E. Morse) 1820.
" *The first Geography published in America*."

———— 1789.   The American Geography.   8°.   pp. 534 (3000 copies), *Elizabethtown* ; 2d. Am. ed. 1793 ; *London*, 1792 ; 2d. 4°. pp. 716, with 25 maps, *Stockdale* ; 3d. ed. 1798 (8°) ; also *Edinburgh, Dublin*, and several editions without acknowledgment of the Author.

———— 1790.   Abridgement of the American Geography.   12°. pp. 322, 1st and 2d ed's.   *Boston*, 1790 ; 10th ed. do. 1810 ; 14th ed. do. 1811 ; 15th, 1812.

" A Geography which has quite superseded all other 'Geographies' in this part of the world." (" The American "). *Blackwood's Mag.* xvii., 184 ; *American Writers* No. V., in *Milton* ii., 1374.   The last states that Dr. M.'s first work was an American Atlas, folio, London, 1775, (when he was 14 years old). The writer has not met this work.

———— A General Hist. of America, and of the late Revolution. Map.   12°.   *Philadelphia*, 1790

1792.

" An Act [Mass. Leg., March 9] for incorporating certain Persons for the Purpose of building a *Bridge* over *Charles River*, from the Westerly part of Boston to Cambridge, and for Extending the Interest of the Proprietors of *Charles-River Bridge* for a Term of Years."   *Other Acts*, see June 30, 1792 : March 28. 1793 ; Feb. 27, 1796 ; Feb. 6, 1800 ; June 20, 1803 ; March 2, 1804.

Holden, Oliver, "Teacher of Music in *Charlestown*."   " American Harmony : | containing, | A Variety of Airs, | Suitable for Divine Worship, on | Thanksgivings, Ordinations, Christmas, | Fasts, Funerals, and other Occasions | " etc.   14 pieces.   " Printed Typographically, at Boston, by Isaiah Thomas, and Ebenezer T. Andrews, Faust's Statue, No. 45 Newbury Street."   *Boston*, 1792
Printed from movable types, apparently a novelty then and there for music.

Hall, Prince.   Masonic Charge at C. June 25, 1792.   *Boston*
Morse, Rev. J.   The American Universal Geography.   2 vols.   8°. (I., Western Continent ; II., Eastern do.).   *Boston*, 1792

2d. ed. 2 vols. 8°, 11 maps, Boston, 1793; 3d. ed. Introduction by Sam'l Webber, 2 vols. 8°, 28 maps, Boston, 1796; 4th ed. (5,000 copies), 1801; 5th ed. (5,000), revised by Sam'l Webber, with 6 maps, and Atlas of the World (4°) with 63 maps. Price $12 50. Without the Atlas, $6.50, Boston, 1805; 6th ed. (5,000), "greatly altered, and with 290 add'l pages, 1812; 7th ed. 2 vols. 8°, Boston and Charlestown, 1819; ed. edited by S. E. Morse.

1793.

" An Act [Mass. Leg. March 27] to incorporate certain Persons by the Name of *The Trustees of Charlestown Free Schools*."   Additional Act March 4. 1800 ; amended ch. 25, Feb. 22, 1811, and Trustees increased from 7 to 11.

An Act [Do. June 22] for incorporating James Sullivan, Esquire, and
others, by the Name and Style of *The Proprietors of the Middlesex
Canal.* Additional Acts, Feb. 28, 1795; June 25, 1798; Jan. 25,
1800; March 2, 1803; ch. 113, 1813. See Works, 1813, 1843
(history). Forfeiting charter, Resolve, ch. 38, 1859; forfeited, ch.
203, 1860.

The terminus of this once important work was in C. The first officers were men
prominent in Boston and C. "The science of Civil Engineering was almost unknown
to any one in this part of the country, and * * many difficulties" were met with "for
the want of requisite scientific knowledge." The survey was completed Aug. 2, 1794;
the Canal, from the Charles to the Merrimac, was navigable in 1803. The income had
to be used for renewals, alterations, etc., "and no dividend could be or was declared until
Feb. 1, 1819." One hundred assessments were laid, Jan. 1794 to Sept. 1, 1819, making
each share cost, with interest, $1,455, and the whole work $1,164,200. Twenty-five
dividends were paid, the last Jan. 30, 1843, averaging 1 ½ per cent per year. In 1830
the Packet Boat left C. "near the B. Hill Tavern," at 8 A. M., and reached Chelms-
ford at 3 P. M. It was an hour by stage thence to Lowell. The railroad ruined the
business. (See Eddy, 1843.)

BARTLETT, Hon. Josiah, M. B. (C. 1759). A Discourse on the Ori-
    gin, Progress, and Design of Freemasonry. Delivered At the Meet-
    ing-House in C., on the Anniversary of St. John the Baptist, June
    24, A. D. 1793, pp. 20; also, A Charge delivered at C. (same day)
    to the Worshipful Master, the Wardens and Brethren of King Solo-
    mon's Lodge. By R. W. William Walter, D. D., pp. 21–31. 8°.
    pp. 31.   *Boston,* 1793
FREEMAN [Rev.] Jas.. Remarks on the American Universal Geog-
    raphy, by J. F., pp. 62. (See Morse, 1792.)   *Boston,* 1793
MORSE, Rev. J. "Tegenwoordige Staat | der | Vereenigde Staaten |
    van | Amerika; | behelzende : | een Algemeen verslag van derzel-
    ver | Grenzen, Meiren, Baaijen, Rivieren, | Bergen, Voortbrengze-
    len, Be- | volkinge, Regeering-form, | Landbouw, Koophandel, |
    Fabrieken, Nevens de | Historie van den | laatsten oorlog. | Door
    | JEDIDJAH MORSE. | Uit het Engelsch." 4 vols. 8°.
                        Pieter den Hengst, *Amsterdam,* 1793–96
TAPPAN. Rev. David (Hollis Prof. Har. Col.). Sermon at C. Apr. 11,
    1793 (Mass. Fast), pp. 31.   *Boston,* 1793

1794.

BARTLETT, Hon. Josiah, M. B. Oration delivered at the Meeting-
House in C. June 17, 1794, before the Artillery Company, pp. 15.
                        Benjamin Edes. *Boston,* 1795
The first " Seventeenth of June" Celebration with an Oration.
BARTLETT, Hon. Josiah, M. D. Oration Dec. 2, 1794, with Address
    of John Soley at Dedication of the Monument on Breed's Hill
    erected by King Solomon's Lodge.
MORSE, Rev. J. The American Geography, etc. 4°. pp. 716, 25
    maps.   Stockdale, *London,* 1794

Since 1784 (in May, 1794), 28,600 copies of Dr. Morse's Geographical works were published in America. (Dr. M. to Prof. Ebeling.)

1795.

DEVENS, Richard. A Paraphrase on some parts of the Book of Job, pp. 39. (See 1797.) *Boston*, 1795

HOLDEN, O. Practical Elements of Music. 4°. *Boston*, 1795

MORSE, Rev. J. "The present Situation of other Nations of the World, contrasted with our own. A Sermon delivered at Charlestown," Feb. 19, 1795, a Public Thanksgiving, pp. 37. *Boston*, 1795

———— Elements of Geography. 12°. *Boston*, 1795

2d ed., 2 maps, 24°, Boston, 1796 ("new and corrected" ed. 8°, Edinburgh, 1795); 3d ed., Improved, 2 maps. 12°. pp. 144. Boston, Feb. 1798.

TAPPAN, Rev. D. A Sermon at C. Feb. 19, 1795, "The Day of General Thanksgiving through the United States." pp. 40.
Boston, 1795

TUCKER, Hon. St. George (Va.). A Letter to the Rev. Jed. Morse, A. M., Author of the "American Universal Geography," pp. 16.
Richmond, 1795

1796.

AN ACT [Mass. Leg. Feb. 2] for the *Preservation* of a *Monument* erected on the *Heights of Charlestown.*"

HARRIS, Rev. Thaddeus Mason. "Masonic Emblems Explained. A Discourse delivered before the Officers and Members of King Solomon's Lodge in C. June 24, 1796, being the Festival of St. John the Baptist." pp. 24. *Boston*, 1796

C. 1768-1842, minister Dorchester 1793-1839. See 1783. He was a very voluminous author. For a nearly full *list of his works see Mass. Hist. Soc. Colls.*, IV., ii., 154. The above was reprinted C. 1801.

MORSE, Rev. J. The Duty of Resignation under Afflictions. * * "A Sermon preached at C. April 17, 1796. Occasioned by the Death of the *Hon. Thomas Russell*, Esq., who died in Boston, Ap. 8, Æ. 56." 4°. pp. 31. *Boston*, 1796

The above, and Burlington, 242-5 (1845), contain full and valuable notes on the distinguished family of Russell.

THACHER, Rev. Peter. Ser. at C. June 19, 1796, occasioned by the sudden death of the *Hon. Nathaniel Gorham*, Esq., Æt. 59. pp. 25.
Boston, 1796

———— Ser. in Brattle St. ch. Boston, Apr. 17, 1796, on the Death of *Hon. Thomas Russell*, Esq., pp. 32. *Boston*, 1796

WARREN, John, M. D. An Eulogy on the *Hon. Thomas Russell*, Esq., etc., delivered May 4, 1796, before the several Societies to which he belonged, in the ch. in Brattle St. 4°. pp. 31, with a Monody set to Music by Hans Gram, pp. 3. *Boston*, 1796

WELSH, Thos. M. D. "An Eulogy, delivered June 29, 1796, at the Meeting-House in C. * * * In Memory of the *Honourable Nathaniel Gorham*, Esquire, who died June 11, 1796, pp. 16. With a Dirge by Rev. T. M. Harris, set to music by O. Holden. *Boston*, 1796

Messrs. Gorham and Russell were two of the most distinguished natives of the town, at any period, and greatly respected. Drs. Welsh and Harris were also distinguished natives, and Mr. Holden was long an active resident, prominent in Music and in the Baptist Church.

1797.

BARTLETT, Hon. J. Address at Warren Hall before King Solomon's Lodge, C. Feb. 22, 1797, with prayer by Rev. J. Morse. pp. 12.   Printed by John Lamson, *Charlestown*, 1797

CARY, Rev. Thomas. A Sermon at C. July 23, 1797. Published at the request of the Hearers, to whom it is respectfully inscribed. pp. 24.   Printed by John Lamson, *Charlestown*, [1797]

C. 1745–1808, minister Newburyport. Two Sermons at N—. 12°. *Boston*, 1773. Ser. Death Rev. S. Webster (Salisbury). 8°. pp. 32. 1801, Ser. at N. Sep. 27, 1801, last service old M-Ho. 8°. pp. 28. See 1768 and 1808.

DEVENS, Richard, Jr., A. M. A Discourse composed for and delivered to the Students in Divinity, at the College in Princeton, N. J., in the year 1777. 8°. pp. 16. (See 1795.) Printed by J. Lamson, near the Bridge.   *Charlestown*, 1797

MORSE, Rev. J. The American Gazetteer, etc. 8°. pp. 600. 7 maps. *Boston*, 1797. 2d ed. 8°. Boston, 1804; 3d ed. 8°. Boston, 1810. (See 1802)

"There is no work within our knowledge that conveys so accurate a picture of what this country was at the period immediately succeeding the Revolution. The names of all the Indian Tribes on the vast frontiers, their numbers and situation, are given with apparent care and accuracy." (S. G. Drake, Sep. 1874.)

RUSSELL, John Miller (C. 1768–1840, son of Hon. T.). Oration at C., July 4, 1797, pp. 16.   *Charlestown*, 1797
——— The same, 2d ed., pp. 15.   *Philadelphia*, 1797

The earliest "Fourth of July" Oration in C. During the first half-century of Am. Ind. similar orations were often delivered and printed. The observance declined or disappeared in many minor places after that period. Twelve orations in C. will be found in this list.

1798.

[AUSTIN, Wm.] Strictures on Harvard University. By a Senior. 12°. pp. 35.   *Boston*, 1798

He was long a resident in C. (H. C. 1798); his style was vigorous.

MORSE, Rev. J. "The Character and Reward of a Good and Faithful Servant illustrated in a Sermon, del. at C. Apr. 29, 1798 * * on *Hon. James Russell*, Esq., who died Apr. 24, Æ. 83. pp. 21.
     Boston, 1798
——— National Fast Ser. May 9, 1798, pp. 29 + 1.   *Boston*, 1798
——— Masonic Ser. at Concord (Mass.) June 25, 1798.
     Leominster, 1798
——— Thanksgiving Ser. at C. Nov. 29, 1798. With an Appendix "exhibiting proofs of the early existence, progress, and deleterious effects of French intrigue and influence in the United States, pp. 79. Published by request.   *Boston*, 1798

1st ed. 1500 copies; 2d ed. 1799. A copy was sent gratuitously by friends to every clergyman in Mass. The work is now scarce.

——— The American Gazetteer, abridged. 12°.   *Boston*, 1798
TAPPAN, Rev. D. Fast Ser. to the Christian Congregation in C., Apr. 5. pp. 31.   *Boston*, 1798

"THE | WORKS | of the late | Dr. Benjamin Franklin. | Consisting of his | LIFE. | written by himself. | Together with | ESSAYS. | Humourous, Moral, and Literary. | chiefly in the manner of the | Spectator. | CHARLESTOWN : | Printed by John Lamson, | for the Principal Booksellers, | in Boston. | 1798." With a portrait of Dr. F. 2 vols in 1. Small 12° size. pp. 300.
The first book and plate engraving printed in C. (?)

1799.

A PRAYER *and* SERMON by Rev. J. Morse, C. Dec. 31, 1799, on the Death of *George Washington*, with a Sketch of his Life ; and Proceedings of the Town by Josiah Bartlett, Esq. pp. 46 + 36 + W.'s Farewell Address 24. *Charlestown*, 1800
——— The same, reprinted, pp. 44 + 36. *London*, 1800

This was one of the few among the numerous Washington eulogies reprinted in England. The Life, etc. were also reprinted in Baltimore, 1800, and sumptuously in 4°, New York, 1835. The 1st (C.) edition was printed at the expense of the town, each family of which was furnished with a copy. It is now rare, — very few copies could be found in C. *Charlestown*, Dec. 31, 1799, "in but seventeen days from the" death of Washington, "was the first town in Massachusetts, and I believe in the United States, that instituted publick funeral honours" on his death. (Dr. B.) "The procession consisted of the male inhabitants, from seven years of age and upwards," 621 persons, including the Magistrates, lodge of Free-Masons, and three military "Companies in uniform. The stores and shops were shut; the flags on the vessels and on shore were displayed *half staff* high, and minute guns were fired from *Breed's* hill. The meeting house was shrouded in black." The procession moved "by a solemn knell, and agonizing peals of cannon to the house of prayer." For a full account see B. H. Aurora, Nov. 10, 1838.

HURD, Isaac, M. D. Discourse in Boston, June 11, 1799, before the Humane Society of Mass. With an Appendix. 4°. pp. 23. *Boston*, 1799
Born C. 1756, physician, Concord.

MORSE, Rev. J. Sermon on the Present Dangers and Duties of the Citizens of the United States. National Fast, Apr. 25, 1799. With Notes in French and English. pp. 50, 2 woodcuts.
Charlestown, 1799

Also N. Y., 1799. This work relates to French Illuminatism (mockery of the holy Supper), and contains a Table of Brethren of Lodge No. 2660, in Portsmouth, Va.

——— Address to the Students of Phillips Academy, Andover, Anniversary Exhibition, July 9, 1799, pp. 16. *Charlestown*, 1799

1800.

AN ACT [Mass. Leg., March 4] " to empower the Selectmen of the Towns of Boston and C., to increase the Number of *Engine-Men* in said Towns and for other Purposes " (see Gen. Act, Feb. 7, 1786).
——— [Do. *June* 17, ch. 26.] " authorizing the *United States* to *purchase* a certain Tract of *Land* in C. for a *Navy Yard*."

Add'l Act, June 18, 1825, ch. 8. Special Laws, vol. 2, p. 506. Ceding Jurisdiction of certain lands in C. to U. S., ch. 195, 1862, and ch. 35, 1867; 249, 1868. The B. H. Aurora (Oct. 27 and Nov. 3, 1838) contains the Town Record with the full instructions by a committee " in the name of the town," to Aaron Putnam, Esq., "who was chosen to repair to the Seat of Government, respecting the Navy and Dockyard," *April, 1800.*

These show that a proposed site at Noddle's Island would be "almost as injurious to this town as a second conflagration. * * * * If [they add] the situation we propose is as good as any other, it may not be amiss to invite ... attention to our unequalled Sufferings in the late revolutionary war: the embarrassments we still experience in consequence ... the want of success in our early application for some compensation * * * the labor * * by which we * * are now enabled by 24 years' industrious application * * to sustain a decent rank with our fellow citizens at large." While the town endeavored to secure the yard, the land-owners asked $73,200 for what sworn appraisers valued at $15,180. — John Harris holding his lot at over eleven times the appraisal. (*Town Rec.* above.) "Between 40 and 50 acres" were ceded to the U. S. by the Leg., "valued by a Jury at $37,280." (*Dr. B.*) A Marine Hospital was erected in 1804. A noble Dry Dock, built of granite, was opened June, 1833. It cost $670,089. (*Barber.*) See Baldwin, 1834. Many large and substantial buildings have at various dates been added.

RESOLVE. Do. 68, Jan. 22, 1800, to appoint a Com. to select and procure land in C. for *State Prison.* Do. 54, June 23, 1802, appointing Com., His Honor Edw. H. Robbins, Hon. Peleg Coffin, and Jonathan Hunnewell, Esq. to carry No. 68 into effect, granting $70,000. Do. 54, June 22, 1803, Chas. Bulfinch, Esq., added to Com. Do. 108, Feb. 23, 1804, Com. appointed (Hon. Sam¹ Sewall, Nathan Dane, Esq.), to establish a proper system for, etc. See Do. 56, 57, in June 1804. *See Account of, 1806.*

BARTLETT, Hon. J. An Oration on the Death of Gen. George Washington, delivered at the request of the Selectmen and Parish Committee before the Inhabitants of C. Feb. 22, 1800, "being the day set apart by the Congress of the United States, to testify the Grief of the Citizens, on that melancholy event." pp. 15.

Charlestown, 1800

This day "was suitably noticed by the town. A procession was formed similar to" that Dec. 31, 1799. (Dr. B.)

HOLDEN, O. "Plain Psalmody, or Supplementary Music," etc. 70 tunes and an Anthem. Ob. 8°. pp. 72. *Boston*, Nov. 1800

Contains (pp. 52-55) Anthem, Ps. 48, "Composed for the Dedication of the New Meeting-House in Charlestown" (1st Baptist, see 1801).

———— Sacred Dirges, Hymns, and Anthems, commemorative of the Death of Gen. Geo. Washington, "by a Citizen of Mass." Ob. 4°. pp. 24. Nine pieces with words and music. *Boston*, [1800]

[MORSE, Rev. J.] A Descriptive and Historical Account of the Isles of Shoals. Mass. Hist. Soc. Collections for 1800, vol. vii. pp. 242-61.

1801.

AUSTIN, William. Oration before the Artillery Company. C. June 17, 1801. pp. 29. (*3d Celebration with Oration.*) *Charlestown*, 1801

HARRIS, Rev. T. M. "Discourses, [12] Delivered on Public Occasions. | Illustrating the Principles, Displaying | the Tendency, and Vindicating | the Design, | of | Free Masonry. | By Thaddeus Mason Harris, | Past Grand Chaplain to the Grand Lodge, | and | Chaplain to the Grand Royal Arch Chapter | of Massachusetts." | [All in capitals.] Printer's mark. "Printed at Charlestown, | By Samuel Etheridge. | (*Copyright secured.*) | Anno Lucis, | 5801." Eng. frontispiece. 8°. pp. 328. [*Charlestown*, 1801]

Contains, also, Masonic Eulogy, Worcester, 1794; Charge, 1795; two other Charges; three Degrees; two Addresses; Fraternal Tribute to Masonic Character of Washington, Dorchester, Jan. 7, 1800 (pub. C. 8°, pp. 13, 1800); three Poems, and Dissertation on the Tessera Hospitalis. Now very rare. *The first octavo volume printed in Charlestown* [?]. For notice of the Printer, see Appendix.

HARRIS, Rev. T. M. A Tribute of Filial Respect to the Memory of his mother, *Rebecca (Mason) Harris* (C. 1738). Discourse at Dorchester, Feb. 8, 1801. pp. 20. *Charlestown*, 1801

MORSE, Rev. J. Sermon before the Humane Society of Massachusetts, June 9, 1801, pp. 53. *Boston*, 1801

———— Revised edition of the Earl of Chesterfield's Elements of a Polite Education, selected from his Letters to his Son. 12°.
Boston, 1801

Article "New England" in Sup. Am. ed. "Encyclopedia Brittanica," developed to Hist. of N. E. See 1804.
Five Articles in the Boston Independent Chronicle (Ebeling letter controversy); see also National Intelligencer, American Mercury Sept. 26, 1799, and Mass. Spy (Worcester) Oct. 9, 1799. The Mercury and New England Palladium, No. 1, Jan. 2. Dr. Morse was actively engaged in the establishment of this paper.

STILLMAN, Rev. Sam¹ "A Discourse, delivered at the Opening of the New Baptist Meeting-House in Charlestown, May 12, 1801." Also a Dedicatory Hymn, Address by J. Morse, D. D., and Recognition Address by Thos. Baldwin, A. M. pp. 31. (For Music of Anthem, see *Holden*, 1800.) *Boston*, [1801]

The First Church had continued substantially the only one in C. until this was organized Sept. 16, 1800, by eleven members (see *History, 1875*). They began Oct. 1, with small means, to build a Meeting-house, which was 65 ft. long, 50 wide, 29 high, and had a cupola and bell. (*Dr. B.*) The Church Records begin March 31, 1801.

1802.

AN ACT [Mass. Leg., Mar. 6] for Incorporating certain Persons for the Purpose of laying out and making a Turnpike Road from *Salem* to *Charles River* Bridge, etc. (*Chelsea Bridge*).

Additional Acts, Feb. 26 and June 18, 1804; June 18, 1825; to make a new draw, etc., ch. 124, Apr. 1, 1853; made a public highway, ch. 309 and ch. 335, 1858. This bridge, built in 1803, had 2 draws and cost $54,000, held in 2,400 shares. It was to revert to the State in 70 years. (*Dr. B.*)

———— to set off Nathaniel Prentiss and others from the Town of C.
* * * and annex them to Cambridge.

MORSE, Rev. J. (and Rev. Elijah Parrish). "A New Gazetteer of the Eastern Continent," etc., "designed as a second volume to the American Gazetteer." Thick 8°. Unpaged. 18 maps.
Charlestown, 1802

The List of Subscribers is very long and remarkable, and for nearly 1,700 copies widely distributed. 2d ed., 1808. See also 1824.

———— and friends, chiefly in the 1st Parish, Nineteen Religious Tracts for general distribution, of which 32,600 copies were circulated. (See *Sprague's Life*, pp. 278–9.)

"There can be little doubt, I think that in 1802, the pastor and people of the First Parish in Charlestown had done more in circulating religious tracts among the poor and destitute in the United States than any other people in New England."—*S. F. Morse, 1867*. In 1802, S. Etheridge printed several tracts in C., probably these.

STILLMAN, Rev. S. A Sermon at C. Oct. 7, 1802, at the Instalment of the Rev. Thomas Waterman as pastor of the Baptist Ch. Also Ch. by Rev. Mr. Baldwin, and Ad. by Mod. of the Council. pp. 28.
Boston, 1802

Mr. Waterman was the first minister of the Baptist Ch. in C., and settled 8 months.

1803.

AN ACT [Mass. Leg., March 2] for incorporating certain persons for the Purpose of laying out and making a *Turnpike* Road from *Medford to C. Neck*, etc.

——— [Mass. Leg., ch. 107, March 5] " to incorporate a Religious Society, by the Name of *The First Parish in the Town of Charlestown*."

Additional Acts, ch. 146 Feb. 28, 1812; ch. 8, June 15, 1822; ch. 27, March 5, 1835, With this Parish belongs the *First Church*, founded 1630, reorganized 1632, and now occupying the original site of the first established worship in this region. See Budington, 1845, Records, 1880.

MORSE, Rev. J. Mass. Artillery Election Sermon, Boston, June 6, 1803, with notes. pp. 32.   *Charlestown*, 1803

——— Sermon at the Ordination of Rev. Hezekiah May, Marblehead, June 23, 1803 (inc. Ch. and R. H.). pp. 32.
Charlestown, 1803

1804.

AUSTIN, WM. " Letters [40] from London: written during the years 1802 and 1803," 8°. pp. 312.   *Boston*, 1804

MORSE, Rev. J. (and Rev. E. Parish). "A Compendious History of New England, designed for Schools and Private Families. Ornamented with a neat map." 12°. pp. 388.   *Charlestown*, 1804

2d ed. 12°, map. Printed at Amherst (N. H.), and published at Newburyport by Thomas and Whipple, Proprietors of the Work. Price, 1.12½, 1808; 3d ed., Charlestown. 12°. pp. 424. 1820. Also London, 1808.

RAND, Isaac, M. D. Observations on Phthisis Pulmonalis, etc.; read at request of Mass. Med. Soc., June 6, 1804. pp. 24.
Boston, 1804

Reprinted, Boston, 1853. Dr. R. born C. 1743, d 1822.

1805.

AN ACT [Mass. Leg., June 15] to provide Regulations for the *State Prison*. See 1806.

In Oct. following, a Board of Visitors was appointed; its first meeting, Nov. 7, "at the Charlestown Hotel."

GLEASON, Benj. Oration pronounced at the Request of the " Charlestown Light Infantry " before the Republican Citizens of Charlestown, July 4th, 1805. pp. 24. Two editions.   *Boston*, 1805

Mr. Gleason, a popular orator in the earlier part of this century, lived in C. (Dr. B.) His numerous publications (pamphlets) have almost disappeared. Also by him, before 1805: Oration at Wrentham (Mass.) Feb. 22, 1800, on the Death of George Washington. 8°. *Wrentham*, 1800. Address at Providence, R. I., June 24, 1802. 8°. *Boston*, 1802. Masonic Address at Reading (Mass.), June 24, 1805. Two editions, *Boston*, 1805.

PUTNAM, Aaron Hall. An Oration pronounced July 4, 1805, at the Request of the Federal Republicans of the Town of C. pp. 18.
Charlestown, 1805

Mr. Putnam was a resident of C. (Dr. B.)

MORSE, Rev. J. The true reasons on which the Election of a Hollis Professor of Divinity in Harvard College was opposed, Feb. 14, 1805. pp. 28.   *Charlestown*, 1805

STATE Prison (Mass.). N. Dane and S. Sewall, Communication to the Legislature; with Bills for the Regulation of the State Prison. pp. 64. *Boston*, 1805

1806.

"AN ACT [Mass. Leg., ch. 70, Mch. 7] to incorporate the *Trustees* of the Charlestown *Charity Fund*."

————— [Do. Mch. 14] "providing for the *Regulation of the State Prison* in Charlestown." See 1811.

————— [Do. June 21] to incorporate the Proprietors of Prison Point Dam Corporation.

COLLIER, Rev. Wm. Sanctuary Waters; or the Spread of the Gospel: Sermon before the Mass. Baptist Missionary Ass'n, Anniversary Meeting, Boston, May 28, 1806. pp. 31. *Boston*, 1806

GLEASON, Benj. Oration before the Bristol Lodge, Norton, June 24, 1806, pp. 22. *Boston*, 1806

MORSE, Rev. J. Sermon at C. on the Sabbath after Interment of *Miss Mary Russell*, who died July 24, 1806, Æ. 53. pp. 18. Printed by J. Howe, n. p. 1806.

————— Sole Editor of "*The Panoplist*," 1806–11 (vols. 1–6), the great early Foreign Missionary organ, predecessor of the Missionary Herald.

"MASS. STATE Prison, Account of the; containing a Description [large plate, an elevation], Plan of the Edifice; The Law, Regulations, Rules and Orders; with a View of the Present State of the Institution. By the Board of Visitors." pp. 48.
Charlestown, 1806

In this work, and two publications mentioned 1811, 1816,—all now very scarce,—will be found three illustrative folding plates and descriptions of the Prison. They state that this structure, with "about 5 acres of ground, including extensive flats," cost "about $170,000. * * Competent judges pronounce" it "to be one of the strongest and best prisons in the world." It was "built of hewn stone" during 1804-5, in "a pleasant and healthful situation, commanding an extensive, rich, and variegated prospect." The main building was 200 ft. long, 28 to 44 wide, and 4 and 5 stories high. The first floor was formed by "a tier of hewn stone, 9 feet long, and 20 inches thick." The work yard was 375 by 260 feet, the building containing workshops, kitchen, chapel, etc., was of brick, 227 by 25 feet, with 2 stories and a basement. Dec. 12, 1805, the first two convicts were received, and by end of 1805, thirty-four. Dr. Bartlett (1814) wrote of the Canal, Navy Yard, and Prison, "we cherish a belief that these * * will be so estimated and conducted, as to answer the publick expectations, and promote the happiness of the town."

1807.

AUSTIN, Wm. An Essay on the Human Character of Jesus Christ. Sm. 8°. pp. 120. *Boston*, 1807

————— "Peter Rugg, The Missing Man," a story very popular during the earlier part of the Century, (first in the "Literary Repository," Boston?) also in "The Boston Book," pp. 28-73, 1841. The writer has not seen it as a separate volume. Also, "Martha Gardner, or Moral Reaction," in N. E. Magazine (?). These are two of the earliest published tales written in C.

GLEASON, Benj. Address, Mason's Hall, Mt. Lebanon Lodge, at Boston, Aug. 11. 8°. pp. 16. Oration at Hingham (Mass.), July 4. Two editions. 8°. *Boston*, 1807

MORSE, Rev. J. Sermon before the Managers of the Boston Female Asylum, Sept. 25, 1807, in Brattle St. ch., pp. 23, and Statement, 1 page. [*Boston*,] 1807

1808.

ANDREWS. Rev. J. A Sermon. Nov. 26, 1808, at the Interment of *Rev. Thos. Cary*, Newburyport, pp. 31. Appendix, pp. 15. (See 1768, 1797.) *Newburyport*, 1808

BROADSIDE, "To the Citizens of Charlestown," with " Extracts from the Payroles, for ten years, commencing in June," chiefly of payments to Representatives to the General Court. " Russell and Cutler, Printers."

MALDEN Bridge, Rules and Regulations of the Corporation of, July, 1808. 16°. pp. 9. (See 1829.) *Charlestown*, 1808

MORSE. Rev. J. Sermon, May 18, 1808, at Ordination of Rev. Joshua Huntington, Marlborough St. Ch., Boston. pp. 32.
Boston, 1808

—— Discourse at the African Meeting-House in Boston, July 14, 1808, in Grateful Celebration of the Abolition of the African Slave Trade, by the Governments of the U. S., Great Britain, and Denmark. pp. 28. Two editions. *Boston*, 1808

—— R. Hand. of Fellowship, Ord. of Rev. E. Pearson, Andover, Sept. 28. In 8°, pp. 39, Boston, 1808, with Dr. Timothy Dwight's Sermon.

1809.

COLLIER. Rev. Wm. Evangelicana ; or Gospel Treasury, containing a great variety of interesting anecdotes, remarkable providences, and precious fragments, selected chiefly from the London Evangelical Magazine. 4 vols. 12°.
Boston, Hastings, Etheridge, and Bliss, 1809
2d ed., 4 vols. 12°. Charlestown, 1810-11.

GLEASON, Benj. Oration at C. July 5, 1809. *Charlestown*, 1809

SOUTHACK, J. Life of, written by himself ; with History of the State Prison in C. 12°. pp. 119.
Printed for the Author, no place, 1809

1810.

" AN ACT 'Mass. Leg., Feb. 15 for the better security of the Town of C. *against fire*." Additional Act, ch. 49, 1821. Repealed, ch. 25, 1824.

BALFOUR. Rev. Walter (in C. 1811–52). Some Observations on searching the Scriptures. 12° size. pp. 72.
Jonathan Howe, *Charlestown*, 1810

BARTLETT, Hon. J. Dissertation on the Progress of Medical Science in Mass. Read before the Mass. Medical Soc. June 6, 1810, pp. 48.
Boston, 1810

" With alterations and additions to Jan. 1, 1813," in M. H. Soc. Coll's, vol. xi.

BROWN, John H. Court Martial at C., Mass., Aug. 14, 1810, upon the Charges of Lot Pool against him. pp. 131. *Charlestown*, 1810

MORSE, Rev. J. Signs of the Times : Ser. at Boston, Nov. 1, 1810. before the Society for Propagating the Gospel among the Indians and others. With an Appendix. pp. 72. *Charlestown*, 1810

" Statement of the Expenses of the Town of Charlestown from May, 1809 to May, 1810 ; " dated April 21, 1810, and signed David Devens, Town Treasurer. *A Broadside*, the *first printed Annual Report of Town expenses*, in a Collection, perhaps unique, in the Public Library of C., formed and presented by Mr. H. K. Frothingham. This style of publication was continued through 1823. A pamphlet form was then adopted. In order to show together the sum total figures of these early and rare Reports, all the Broadsides are mentioned under this date. The titles to all are similar to that quoted above. The sizes gradually increase.

				Appropriations.	Expenditures.
1810.	May 1809 to May	1810.		$ 8,360,00	$ 7,269.60
1812.	" 1811 " "	1812.		12,380.00	11,342.16
1814.	" 1813 end April 1814.			9,830.00	11,527.36
1815.	" 1814 " "	1815.		12,870.00	13,392.84
1816.	" 1815 " "	1816.		14,817.00	13,492.13
1817.	" 1816 " "	1817.		14,900.01	16,368.90
1818.	" 1817 " "	1818.		13,448.90	14,032.12
1819.	" 1818 " "	1819.		21,939.00	22,342.68
1820.	" 1819 " "	1820.		21,359.00	23,120.70
1821.*	" 1820 " "	1821.		18,489.15	17,213.83
1822.*	" 1821 " "	1822.		16,100.00	17,613.62
1823.*	" 1822 " "	1823.		17,086.00	17,718.18

For the next annual report see 1824.
* A Broadside Statement of Overseers of the Poor was published in each of these years, which see.

1811.

" An Act, [Mass. Leg. ch. 100, Feb. 27] to incorporate Moses Hall and others into a religious Society by the name of the *First Universalist Society* in C.

Dr. Bartlett states that " A Universal meeting-house, 62 feet long, 62 feet wide, and 34 feet high, was built with brick in 1810. It is commodious and handsomely finished." The third prominent Religious Society in C., and still occupying its early site near " Thompson Square."

———— [Do. June 21] to annex Peter Tufts and a part of his Estate to C.

———— [Do. do., ch. 32] providing for the Government and Regulation of the *State Prison*. See 1800, 1805, 1806 ; June 16, 1813, (47) March 1, 1815. Subject continued 1857.

Collier, Rev. W. The Evangelical Instructor ; designed for the use of Schools and Families. 12°. *Charlestown*, 1811

Kneeland, Rev. Abner, Universalist Ch. 1811–14, several works 1804–44. He was an editor (1811 and after) of the Gospel Visitant. 8° quarterly, the first regular Universalist periodical in the U. S., published at Salem. The no. for March, 1812, at C. (See *Streeter*, Salem press (1856), p. 23.)

Lathrop, John, jun. Address before King Solomon's Lodge, C. June 24, 1811. pp. 23. *Boston*, 1811

Lyman, Rev. Jos., D. D. (Hatfield, Mass.). Sermon on the Saviour, First Ch. C., Nov. 3, 1811. pp. 23. S. T. Armstrong. *Boston*, 1811

Massachusetts State Prison, Rules and Regulations for the Government of the. By the Board of Directors. With a description of the Edifice (3 folding plates), Remarks on the Present State of, etc. pp. 23. *Boston*, 1811

1812.

COLLIER, Rev. W. A New Selection of Hymns, designed as a Supplement to Dr. Watts's Psalms and Hymns. 12°. *Boston*, 1812

EVARTS, J. Oration at C., July 4, 1812. pp. 32. *Charlestown*, 1812

GLEASON, Benj. Masonic Oration June 24, 1812, at Montreal, L. C. Two editions. 8°. *Boston*, 1812

LOWELL, Rev. Chas. Sermon at the State Prison, Nov. 29, 1812. 12°. pp. 14. *Boston*, 1812

Reprinted (No. IV.) in Sermons. 12°. Boston, 1855.

MORSE, Rev. J. A Sermon at C., July 23, 1812, on State Fast at Declaration of War with Great Britain. In Two Parts. pp. 32. Published at the request of the hearers. *Charlestown*, 1812

————— A Sermon before the Convention of Congregational Ministers in Boston, at Anniversary Meeting, May 28, 1812. *Boston*, 1812

1813.

" EXPENSES *and Funds of the Charlestown Free Schools.*" for 1812, dated April 22, 1813, and signed Nehemiah Wyman, Treasurer to the Trustees. A Report made " Conformably to a Vote of the Town, passed July 30, 1812." *A Broadside, the first printed annual Statement of the expenses of the Schools.* This, and the following to 1823 inclusive, are in the Collection in the Public Library mentioned under 1810, and are similarly arranged. The titles or headings, except dates, are like that above. The size is that of a medium 4° leaf.

				Receipts.	Expenditures.	Trustees' Funds.
1812,	dated	April	22, 1813.	$3,824.96	$3,462.20	$5,085.94
1813,	"	"	23, 1814.	4,145.36	4,137.00	5,081.85
1814,	"	"	23, 1815.	4,821.07	4,722.04	5,085.94
1815,	"	"	24, 1816.	5,117.03	4,845.01	5,001.50
1816,	"	"	—, 1817.		wanting.	
1817,	"	"	21, 1818.	4,535.50	2,755.05	5,001.50
1818,	"	"	12, 1819.	4,987.24	5,059.05	5,001.50
1819,	"	"	19, 1820.	4,572.09	4,372.09	5,001.50
1820,	"	"	28, 1821.	3,627.49	3,812.56	5,001.50
1821,	"	"	10, 1822.	4,449.42	4,177.35	5,001.50
1822,	"	"	—, 1824.	3,846.17	3,454.44*	5,001.50

* In April, 1823, all bills had not been presented.
For the next annual report, see 1825, in 8° then and afterward.

" AN ACT [Mass. Leg., ch. 63, June 16] to incorporate Sundry persons in C. in the Co. of Middlesex, by the name of *The Washington Hall Association.*" See Bartlett, 1814.

BALDWIN, Rev. Thos. A Sermon at C., Sept. 26, 1813, occasioned by the Death of *Mrs. Abigail*, wife of Rev. Wm. *Collier*, pastor First Baptist Ch. in C. With her diary, etc. pp. 32. *Boston*, 1813

BALFOUR, Rev. W. Support of religious teachers considered. 8°. *Charlestown*, 1813

BARTLETT, Hon. J. Address before the C. Branch of the Washington Benevolent Society of Mass., Feb. 22. With an Ode by Henry Small, List of Officers, etc. pp. 15. *Charlestown*, 1813

THE CHARLESTOWN Association for the Reformation of Morals: Discourse at Organization (May) by Rev. J. Morse, D. D.; Constitution and List of Officers and Members; Rules, etc.; Laws of Mass. for Suppression of Vice. 12°. pp. 48. *Boston*, 1813

The Preface states that "some late occurrences having attracted the attention of many respectable citizens of this town to the state of morals among the children and youth, it was found that extraordinary means were necessary to guard the rising generation." Of the Soc., Dr. Morse (1st Ch.), was chairman: Dea. D. Goodwin (Baptist), Treas.; Rev. Mr. Collier (Baptist), Rev. A. Kneeland (Univ.), Deacons J. Carter, T. Miller, M. Hall, A. Tufts, and 18 others, Standing Committee. Names of 99 members, showing all classes and beliefs, are given. See Circular Letter of this Soc., Panoplist, Dec., 1813. Similar Societies were formed in Newburyport and other towns.

GLEASON, Benj. Oration before the Republican Citizens of C., July 5, 1813. pp. 16. *Boston*, 1813

SULLIVAN, John L. Remarks on the Importance of Inland Navigation from Boston by the Middlesex Canal, etc. pp. 22.

Boston, 1813

Also, Letters in Answer to Inquiries relating to, etc., 1818; Reports on the Canal, 1805, 1809, 1811, 1812, etc., and several pamphlets on other Canals.

1814.

" AN ACT [Mass. Leg., Feb. 18] to provide for the safe *keeping* of *Gunpowder* in the town of C."

ADAMS, Hannah. " A Narrative of the Controversy between the Rev. Jedidiah Morse, D. D., and the Author." pp. 31. " Some Notice of the Remarks on S. Higginson, jun., contained in Dr. Morse's Appeal to the Publick," by Stephen Higginson, jun. pp. 3. . " Review of Dr. Morse's " Appeal to the Publick," principally with reference to that part of it which relates to Harvard College. By a friend of that college [John Lowell]." pp. 42. 1 vol.

Boston, 1814

" REMARKS on the Controversy between Doctor Morse and Miss Adams, together with Some Notice of the Review of Dr. Morse's Appeal." pp. 33. Two editions. *Boston*, 1814

Defence of Dr. M., and a pretty strong one : see pages 6, 7, etc.

MORSE, Rev. J. " An Appeal to the Public, on the Controversy respecting the Revolution in Harvard College, and the Events which have followed it ; occasioned by the use which has been made of certain Complaints and Accusations of Miss Hannah Adams, against the Author." pp. 192. *Charlestown*, 1814

This long, intricate, and unhappy controversy, treated in the above works, included a charge of literary piracy by Miss A. against Dr. M., and severe censure of him, together with some of the theological strife of the times. "The charge was met at last, as it should have been at first, by an examination and comparison of the two works." (Histories of N. E.) This showed "the astounding fact, that Miss Adams * * as an author was herself guilty of a real and gross violation of the rights of another author; she having copied verbatim, or with only colorable alterations, nearly one third of her whole work, 160 out of 513 pages, from Dr. Ramsay's History of the American Revolution." (S. E. Morse, 1867, in Sprague's Life of Dr. M., N. Y., 1874, p. 277.) This fact appeared, and the attack on Dr. M. ended.

MORSE, Rev. J. (assisted by S. E. Dwight). Compendious and Complete System of Modern Geography. pp. 500. (Edition 5,000 copies.) *Boston*, 1814

BARTLETT. Hon. Josiah (M. D.). "An Historical Sketch of Charlestown, in the County of Middlesex, and Commonwealth of Massachusetts. Read to an Assembly of Citizens at the opening of Washington Hall, Nov. 16, 1813, and afterwards prepared, with notes, for the Massachusetts Historical Society." Printed in its Collections, Series II. vol. ii. pp. 163–84 (1814).

Also *reprinted* with the same type (without change, even in a few evident errors), with a title-page added, worded as above to "1813," and a preface of six lines; Inscribed to the Citizens of C. 8°. pp. 24. John Eliot, *Boston*, 1814. This pamphlet is now rare, especially in C. A recent Sale Catalogue shows that a dealer holds one at $10. Also reprint 1880 (larger paper).

Washington Hall was a "handsome, convenient" brick building, 53 feet long, 29 wide, 3 stories high, on Main St., near the Square, "with a handsome rear entrance from Town Hill." The property, held in 50 shares, subscribed by 34 persons, cost $6,259. The W. H. Association (annual pay't $5) had there newspapers, books, etc. (2d story). "An elegant druggist's store" was in the first (long occupied by Messrs. Kidder and White, and 1880 by Mr. Stowell). A hall was in the third, and in the yard "an office about 15 ft. square," occupied by Jas. Frothingham (Dr. B.), the artist, who became one of the most prominent of C., some of whose works are now to be found there. Dr. Bartlett, chiefly in his notes, gives a full *Review* of the institutions, etc., *of the Town in 1815*. It had 3 militia companies, and the Artillery (formed 1786), Warren Phalanx, and Light Infantry (1804), that long lived; 3 churches (see above); 6 attorneys at law; 2 doctors; 7 school-teachers; 2 reading societies; and a population of about 5,000. The value of the annual manufactures was about a million and a quarter of dollars, chiefly of bricks, morocco and cordage.

Dr. BARTLETT died 1820. Memoir by R. Frothingham, in Mass. Hist. Soc. Proc., 1791–1845, pp. 323–50. Besides Monographs above, see (R. F.) Article on Freemasonry, Mass. Mercury, Sept. 7, 1798 (and reply by Hon. Saml. Dexter); Case of Calculi, 1808; Address, St. Andrew's Lodge, April 12, 1812, at Old Green Dragon Tavern, Boston (in Freemason's Monthly Mag. xxxii.).

GLEASON, Benj. Geography on a new and improved plan. 12°. 2d ed. Map. pp. 148. *Boston*, 1814

TUFTS, Jos., Jr. Oration before the Federal Republicans of C., July 4, 1814. With Ode and Hymn by Henry Small. pp. 16. *Charlestown*, 1814

The author (C. 1783, H. C. 1807) was an attorney at law in C. (Dr. B.)

TURNER, Rev. E. Substance of Two Discourses, May 22, 1814, Salem, Mass., by E. T., "minister elect" of the Universalist Society in C. pp. 24. *Charlestown*, 1814

Settled in C. 1814–25. Oration, Philanthropic Lodge, Marblehead, June 24, pp. 23. *Salem*, 1810. Discourse, Portsmouth, N. H., Ins'n Rev. Hosea Ballou, Nov. 8, pp. 16. *Portsh*, n. d. Do. Univ. Meeting-house, Boston, Aug. 19, Re-Ins'n Rev. Paul Dean, pp. 20. *Boston*, 1815.

1815.

ANCIENT Fire Society. Rules and Regulations of the. 12°. pp. 10. *Boston*, 1815

Instituted at C., Nov. 8, 1743. This pamphlet has a List of all the members, many well-known names, to date, and in present copy in MS. to June, 1832. There were, in 1814, three other Fire Societies in C., Phœnix (1795), Washington (1800), and Jefferson (1810). (Dr. B.)

BARTLETT, Hon. J. Oration on the Death of John Warren, M. D., before the Grand Lodge of Mass., June 12, 1815. pp. 24. *Boston*, 1815

[LOWELL, J.] Review of Dr. Morse's "Appeal to the Publick." pp. 42. No imprint. ? *Boston*, 1815

MORSE, S. F., with N. Willis and Rev. J. Morse. "The Boston Recorder" (weekly) established; "the first religious newspaper ever published in the land." (Rev. J. Todd in Sprague's Life of Morse, p. 313.)

MORSE, Rev. J. Review of American Unitarianism (Rev. T. Belsham's book. *London*, 1812, rep. *Boston*, 1815. 5 editions). pp. 32. Pub. by S. T. Armstrong, from the Panoplist, June, 1815 (vol. ii.).

See Rev. Samuel Worcester's Letter to Wm. E. Channing on the above: also, his "Second Letter" to him, 2 eds. of both. *Boston*, 1815. "Third Letter," 8°. pp. 81. *Boston*, 1815. Also, Rev. W. E. Channing's Remarks on Letter, 2 eds., and on Second do.: also, Letter to Samuel C. Thacher on above Review; the three, *Boston*, 1815. Review of the late Correspondence (W. with C.), by a "Serious Inquirer." *Boston*, 1817. The above reviewed, Panoplist, April and May, 1816.

────── The Gospel Harvest, A Sermon delivered before the Society for Foreign Missions of Boston and Vicinity, Jan. 2, 1815. pp. 28.
Boston, 1815

PRINCE, Jas. Address in the Chapel at the State Prison, April 6. 12°. pp. 22. *Boston*, 1815

TRIAL of Geo. Travers for murder of Jas. McKim and Thos. Hazey, at the U. S. Navy Yard, C., Nov. 27, 1814. pp. 88. *Boston*, 1815

TURNER, Edward. Thanksgiving Sermon at C., April 13, 1815.
Charlestown, 1815

1816.

"AN ACT 'Mass. Leg., ch. 74. Feb. 9, 1816] to incorporate (Nath. Austin, jun., Ben. Swift, Seth Knowles, Jacob Foster, and Jos. Phipps, jun., and others) the *Second Congregational Society* in C." (Unitarian). See 1819 and 1837.

The fourth prominent religious society in C. See its *History*, 1880.

BOYLSTON, Thos. (of London), The Will of. pp. 16.
[Boston?] n. p. [1816]

A resident of London, and an owner of real estate in C.

BRADFORD, G. (Warden 1812-24). Description and Historical Sketch of the Massachusetts State Prison, with the Statutes, Rules and Orders, for the Government thereof. Published by order of the Board of Directors. pp. 38, and 2 sheets of Statistics.
Charlestown, 1816

JOY, B. "A True Statement of Facts, in reply to A Pamphlet lately Published by Messrs. Charles Barrell, Henry F. Barrell, George Barrell, and Samuel B. Barrell." pp. 17. *Boston*, 1816. "Statement of Facts relative to the conduct of Mr. Benjamin Joy, Executor of the Last Will and Testament of the late Joseph Barrell, Esq., of Charlestown, August. 1816." pp. 20.

Mr. Barrell had a large and beautiful estate. "Poplar Grove," purchased from his executor for the McLean Asylum, and still occupied by it, and showing features that he gave it. See *Drake's* Fields of Middlesex, 177; also 1818.

MORSE, Rev. J. Sermon at Brookfield at the Ordination of Rev. Eliakim Phelps, Oct. 23, 1816. pp. 24.

1817.

Turner, Rev. E. Editor of the Gospel Visitant, 1817–18.

Ware, Rev. Henry. A Sermon preached at the Interment of the Rev. *Thomas Prentiss* (2d Cong. Ch. C.), who died Oct. 5, 1817, Æ. 25, pp. 16. *Charlestown*, 1817

Mr. Prentiss was the first minister in the Unitarian church in C.

1818.

" An Act [Mass. Leg., ch. 12, June 12, 1818] authorizing the town of C. to establish a *Board of Health*." Additional Act, ch. 150, March 20, 1832.

McLean Asylum for the Insane in C. (from John McLean, an honored merchant of Boston, d. 1823, æ. 61; opened Oct. 6, 1818). See Hayward's Mass. Directory, Barber's Hist. Coll.'s Mass. p. 366. By-Laws ; with Rules and Regulations, etc. pp. 24. *Boston*, 1821. Do., adopted Dec. 1, 1822. pp. 10. *Boston*, 1822. Fuller, Robert, An Account of his Confinement, etc., 1832. pp. 30. *Boston*, 1833. Stone, Eliz? T. A Sketch of her Life, and do., pp. 42, *n. p.* 1842. See Ellis, 1863.

See Joy, 1816. Since 1842, in Somerville.

Sullivan, John L. Letters first published in the Boston Daily Advertiser in answer to certain Inquiries relative to the Middlesex Canal. *Boston*, 1818

Turner, Rev. E. A Discourse delivered at the Universalist Meeting-House in C., Mass, on Thanksgiving Day, Dec. 3, 1818. pp. 12. *Charlestown*, 1818

1819.

" An Act [Mass. Leg., ch. 62, Feb. 11, 1819] for changing the name of the Second Congregational Society in C." to " *New Church in C.*" (1817). See 1837.

Act establishing the Charlestown Board of Health, and Rules, Orders, etc. of the Board. pp. 20. *n. p.* 1819

Collier, Rev. Wm. The Minister's Hope, and its Influence on his Preaching and Character. Sermon at Ordination of Rev. Geo. W. Appleton, Lyme (Conn.). pp. 24. *Boston*, 1819

Also, Report of (his) Ministerial Labors, to Boston Soc. for Religious Purposes, at An. Meeting, Jan. 1824, with Ser. J. Saurin. pp. 36. Boston, 1824.

Gleason, Benj. Oration before the Republican Citizens of C. July 5, 1819. pp. 16. Published by request.
Printed and published by T. Green, *Charlestown*, 1819

Morse, Rev. J. *Resigned pastorship Aug.* 1819. The following works by him were *afterward* published. Sermon before the A. B. C. F. M. at Springfield. *Boston*, 1821. A Report to the Secretary of War of the U. S. on Indian Affairs, with Narrative of a Tour in 1820 under com'n of the President of the U. S. pp. 96 + 400. *New Haven*, 1822. (With R. C. Morse). Traveller's Guide of the U. S. 18°. *New Haven*, 1823. Do. do. Universal Gazetteer. Roy. 8° with Atlas. Annals of the American Revolution, account settlement of the Country, Indian wars, remarks on the Constitution, and Biography of Revolutionary Officers, 6 plates. pp. 400 + 50. *Hartford*, 1824. New System of Ancient and Modern Geography (J. and S. E. Morse), 25th ed., *Boston*, 1826. Geography for small children, 24°, his last geographical work, 1825.

MORSE, Rev. J. Memoir. See Sprague. 1874. A large vignette portrait (about 7½ × 9½ in.), "Annin & Smith Sculpt. Lith. Co.," showing gray hair and ministerial robes.

MORSE, S. F. B. (C. 1791, N. Y. 1872). Key to Morse's picture in the House of Representatives. pp. 4. 1823. First Annual Discourse, National Academy of Design. *New York*, 1827. Reply to N. A. Review on Academy of Arts. 8°. pp. 45. *New York*, 1828. Foreign Conspiracy against the United States. *New York*, 1835. (7th ed. 18??. N. Y., 1847.) Biographical Sketch of Lewis Clausing. *New York*, 1846. *Magnetic Telegraph*. Controversy. Lord Campbell, and Prof. M., pp. 8, 1848. Report of Case, Bain r. Morse, before Judge Cranch, pp. 106, 1849. Argument of S. P. Chase, O'Reilly et al. r. Morse, pp. 45, 1853. Do. of Geo. Gifford, Case of O'Reilly r. Morse, Smith, et al., pp. 94, 1853. Decision of Supreme Court of U. S. on Patents of M., pp. 23, 1854. Mémoire de Morse aux Governments Européen, pp. 10, 1857. Report of the Dinner, Aug. 17, at Paris, to Prof. M. on completion of the Atlantic Tel., pp. 70, *Paris*, 1858. Tefft's remarks at Dinner to M. in Paris. Chas. Morton's Argument in M.'s Extension Case, pp. 30, 1859. O'Reilly and Speed against Exten. Tel. Patents (Broadside), 1861. Methode Mnemonique de L'Ecriture Tel. de Morse, par Garnier, 1862. *S. F. B. Morse*; Some Errors of Dates, etc., pp. 50, *Paris*, 1867; Do. Memoir, showing grounds of my claim, do. 1867; Do. Examination of Tel. Apparatus, etc., pp. 166, 1869; Do. Full Exposure, etc., pp. 16; Modern Telegraphy, pp. 58; Do. Full Exposure of C. T. Jackson's pretensions to Invention, pp. 80, *Paris*; Do. Dep. of J. Henry, with Critical Reviews, pp. 111, *Paris*; Memorial of Bradley against Extension of Patent, etc., pp. 55; Smithsonian Institute in relation to Mag. Tel., pp. 35.

For Memorials of Prof. Morse, see 1875 (also 1854).

MORSE, S. E. (C. 1794, N. Y. 1871). Geographical View of Greece, etc., map. 12°. pp. 24. [*New Hav n*, 1824]

MORSE, R. C. (C., 1795). With S. E., The New York Observer (still published, 1880). Established, 1823.

S. E. and R. C. Morse continued the Geographical works of Dr. M., 1821 and after, especially developed in School Geography, N. Y., 1844. "More than 100,000 copies were put into the market during the first year, and the work continued to be disposed of at this rate for a number of years." (Sprague's Life of Dr. M., p. 222.)

The contributions of this distinguished family to periodical literature, etc., have been far too numerous for mention here.

TURNER, Rev. E. Discourses (2) on Doctrinal and Practical Subjects. pp. 25. Discourse, Fast Day, April 1, 1819. pp. 13, n. d.
Bellamy and Green, Printers, *Charlestown* [1819]

1820.

" AN ACT [Mass. Leg., ch. 116, Feb. 15, 1820] to incorporate the Trustees of the *Methodist Religious Society*, in C." Nine named. (Fifth religious society.)

The residence of ministers of this ch. in C. has been generally brief, and mention has been omitted of their works except of a few that the writer has found, delivered while they were in C. 1st min., Rev. Wilbur Fisk, 1820-21 (Mass. Election Ser. 1829, and several other works. See Allibone, 599); 1820-39, President of the Wesleyan University, Middletown, Conn.

FIRST CHURCH. "Love of Popularity. A Sermon delivered, Feb. 23, 1820, at the Installation of the Rev. Warren Fay, as Pastor of the First Cong. Ch. and Soc. in C.," by Leonard Woods, D. D. Charge by Rev. Wm. Greenough (2d Cong. Ch., Newton); R. H. by Rev. Mr. Dwight (Park St., Boston); Ad. to People by Prof. Stuart, Andover. pp. 41. Published by G. Clark & Co. (David Wilson, Printer.) *Charlestown*, 1820

WALKER, Rev. J. Sermon in C., March 6, on the Death of Miss *Mercy Tufts*. 8°. pp. 8. (E.) *Charlestown*, 1820
. Second minister of the Unitarian Ch., 1818-39.

1821.

" AN ACT [Mass. Leg., ch. 17, June 15, 1821, Sec. 2.] " to change the name of the Second Social Library in C." (founded Dec. 21, 1820) to " *Charlestown Union Library*."

This Library, after growing to considerable size (in 1828, 2500 vols.), was dispersed by its proprietors March 21, 1842, by sale, and by lot. (Record of C. U. L.) Its "Catalogue" with a brief history, etc., 8°, pp. 31, is without place or date.

" AN ACT [Do., ch. 28, June 16, 1821] to incorporate [Amos Binney, George Bond and others] the Proprietors of the *Charlestown Bleachery*."

Additional Acts, ch. 5, June 10, 1823, and ch. 85, Feb. 22, 1824.

DWIGHT, Tim° Travels N. E. and N. Y., New Haven, 1821. See Vol. I. pp. 166 and 476, on C.

FAY, Rev. Warren. Sermon at the Installation of Rev. Calvin Hitchcock, at Randolph (Mass.), Feb. 28. pp. 32. *Boston*, 1821

Minister First Ch., Feb. 23, 1820, to Aug. 16, 1840. A portrait of him, "Mrs. Turner, del. Pendleton's Lithog." on India paper.

———— Sermon, March 7, at the Ordination of Rev. E. Demond at West Newbury (Mass.), etc. pp. 31. *Boston*, 1821

Ordination Rev. W. Fay at Brimfield, Nov. 3, 1808. Sermon by Rev. Saml Austin, Worcester, 1809. Rev. W. Fay, Sermon at Monson, at the funeral of Mrs. N. Ely, Hartford, 1812. Do., Two Sermons at Harvard, Jan. 30, 1814, being the first Sabbath after his Installation. pp. 23. *Boston* [1814].

STATEMENT of the Overseers of the Poor, Receipts and Expenditures May, 1820, ending April, 1821. *A Broadside*.

TURNER, Rev. E. Discourse Univ. Ch. C., May 20, 1821. pp. 12. *Boston*, 1821. Do. Dedication 1st Univ. meeting-house Westminster, Mass., July 3, 1821. pp. 16. *Boston*, 1822. Also engaged on The Univl Hymn Book. 12°, 1821.

WILLARD, Paul. Oration at C., July 4, 1821, at the request of the Republican Citizens of C., with remarks by Nath. Hall Loring. pp. 16. *Boston*, 1821

The former, a Counsellor at Law (H. C., 1817), was many years resident of C.

1822.

AN ACT [Mass. Leg., ch. 49, Feb. 5], in addition to an Act entitled " An Act for the better *security* of the *Town* of C. *against Fire*." (See 1809.)

BROADSIDE. "Statement of the Overseers of the Poor, April, 1822."

FAY, Rev. W. Sermon Jan. 1, 1822, at Ordination of Rev. Joseph Bennet, Woburn (Mass.), and other parts. pp. 39. *Boston*, 1822

———— Sermon at the Installation of Rev. Nathl Cogswell at Yarmouth (Mass.), April 24. pp. 36. *Boston*, 1822

LORING, Nathl Hall. An Address at request of Republican Com. of Arrangements, July 4, 1822, at C. pp. 24. *Boston*, 1822

TRIAL of Capt. John Shaw by Gen. Court Martial, U. S. Ship Independence, Navy Yard, C., on charges by Capt. Isaac Hull, U. S. N. pp. 88. *Washington*, 1822

TURNER, Rev. E. Substance of a Discourse, 1st Universalist Ch., Roxbury, Jan. 4, 1822, pub. by request of the ch. pp. 15. J. Howe, *Charlestown*, 1822. Discourse to Female Benevolent Soc., C., Nov. 5, 1822. pp. 12. *Boston*, 1822

1823.

" AN ACT [Mass. Leg., ch. 1, June 7] to *incorporate* the *Bunker Hill Monument Association*." Add. Acts, Feb. 26, 1825, ch. 122 (see June 16, ch. 1). Do. to rebuild Beacon Hill Mon't, ch. 110, 1865. See B. H. M. Ass'n (above).

BROADSIDE. " Statement of the Overseers of the Poor, April, 1823."

TURNER, Rev. E. A Discourse, Universalist Meeting House in C., Feb. 23, 1823. pp. 16. J. Howe, *Boston*, 1823

1824.

" AN Act [Mass. Leg., ch. 125, Feb. 20] *repealing* all Acts imposing *restrictions* on the erection of *buildings* in the town of C." (Act, 1810, ch. 44, repealed). [Do. June 12, ch. 16] " An Act to regulate the *Side-walks* in the town of C." (Add. ch. 11, Feb. 7, 1855.)

TOWN Doc. Reports of Receipts and Expenditures, and of Overseers of the Poor, May, 1823, to April, 1824. pp. 8 + 2. The *first* 8° *financial* Town Report.

BALFOUR, Rev. W. An Inquiry into the Scriptural Import of the Words, Sheol, Hades, Tartarus, and Gehenna : all translated Hell in the Common English Version. pp. 8 + 448.
Geo. Davidson, *Charlestown*, 1824

2d ed. 12°. pp. 348. Same printer and place. 3d ed. 8°. *Boston*, 1832. See 1825 and 1854.

WALKER, Rev. Jas. Sermon at Brooklyn (Conn.), at Installation of Rev. S. J. May, Nov. 5, 1823. pp. 40. *Boston*, 1824

Sermon on Smooth Preaching. 12°. pp. 12. *Boston*, 1823; *New York*, pp. 20; *Glasgow*, 1825. (H. H. E.)

1825.

" AN ACT [Mass. Leg., ch. 78, Feb. 15] regulating the *transportation* of *Gunpowder* in and through the town of C."

———— [Do., ch. 40, June 18] to incorporate the *Trustees* of the *Poors' Fund* in the town of C." (Amended, ch. 301, 1868.)

———— [Do., ch. 55, June 18], to *incorporate* the President, Directors, and Company of the *Bunker Hill Bank*.

Add. Acts, 1825, ch. 108 (Feb. 28, 1826), and 1841, ch. 58. Capital increased, ch. 123, March 26, 1847. Do., ch. 136, March 28, 1854. Charter extended to Jan 1, 1875, ch. 217, 1849.

TOWN Doc. Reports of Receipts and Expenditures, and of Overseers of the Poor, and of Schools, May, 1824, to April, 1825. pp. 12.

BALFOUR, Rev. W. (Rev. Jas. Sabine. Reply to an "Inquiry," etc. See 1824. pp. 132. *Boston*, 1825.) Reply to J. Sabine's Lectures on the "Inquiry." pp. 136.   *Boston*, 1825

EMMONS, W. Oration. See Bunker Hill Celebrations.

FAY, Rev. W. Sermon before the Auxiliary Foreign Mission Society of Boston and Vicinity. at 13th An. Meeting, Jan. 3, Old South Ch., Boston (with Constitution and Rep. of the Soc., etc.). pp. 40.   *Boston*, 1825

MELLEN, G. Poem. See B. H. Celebrations.

REASONS principally of a Public Nature against A New Bridge from C. to Boston. pp. 32.   *Boston*, 1825

Several pamphlets on this once exciting subject were issued between 1825 and 1841, which last see.

WEBSTER, D. Oration. See B. H. Celebrations.

1826.

"AN ACT [Mass. Leg., ch. 97, Feb. 22 to empower the Inhabitants of the town of C. to choose *Assistant Assessors*." [Do. ch. 21, June 20] "An Act authorizing the Selectmen of C. to appoint a Company of *Hook and Ladder Men*, and additional *Engine-Men*."

TOWN DOC. Reports of Receipts and Expenditures of Overseers of the Poor, and Schools, May, 1825, to April, 1826. pp. 12.

EVERETT, Hon. Edward. An Address at C. Aug. 1, 1826, In Commemoration of John Adams and Thomas Jefferson (with action of Com. on " the funeral solemnities at C."). pp. 56.   *Boston*, 1826

Mr. Everett lived nearly 15 years in C., on Winter Hill, and in Harvard St., near the Square. His "Orations and Speeches," 4 vols. *Boston*, 1850, show that he delivered about fifty, all given therein, while he lived in the town. He also made large contributions to the North American Review, and wrote or published other works.

FAY, Rev. W. Sermon at the Ordination of Rev. Rufus Anderson, also of Rev'ds M. M. Josiah Brewer, Eli Smith, Cyrus Stone, and Jeremiah Stow, Missionaries, at Springfield, May 10. and other parts. pp. 40.   *Boston*, 1826

WALKER, Rev. J. Causes of Progress of Liberal Christianity in N. E. Am. Unit. Ass'n Tracts, I. 9. 12°. pp. 16. Discourse, Groton, Mass., Nov. 1, do. I. 39. (3d ed. 1832.)   *Boston*, 1826

1827.

AN ACT [Mass. Leg., ch. 49, Jan. 27] to authorize Ebenezer Baker to dispose of certain real estate in C., and to invest the proceeds thereof in other real estate.

TOWN DOC's. Reports of Receipts and Expenditures. Overseers of the Poor, and of Schools, May, 1826, to April, 1827. pp. 12. Expenditures for Support of the Poor, and Repairs of Highways, April, 1825, to April, 1827. pp. 18.
       G. Davidson, *Charlestown*, 1827

REVIEW of the Case of the Free Bridge between Boston and C., including the Public Documents. pp. vi. + 106.   *Boston*, 1827

REPORTS and Documents (Ho. of Rep., Mass., No. 71) on the
Charles-River Bridge. pp. 36.

Contains a List of the 63 holders of the 150 shares, Jan. 1, 1827, about one quarter of
the whole in trusts; Peter C. Brooks and the estate of S. Buck were the largest holders,
— 11 shares each. Also, the dividends from the opening June 17, 1786, to Jan. 1, 1827,
from £3 per share, 1788, to $148, in 1824. Also, of values, etc. The project of the
new (Warren) Bridge caused the Stock to decline from $1,550 per share, Oct. 4, 1823,
to $825, April 27, 1824. See 1786.

BUNKER-HILL AURORA: | and Farmers' and Mechanics' Journal. |
Published every Thursday by William W. Wheildon and George
Raymond, at Austin's Stone Building, Main-Street, Charlestown. |
No. 1, Thursday Morning, July 12, 1827. Vol. I."

The publication of this paper was continued until Sept. 24, 1870, and ceased with
No. 39, Vol. 44 (per C. Pub. Library file from W. W. W.). This paper contains a very
large amount of materials for the history of C., much more than any other one publication during this Town Period. A copy is in the C. Public Library.

GARDNER, Rev. Calvin (Univ. Ch. 1825-27). Nothing while in C.?
Two Sermons in "Original Sermons." 3 vols. 8°. (1831-33.)
Gardiner, Me., n. d.

[WALKER, Rev. J.] Sermon at Harrisburg, Penn., Feb. 4, A. U. A.
Tracts, I. 11. 12°. pp. 24. *Boston*, 1827

1828.

AN ACT [Mass. Leg., ch. 127, March 12] to establish the *Warren
Bridge Corporation* (John Skinner, Isaac Warren, John Cofran,
Nath! Austin, Ebenezer Breed, Nathan Tufts, and their associates).

Add'l Acts, 1832, ch. 170; 1834, ch. 219; 1834, ch. 131; 1835, ch. 155; 1836, Resolve
April 16. See 1841. This bridge, opened in 1828, was 1,390 feet long and 44 wide.
Barber Hist. Col., 365.

TOWN DOC'S. Reports of Receipts and Expenditures, and Overseers
of the Poor, May, 1827, to April, 1828. pp. 14.

BALFOUR, Rev. W. Letter to Dr. Allen in Reply to his Lecture on
the Doctrine of Universal Salvation. pp. 72.
G. Davidson, *Charlestown*, 1828

———— Three Essays on the Intermediate State of the Dead, etc.,
with Remarks on Mr. Hudson's letters, etc. 12°. pp. 360.
G. Davidson, *Charlestown*, 1828

EVERETT, Hon. E. An Oration before the Citizens of C. on the 52d
Anniversary of the Declaration of the Ind. of the U. S. A. pp. 43.
Charlestown and *Boston*, 1828

———— An Address at the Erection of a Monument to John Harvard,
(Old Burial Ground, C.), Sept. 26, 1828. pp. 24. *Boston*, 1828

THE Proprietors of Charles River Bridge, in Equity *vs.* The Proprietors of the Warren Bridge, with Documents, Supreme Judicial
Court, Suffolk, March, 1828. 4°. pp. 72.

SPRAGUE Family in Hingham * * with the addition of Ralph Sprague's
Family of C., Mass. pp 68.

Very rare, Cook $13, Elliott (1880) $6.

WALKER, Rev. Jas. Mass. Election Sermon, May 28, 1828, pp. 16.
Boston, 1828. Discourse at Saco, Nov. 21, 1827. 12°. pp. 54.
Kennebunk, 1828

1829.

AN ACT [Mass. Leg., ch. 70, Feb. 21] to incorporate the *Warren Institution for Savings*, in the Town of C (David Stetson, John Sweetser, Loammi Kendall, Elisha L. Phelps, Joseph Hunnewell, John M. Robertson, Lot Poole, James K. Frothingham, and others).

Addl. Acts to hold $20,000 real estate, March 22, 1851; March 31, 1854; these two repealed, amount made $60,000, ch. 195, 1859; March 19, 1855, Trustees choose Treas., ch 74, 1855. This, among the earlier Savings Banks in the State, has maintained a high character, and has become also one of the most important. At the end of the first year's business the balance due Depositors was $6,145. This amount now (1880) is about four and a quarter millions of dollars.

"AN ACT Do, ch. 21, June 12 to *establish a Fire Department* in the Town of C."

TOWN DOC. Receipts, Expenses, Overseers of the Poor, Schools.

BALFOUR, Rev. W. A Letter to the Rev. Dr. Beecher. 12°. 2d and 4th editions. *Boston*, 1829

———— Letters on the Immortality of the Soul and a Future Retribution in reply to Mr. Chas. Hudson, Westminster, Mass. 12°. pp. 360. G. Davidson, *Charlestown*, 1829

"MALDEN Bridge to the People." pp. 20. *Boston*, 1829

A defence of chartered "rights" against a project on foot to ruin Malden and Chelsea bridges," an interesting chapter in the controversy about the bridges.

THOMPSON, Rev. J. S. (Univ. Ch. 1827–29). Nothing while in C.?

Critical Lectures, 8°, Rochester, 1824; Editor of the Universalist, 1825; Christian Guide to Scriptures, with Memoir of Author, 8°, Utica, 1826; The Monotessaron, 8°, Baltimore, 1829; The Reformed Christian Guide, 12°, pp. 72, New York, 1831.

WARREN Ins. for Savings. Plan, By-Laws, etc. 12°. pp. 12. G. Davidson, *Charlestown*, 1829

Also two pages of Amendments, Feb. 10, 1847, added.

1830.

"AN ACT [Mass. Leg., ch. 8, June 5] to incorporate the *Charlestown Fire and Marine Insurance Company*."

Time Walker, David Devens, Sam'l Devens, Isaac Warren, Thos. J. Goodwin, Chester Adams, eight others and associates. Add'l Act, ch. 25, June 15, 1851, to change name to *Neptune* Ins. Co., *Boston*, and to establish it there. (Continued, 1880.)

———— [Do., ch. 65, March 4, 1831] to incorporate the *Lyceum Hall* in the Town of C. (17 corporators named). See Walker, 1830.

TOWN DOC. Receipts, Expenses, Overseers of the Poor, Schools.

CHARLES RIVER BRIDGE. Case of the Proprietors of, against the Proprietors of Warren Bridge, argued and determined in the Supreme Judicial Court of Mass. *Boston*, 1830

———— *vs.* Warren Bridge, New York Review, Vol. II.

EVERETT, Hon. E. An Address June 28, 1830, the Anniversary of the Arrival of Gov' Winthrop at C., at the request of the C. Lyceum. pp. 51. *C.* and *Boston*, 1830

———— A Lecture on the Working Men's Party, Oct. 6, before the C. Lyceum. Published at their request. pp. 27. *Boston*, 1830

JACKSON, Rev. Henry. Sovereignty of the Divine Government. A Discourse in the First Baptist Meeting House, C., Nov., 1829. pp. 36. *Boston*, 1830

First Bap. Ch. 1822–36. Also, account of the Churches in Rhode Island, *Providence*, 1853. A large lithographic portrait of him ; pub. while in C.?

WALKER, Tim? Address at Opening of the C. Lyceum, Jan. 5, 1830.
12°. pp. 24. *Cambridge*, 1830

The Preface refers to "the earnest efforts, now making in every part of the State, to increase the number and utility of Lyceums."

1831.

TOWN DOC. Receipts, Expenses, Overseers of the Poor, Schools.

BALFOUR, Rev. W. Reply to Prof. Stuart's Exegetical Essays on several words relating to future punishment. 12°. pp. 238.
Boston, 1831

———— Four Days' Meetings, etc. Sermon at Boston, Sept. 25, 1831.
pp. 36. *Boston*, 1831

———— Mr. Balfour's Opinion of the Devil carried out. pp. 14.

First published in the Christian Magazine.

CHARLESTOWN Directory (*the first*). 16°. pp. 113 + 12.
Waitt & Dow, *Charlestown*, 1831

———— Female Seminary. Prospectus. (See Acts, 1833.)

Opened (under Baptist auspices) May 9, with about 40 pupils.

EVARTS, Jeremiah. A Tribute to his Memory by Gardiner Spring, D. D. pp. 32. *New York*, 1831. A Sermon on his Death by Leonard Woods, D. D., in Andover, July 31, 1831. pp. 27.
Andover, 1831

Member of the First Ch. under Dr. Morse, and resident of C. several years. Father of Hon. Wm. M. Evarts, Sec. of State of the U. S. He edited the Panoplist and Missionary Herald, wrote 10 Reports of the Am. Board, 24 Essays (under signature of Wm. Penn) on the rights of the Indians, periodical articles, etc., — showing forcible style and much ability.

EVERETT, Rev. L. S. An Exposure of the Principles of the "Free Inquirers." pp. 44. *Boston*, 1831

Minister Univ. Ch. 1829-36. Reply to Rev. M. H. Smith's renunciation of Universalism, etc. Salem, June 7, 1840. pp. 24. *Middletown*, Conn., 1840. Sacred Songs for Children in Sabbath Schools. 18°. *Boston*, 1843.

FESSENDEN, Thos. G. Address before the C. Temperance Soc., Jan. 31. pp. 46. *Charlestown*, 1831

SUMNER, Wm. Address to the C. Artillery Co., Nov. 23, 1831.
Charlestown, 1832

WALKER, Rev. J. An Introductory Lecture delivered in Boston, before the American Institute of Instruction, Aug. 25, 1831. pp. 14.
Boston, 1831

1832.

AN ACT [Mass. Leg., ch. 32, Feb. 16] to incorporate the *C. Dock Company* (John Skinner, Nath¹ Austin, Benj. Brintnall, Wm. B. Sweet and ass's).

———— [Do., ch. 125, March 13] to incorporate the President, Directors, and Company of the *Charlestown Bank*, in C. (nine corporators). Capital reduced, ch. 31, March 12, 1840.

———— [Do., ch. 126, March 13] to incorporate the President, Directors, and Company of the *Phoenix Bank*, in C. (five corporators). Repealed, ch. 106, March 6, 1845.

———— [Do., ch. 150, March 20] *Board of Health* (1819), add'l act.

Town Doc. Receipts and Expenses, Town Schools (March, 1831, to April 21, 1832), Exp. for Poor, and Repairs of Highways, March, 1831, to March 1, 1832. pp. 24.

Luther, Seth. Address to the Working-Men of N. E., etc., del. at C. pp. 39. *Boston*, 1832

Walker, Rev. J. Discourse at Ordination of Rev. E. Peabody, First Cong. Ch. Cincinnati, May 20, 1832. With charge, etc., by Rev. F. Parkman, of Boston. pp. 45. *Cincinnati*, 1832

—— On the Exclusive System: tract Am. Unit. Ass., I. 39. 12°. pp. 34. 3d ed. *Boston*, 1832. Same title, Saco, Nov. 21, 1827. 12°. pp. 34. *Kennebunk*, 1828 (E.)

1833.

An Act [Mass. Leg., ch. 54, March 1] to incorporate the *Winthrop Society* in C. (Chester Adams, Jos. F. Tufts, Eliab P. Mackintire, and associates).

First Ch. edifice Union St., E. side, near Washington; 24, Green St. See 1849.

—— [Do., ch. 61, March 1] to incorporate the Trustees of the *Charlestown Female Seminary* (Henry Jackson, Benj. Badger, jun., Oliver Holden, John W. Valentine, Dan! White, and ass's.) Add'l Act to hold $30,000 Real Estate, ch. 44, Feb. 14, 1848. See 1851.

Town Doc. Receipts and Expenses, Town, Schools, Poor, March, 1833. pp. 28.

W. Darby and T. Dwight, jun. A New Gazetteer of the U. S. 8°. *Hartford*, 1843. p. 93, account of C.

Walker, Rev. J. Sermon, Ordination of Rev. J. K. Waite, Fitz-william, N. H., May 22. *Boston*, 1833 (E.)

1834.

An Act [Mass. Leg., ch. 135, March 28] to incorporate the *C. Infant School Society* (Catherine Walker, Maria T. Jackson, Elizabeth T. Hurd, Ann L. Holden, and ass's). Amended, ch. 135, 1869, name changed to "The Infant School and Children's Home." For reports of latter, see 1870–80.

Town Doc. Receipts and Expenses, Town; Exp. Poor, March, 1833, to March, 1834. pp. 24.

—— Annual Report of the Trustees of the C. Free Schools, May, 1834. pp. 11. Signed Benj. Thompson, Sec. Aurora Office, 13, C. Square. [1834]

The *first* printed School *Report*.

Directory (2d). Map. 16°. pp. 76.
A. Quimby, *Charlestown*, 1834

Austin, A. W. A Memorandum concerning the C. Post Office. pp. 23. n. p. [1834]

Baldwin, Loammi. Report on the subject of introducing Pure Water into the City of Boston. pp. 78. Dated C., Oct. 1, 1834. *Boston*, 1834

Died C. 1838, engineer of the Dry Dock, C. Navy Yard, etc. Also, Thoughts on the Study of Political Economy, etc. pp. 75. *Cambridge*, 1849; Report on the Brunswick Canal and R. R. Glynn Co., Ga. pp. 42. *Boston*, 1836; Do. do. with Appendix, pp. 48. *Boston*, 1837.

BALFOUR, Rev. W. Letter to B. Whitman on the term Gehenna. 12°. pp. 95. *Boston*, 1834.

———— Cooke, P. Modern Universalism Exposed; Examination of the writings of Balfour. 12°. *Lowell*, 1834.

CROSBY, Rev. Daniel. Sermon, Dec. 25, 1833, at Ordination of Rev. Henry Adams, Worthington, Mass. pp. 23 + 1. *Boston*, 1834.

Winthrop Ch., 1833-42. This Sermon, entitled "Good Men Love the Sanctuary, was also preached, with some alterations, at the dedication of the new house of worship erected by the Winthrop Society." Ser. at Ord. of Rev. D. C. at Conway, Mass., Jan. 31, 1827, by Rev. Justin Edwards. pp. 21. *Andover*, 1827: Thanksgiving Discourse Nov. 29, 1832, by Rev. D. C., pub. by req. of the Conway Temperance Soc. pp. 24. *Amherst*, 1833.

LUTHER, Seth. Address before the Union Ass'n of Working Men, Town Hall, C., Jan. 30, 1834. pp. 43. *Boston*, 1834

TRIAL of Lieut. E. B. Babbitt on charges by Com. Jesse D. Elliott, Naval Court Martial, Navy Yard, C., Oct. 13, 1834. pp. 120.

URSULINE CONVENT, *Mount Benedict.*

This Institution (Order of St. Ursula, established 1536) was founded in 1820 by Drs. Matignon and Cheverus, "with funds given by a native citizen of Boston." The community removed to C. 1826, and occupied a farm-house at the foot of Mt. B. once a commanding eminence, — "until the main building (of brick, two stories high) on its summit was finished," 1827. (See Report below.) It was a well-known Seminary. Certain reports about it having been circulated, it was burned by a mob at night, Aug. 11, 1834. The event occasioned great excitement; and a number of (now rare) publications, for which see below, and 1835, 1837, 1842, 1847, 1852-55, 1870, 1877.

Account of the Conflagration of the ———— by a Friend of Religious Toleration. 12°. pp. 35. *Boston*, 1834

Austin, Jas. T. Argument as Attorney-General of Com[h] before the Supreme Judicial Court of Middlesex; Case of John R. Buzzell (see *Trial*). pp. 44. *Boston*, 1834

Report of the Committee appointed at Faneuil Hall, meeting Aug. 12, relating to the Destruction of. pp. 16. *Boston*, 1834

Reprinted in "Documents," etc., 1842.

Stetson, Rev. C. A Discourse on the duty of sustaining the laws, at Medford, Aug. 24, 1834, occasioned by the burning of the Convent. pp. 18. *Boston*, 1834

[Norton, A.] The burning of the Convent, pp. 6, in Christian Examiner, Vol. 17, Sept., 1834.

The Trial of the persons charged with burning the Convent in C., before the Supreme Judicial Court. E. Cambridge, Dec. 2, 1834. 2 parts. pp. 34. This is the Trial of John R. Buzzell of C., found Not Guilty. [*Boston*, 1834]

———— of Wm. Mason, Marvin Marcy, jun., and Sargent Blaisdell, same Court, Dec. 12-20, 1834, for same. pp. 20.
Allen & Co., *Boston* [1834]

Thacher, Hon. P. O. Charge to Grand Jury of Suffolk Co, Dec., 1834. pp. 23. *Boston*, 1834

WALKER, Rev. J. Sermons at the Dedication of the 2d Cong. Ch. in Leicester, and Ordination of Rev. S. May, jun., Aug. 12 and 13, 1834. pp. 14. *Worcester*, 1834

———— The Philosophy of Man's Spiritual Nature, etc., a Tract (No. 87) for the American Unitarian Ass'n. 12°. pp. 22.
Boston, (Sept.) 1834

WINTHROP CHURCH. Articles of Faith, List of Members, etc. 16°.
pp. 12.   *Boston*, 1834

1835.

" AN ACT [Mass. Leg., ch. 111, April 4] to establish the *Charlestown
Branch Rail-road Corporation.*" Repealed April 9, 1836, which see.
TOWN DOC. Receipts and Expenses, March 1, 1834, to March 3,
1835, and Statement of Overseers of the Poor. pp. 23. Rules
and Regulations of the Board of Health, May 21, 1835, and Act of
Leg., 1818. pp. 8. School Report to May, pp. 4.
REPORT of Joint Committee of the Legislature on Warren Bridge.
Senate Doc. 58. pp. 52.
FAY, Rev. W. A Sermon at the Funeral of Rev. Benj. B. Wisner,
D. D. (Old South Ch.). pp. 31.   *Boston*, 1835
URSULINE CONVENT. *Argument* [Richard S. Fay] before Committee
of House of Representatives on Petition of Benedict Fenwick and
others. pp. 75. (Report, House Doc. 37.)   *Boston*, 1835
Reed, Rebecca T. Six Months in a Convent; or, The Narrative of
Miss R., an Inmate of the Ursuline Convent at Mt. Benedict, in
C. 18'. pp. 192.   *Boston*, 1835
An Answer to the above, " exposing its falsehoods and manifold absurd-
ities. By the Lady Superior [Mary Anne Ursula Moffatt, called
Mary Edmond Saint George], with some Preliminary Remarks."
pp. 38 + 66.   *Boston*, 1835
A Review of the Lady Superior's Reply to " Six Months in a Con-
vent," being a vindication of Miss Reed. pp. 51.   *Boston*, 1835
Supplement to Six Months in a Convent, confirming the above Narra-
tive by more than 100 witnesses. Also an Account of the Elope-
ment of Miss Harrison. 12°. pp. 264.   *Boston*, 1835
The Ursuline Convent, a poem. 16°. pp. 46. *Louisville* (*Ky.*), 1835
A Few Chapters to Brother Jonathan, concerning Infallibility.
                                             Louisville (*Ky.*), 1835

1836.

" AN ACT [Mass. Leg., ch. 64, March 23] to incorporate the *Charles-
town Mutual Fire Insurance Company.*" Add'l Act, ch. 8, Feb.
13, 1838. Sundry Annual Reports were printed.
————— [Do., ch. 119, March 31] " to incorporate the *Charlestown
Wharf Company* in C." Add'l Act to extend wharfs, ch. 213,
April 19, 1837. Do., ch. 35, Feb. 23, 1841.
————— [Do., ch. 187, April 9] to establish the *Charlestown Branch
Rail-road* Company.

Henry Jaques, Abijah Goodridge, Hamilton Davidson, and ass's and successors.
Add'l Act, extension of time, ch. 94, March 25, 1837, and ch. 126, April 8, 1839. To
extend road, ch. 108, March 17, 1841. Same amended, ch. 12, Feb. 21, 1842. To
straighten, etc., ch. 176, March 16, 1844. To build a branch, ch. 255, March 26, 1845.
Fitchburg R. R. to succeed, ch. 24, Feb. 7, 1846. The Wharf Co. was authorized to
hold the water front of the town from the State Prison to the Navy Yard, and did hold
much of it. The R. R. began at Swett's wharf in C., and extended to the Lowell R. R.
near the McLean Asylum. The railroad and much of the land became part of the [Bos-
ton and] Fitchburg R. R. property, and an important aid to it. See 1842.

————— [Do., ch. 216, April 13] " to incorporate the *Charlestown
Steam Cotton Factory.*"

An Act [Do., ch. 265, April 16] "to incorporate the *Middlesex Mill-Dam Company* in C." (Henry Jaques, A. Goodridge, Thomas Hooper, and ass's).
—— [Do., ch. 271, April 16] to "incorporate the Proprietors of *Swett's Wharf* in C." (Sam¹, Wm. B., and Tasker H. Swett).
Town Doc.   Receipts, Expenses, Overseers of the Poor, Schools.
Balfour, Rev. W.   A Discourse, Boylston Hall, Boston, July 18. pp. 16.   *Boston*, 1836
By-Laws of Engine Co. No. 4.   Adopted May 16, 1836.   16°.   pp. 8.
                                                                Charlestown. 1836
C. Wharf Company.   Act of Inc. and By-Laws.   12°.   pp. 29.
                                                                Charlestown, 1836
Directory (3d).   16°.   pp. 75 + 18.
                                      S. Rodenburgh, *Charlestown*, 1836
Everett, A. H.   See Bunker Hill Celebrations, 1836.
First Church, Articles of Faith, Covenant. List of Members.   12°. pp. 12.   Another. pp. 19, 1842; do. pp. 20, 1856.   All *Boston*.
King, Rev. Thos. F. (Univ. Ch. 1836–59).

Sermons at *Portsmouth*, *N. H.*, Nov. 23, 1828, pp. 16.   *P.*, 1828; April, 1831. pp. 16. *P.*, 1831; March 24, 1834, 12°, pp. 12.   *P.*, 1834; March 30, 1834, 12°, pp. 19.   *P.*, 1834.   See "Original Sermons by Universalist Ministers."   [Have met none separate in C.]

Mass. State Prison, Laws of the Commonwealth for Government of, etc.   *Boston*, 1836

1837.

" An Act [Mass. Leg., ch. 77, March 16] for changing the name of the New Church Soc. in C. (Unitarian) to *Harvard Ch.* in C." See 1816, 1819.
—— [Do., ch. 232, April 19] "authorizing the Proprietors of Harris' Wharf [between Swett's and Gray's] to extend the same."
Town Doc.   Receipts and Expenses, and Exp. Poor, March, 1836, to March, 1837.   pp. 23.
Charles River Bridge.   Opinions of the Judges of the Supreme Court of the U. S. in the Case of the Proprietors of *vs.* the Proprietors of Warren Bridge *et als.*, Jan. Term, 1837.   pp. 115.
                                                                Boston, 1837
Edes. Peter.   A Diary of, during his confinement in Boston by the British, 107 days, in 1775, immediately after the battle of B. Hill, Written by himself.   pp. 24.   *Bangor*, 1837

See Forster, 1870, for Diary of his companion.

Franklin Fire Society, instituted at C. Aug. 10, 1830.   Constitution revised Nov. 3, 1836.   Members' Names. (16° size.)   pp. 11.
                                                     C. Power Press, 1837
" The Chronicles of Mount Benedict.   A Tale of the Ursuline Convent.   The Quasi production of Mary Magdalen."   18°?.   pp. xv. 191.   Printed for the Publisher, *Boston*, 1837
Warren Ins. for Savings, Plan, By-Laws revised, etc.   12°.

1838.

" An Act [Mass. Leg., ch. 149, April 18] to incorporate the *Milk Row Bleachery* Company " (in the town of C.). Add'l Act, ch. 111, April 17, 1848.

———— [Do., ch. 174, April 24] in relation to a *Highway* from *Prison Point* to *Lechmere's Point* " (to lay out Prison Pt. Bridge). Widening draw, ch. 311, 1869 ; draw and maintaining, ch. 300, 1870.

Town Doc.   Report of Treasurer, and Overseers of the Poor. pp. 23.   Year to March 1, 1838.

By Town vote, March 27, 1837, the interest of the Town's portion of the State Surplus Revenue was appropriated for Support of the Schools. Amount received of State Treas. this year, $19,230.34, interest on same to Jan. 1, 1838, $681.58, paid to Trustees of Schools. The Town Debt this year, exclusive of $10,500 held in Town Notes by Trustees and Overseers of the Poor, " is now reduced to $30,000."

———— By-Laws of the Town of C. adopted June 20, 1838.   12°. pp. 24.   *Charlestown*, 1838

Directory (4th), Rodenburgh's.   16°.   pp. 102 + 14.

Published by John Harris, *Charlestown*

Bunker Hill Aurora.   Extracts from Early Town Records of C., by Wm. Sawyer.

These numerous and ample selections are important contributions in print to the history of the town from 1646 to 1814. They are in papers from Jan. 20 to Dec. 15, including (Aug. 11) the Votes May 28, 1776, for Independence (Aug. 18). Petition to Congress for aid July 30, 1776; (Aug. 25) Report on it, May 16, 1777; (Nov. 10) Obsequies of Washington; and (Oct. 27, Nov. 3) establishment of the U. S. Navy Yard, 1800-1.

Report accepted by the C. Wharf Co., June 5, 1838.   With a very large Plan of the Property of the Co., and a smaller of the C. B. Railroad.   pp. 24.   *Boston*, 1838

1839.

An Act [Mass. Leg., ch. 58, March 20, 1839] to incorporate the *C. Mechanic Union Charitable Association* [Rich. C. Bazen, Sam'l Brintnall, Wm. D. Butts, and ass's).

Mass. Leg. Documents, Senate 56, Report and Bill, C. R. and W. Bridges, pp. 30 ; House, 29, Expenses W. Bridge, pp. 7 ; Do., 35, Returns of Proprietors do.   1829-33, pp. 12.

" Annual Statement of the Expenses of the Town of C.," March, 1838, to March, 1839, pp. 23.   1839.

"Printed at the Aurora Office," first time, a full title-page.

" Annual Report (pp. 32) of the Trustees of the C. Free Schools, made in pursuance of the Act of 1838, together with the Report of the Treas. of the Board."   pp. 8.   Aurora Office, 1839.

The School Reports after this are all 8°, and published annually.

C. Debating Society, Constitution and By-Laws.   Adopted Nov., 1838.   Names of Members.   (16° size.)   pp. 12.

B. H. Aurora Office, 1839

Report of the Committee appointed by the Stockholders of the C. Wharf Co., at the last Annual Meeting, July 5, 1839.   pp. 16.

Boston, 1839

With prospects of development of Co.'s property not yet (1879) fully realized.

CONDITIONS OF SALE of House-Lots, B. H. *Monument Grounds*, at Public Auction, Wed., Sept. 25, 1839, etc., by Coolidge & Haskell. pp. 8, and large map by S. M. Felton. n. p. or d.

WALKER, Rev. J. A Discourse in Harvard Ch., C., July 14, 1839, on taking Leave of his Society. Printed by request. pp. 40.
Cambridge, 1839

With Letter of Members of the Soc. by a Committee, to their pastor.

———— A Farewell Discourse to the Children in his Soc. delivered in Harvard Ch., C., June 23, 1839. 18°. pp. 24. *Cambridge*, 1839

For list of works after leaving C., see History of this church, 1880.

SEWALL, Rev. Samuel (Burlington, Mass.). A Brief Survey of the Congregational Churches and Ministers, Middlesex Co., and Chelsea, in the American Quarterly Register, Vol. XI. (1839) 48–51, and XIII. 37, 43–48, much historical and biographical matter about First Ch. and C., — a pioneer work on Church history in C.

1840.

AN ACT [Mass. Leg., ch. 2, Feb. 15] *establishing a Fire Department* in the town of C.

———— [Do., ch. 86, March 23] authorizing John Harris to construct a wharf in C.

SENATE DOC. No. 22, N. Austin, Rep. as Agent for Warren Bridge. pp. 4. Do. No. 40, pp. 13.

TOWN DOC's. Annual Statement of Expenses, March, 1839, to March, 1840, inc. Poor. pp. 24. Ann. Report Trustees C. Free Schools, pp. 24, and Treasurer's Report, May, 1839, to May, 1840, pp. 25–31. Both at Aurora Office, 1840. Rules and Regulations of the Fire Department. 12°. pp. 24. *Boston*, 1840

Includes State Laws. First publication after establishment of this Department.

DIRECTORY (5th). 16°. pp. 109 + 18.
C. P. Emmons, *Charlestown*, 1840

BUNKER HILL Declaration of the Principles of the Whig Party, Sept. 10, 1840. pp. 12. No imprint.

Set forth at B. H. by "fifty thousand of the free electors of the N. E. States * * and from nearly every other State in the Union," in the largest political meeting ever held in C., preceded by an immense procession.

CROSBY, Rev. D. The Death Scene of the Aged Saint. A Sermon, Dec. 8, 1839, Winthrop Ch., on the Death of *Dea. Amos Tufts.* pp. 16. *Boston*, 1840

ELLIS, Rev. George E. (Unitarian Ch. 1840–69). The Preacher and the Pastor. Two Discourses in Harvard Ch., C., March 15, 1840, on the Commencement of his Ministry. pp. 47. *Boston*, 1840

———— An Individual Faith, Tract A. U. Ass., 1 ser., 160. 12°. pp. 28. *Boston*, Nov. 1840

FROTHINGHAM, Richard. Address at Dedication of the Warren School-House, April 21, 1840. See B. H. Aurora, May 16, 1840.

MARSHALL, J. F. B. (M. Calkin and F. Johnson). Hawaiian Collection of Church Music, compiled for the use of Foreign Communities at the Sandwich Islands. Ob. 8°. pp. 147. *Honolulu*, 1840

A singing-book was needed as above, and Mr. Marshall of C., then a merchant at Honolulu, assisted in preparing this work, and thus had it in use a year sooner than it could have been ordered and obtained from the U. S.

THIRD Grand Rally of the Workingmen of C., Oct. 23, 1840, and their Address. pp. 18.

YOUNG, Rev. Alex. The Church, the Pulpit, and the Gospel. A Discourse at the Ordination of Rev. G. E. Ellis, March 11, 1840. pp. 64. *Boston*, 1840

Includes Notes; Charge, Rev. E. S. Gannett; R. H., Rev. S. Osgood; Ad., Rev. J. Walker. This was an *Annus mirabilis* of the ministry in C. During it, three clergymen were settled in the town, each young, each to attain marked eminence, — Dr. W. I. Budington, Trinitarian, at the First Ch.; Dr. E. H. Chapin, Universalist; Dr. G. E. Ellis, Unitarian.

1841.

AN ACT [Mass. Leg., ch. 42, Feb. 27] authorizing Hamilton Davidson to extend his Wharf.

———— [Do., ch. 88, March 17] relating to *Charles River Bridge* and *Warren Bridge.*

See House Doc. 40, pp. 8. Add'l Act, ch. 48, March 3, 1842, and ch. 84, Feb. 27, 1845. Duties of Agent, ch. 30, March 22, 1843. Compensation of Do., ch. 250, March 26, 1845. Agent may lease a wharf, ch. 40, Feb. 25, 1850; to build floating bath, ch. 105, May 7, 1851. See 1855. A settlement of the great Bridge controversy. For beginning see 1825 and 1828.

TOWN DOC's. Receipts and Expenses, and Poor. March, 1840, to March, 1841. pp. 31. Report of Trustees of C. Free Schools, and Treas. of the Board. pp. 32. Report of the Com. of Finance for the Town of C., accepted May 3. 16°. pp. 8. *Charlestown*, 1841

CHAPIN, Rev. E. H. Discourses on various Subjects. 18°. pp. 213. *Boston*, 1841

Universalist Ch. 1840–46. Lecture Oct., 1824, in Chapel of Waterville, Col., pp. 31, W., 1824. Universalism, etc., Dis. Richmond, Va., Aug. 12 and 24, 1825, 12°, pp. 23, *Utica*, 1838. Address on True Greatness, to Madison Debating Soc., pp. 24. Oration, July 4, 1840, to Military Co's., pp. 32. Both, *Richmond*, 1839. Duties of Young Men, 18°, *Boston*, 1840; (2d ed. 32°) pp. 208, B., 1846; 3d, 18°. B., 1850.

———— The Responsibilities of a Republican Government. Discourse Fast Day, April 8. pp. 18. *Boston*, 1841. Christian Union. Discourse Univ. Ch., C., pp. 17. *Charlestown*, 1841

CHARLESTOWN CHRONICLE. Published weekly at the office : Square, corner of Chelsea Street. Caleb Rand, publisher and proprietor. No. 1. Sat., Feb. 6, 1841. Continued about three years. No complete file known to the writer.

ELLIS, Rev. G. E. See Bunker Hill Celebrations.

THOMPSON, Dr. A. R. Eulogy before the Citizens of C., April 19, on the Decease of Wm. Henry Harrison, late President of the U. S. pp. 15. *Boston*, 1841

1842.

"AN ACT [Mass. Leg., ch. 16, Feb. 21] authorizing First Baptist Ch. and Soc. to sell lands.

———— [Do., ch. 24, Feb. 25] *to annex a part of C. to West Cambridge.*

"All that part of C. which lies northwesterly of 'Little river,' so called."

———— [Do., ch. 76, March 3] *to incorporate the Town of Somerville.*

Formed from the westerly part of C., to Cambridge, West Cambridge, and Medford.

" AN ACT [Do., ch. 84, March 3] to establish the *Fitchburg Railroad Company.*
Succeeding to C. Branch R. R., with terminus in C. See 1836. Add'l Act, ch. 218, March 25, 1845. Act of succession to C. B. R. R., ch. 21, Feb. 7, 1846. To authorize F. R. R. Co. to extend to Boston, ch. 200, Apr. 20, 1847.

MASS. LEG.   See Senate Doc. No. 16 (pp. 8), 29 (pp. 7), 32 (pp. 17), 40 (pp. 4), 45 (p. 1).

TOWN DOC'S.   Receipts and Expenditures, March 1, 1841, to March 31, 1842, pp. 29, and Poor, pp. 3. Report Trustees C. Free Schools and Treas., do., pp. 32.

DIRECTORY (6th).   16°.   pp. 120 + 16.
John Harris, *Charlestown,* 1842

BUDINGTON, Rev. W. I.   Winter of 1842–43, Nine Lectures, History of First Church. See 1845.

CHAPIN, Rev. E. H.   Sermon at Ins'n Rev. Henry Bacon, 1st Universalist Soc., Providence, R. I., March 17, 1842.   pp. 20.   *Providence,* 1842. The Idea of the Age, Oration to Mercantile Lodge, No. 47, I. O. of O. F., Jan. 14.   12°.   pp. 24.   *New York,* 1842

ELLIS, Rev. G. E.   Regeneration and Sanctification. Two Sermons in Harvard Ch., March 6, 1842.   pp. 30.   *Charlestown,* 1842. Sermon in do., Oct. 9, 1842, on Death of Rev. Wm. E. Channing, D. D., pp. 24.   *Boston,* 1842.   Address at Ordination of Rev. F. D. Huntington, Oct. 19, 1842.   *Boston,* 1842

FITCHBURG R. R. Co.   Report Com. of Directors on prospects of proposed R. R., Sept. 26.   pp. 16.   *Boston,* 1842

HARRIS, Rev. T. M. (b in C., 1768. See 1796, 1801).   Address in 1st Ch., Dorchester, April 7, 1842, at his Funeral, by Rev. Nath! Hall.   pp 28.   *Boston,* 1842.   Eulogy at Masonic Temple, May 4, by Rev. Benj. Huntoon.   pp. 16.   *Boston,* 1842.   Memorial, 1842, and Memoir by Rev. N. L. Frothingham (Mass. Hist. Soc., IV. 2), pp. 28.   *Cambridge,* 1855

PROTESTANT EPISCOPAL CHURCH, Annual Convention of Eastern Diocese at St. John's Church, C. Journal, Bishop Griswold's Add., etc.   pp. 32.   Sermon do., Sep. 28, by Rev. G. M. Randall. pp. 20.   Both *Boston,* 1842.

URSULINE CONVENT, Documents relating to — Reprint of Report, 1834, and Report to House of Representatives, Mass. (Doc. 50) for Com. of House by Geo. T. Curtis.   pp. 32.   *Boston,* 1842

1843.

TOWN DOC'S.   Receipts and Expenditures, and Poor, March 31, 1842, to March 1, 1843.   pp. 27.   *Charlestown,* 1843

BUDINGTON, Rev. W. I.   Capital Punishment. A Discourse, occasioned by the Murder (June 14) of *Charles Lincoln,* late Warden of the Mass. State Prison, 1st Ch., Appendix.   pp. 32.   *Boston,* 1843

CHAPIN, Rev. E. H.   Three Discourses upon Capital Punishment. 18°.   pp. 72.   *Boston,* 1843.   Lectures.   18°.   pp. 156.
New York, 1843

CHARLESTOWN Branch Railroad.   Act. Inc., By-Laws, Aug., 1843. 12°.   pp. 37.   *Boston,* 1843

EDDY, Caleb. "Historical Sketch of the Middlesex Canal, with Remarks for the Consideration of the Proprietors." pp. 53.
Boston, 1843

See 1793 (Incorp. and hist. note); and 1813, Sullivan, for Reports, etc.

ELLIS, Rev. G. E. The Bible, or the Church, or " Puseyism," a Discourse. pp. 32. *Boston*, 1843. See Bunker Hill, Monographs.

GREEN, Rev. D. Sermon at the Funeral of *Rev. Daniel Crosby*, late Pastor of the Winthrop Ch., C., March 3, 1843. pp. 39.
Boston, 1843

GREENLEAF, Rev. P. H. (St. John's Episcopal Ch., 1841–51). The Christmas Festival. A Sermon in St. John's Ch., C. pp. 22.
Boston, 1843

WEBSTER, D. See Bunker Hill Celebrations.

1844.

TOWN Doc's. Receipts and Expenditures March 1, 1843, to March 1, 1844, and Rep. on Poor, etc. pp. 24. An. Rep. Trustees of C. Free Schools.

———— List of Persons assessed a State, Town, and County Tax in the Town of C. for the year 1844. Published by Order of the Town. pp. 31. *Charlestown*, 1845

CHAPIN, Rev. E. H. The Catastrophe of the Princeton, a Discourse at the Universalist Ch., C., March 3, 1844. pp. 16. Ann. Mass. Election Sermon. Jan. 3. pp. 36. The Philadelphia Riots, a Discourse in the Universalist Ch., May 12, 1844. pp. 16.
All, *Boston*, 1844

ELLIS, Rev. G. E. Obligations of Christians to the Heathen. 12°. Tract Am. Unit. Ass'n, No. 199, 1st Ser. pp. 22.
Boston, Feb., 1844

LIFE of John Mason (Conn.) In Sparks's Am. Biography, II., iii., 307–438.

FITCHBURG R. R. Report (2d) to Stockholders, Jan., 1844. pp. 15. Annual Reports continued from this time. *Boston*, 1844

GIFFORD, Geo. P. Address to B. H. Native American Ass'n, Town Hall, C., Sept. 17, 1844. 12°. pp. 12. n. p.

1845.

TOWN Doc's. Receipts and Expenditures March 1, 1844, to March 1, 1845 (pp. 24), with Tax List of 1844. pp. 56. An. Rep. Trustees of C. Free Schools. pp. 14.

DIRECTORY (7th) Emmons's. 16°. pp. 108 + 13.
Published by Chas. P. Emmons & Co., *Charlestown*, 1845

BUDINGTON. Rev. W. I. The History of the First Church, Charlestown, in Nine Lectures, with 60 long Notes. Portrait of Rev. John Wilson. pp. 259. *Boston*, 1845

The most valuable work on C. that had appeared at this date, and still, with Mr. Frothingham's Hist. (1845–49), unsurpassed in value. The lectures were delivered in the First Ch. to large audiences. The Edition, about 500 copies (now scarce), was issued to subscribers, and the balance was paid for by the Parish, that still holds a few copies.

CHAPIN, Rev. E. H. The Mission of Little Children, a Discourse. pp. 16. Occasional Sermon to U. S. Gen'l Convention of Universalists, Sept. 17. pp. 20. Hours of Communion. 32°. pp. 160.

All, Boston, 1845

ELLIS, Rev. G. E. Address at the Installation of Rev. H. Alger, Marlboro'. Jan. 22. pp. 38. Sermon at Dedication of First Ch., Somerville, Sept. 3. pp. 24. A Collection of Psalms and Hymns for the Sanctuary. 12°. pp. 585. 2d ed. + pp. 81, 1860 (E.). All, *Boston*, 1845. Life of Anne Hutchinson, in Sparks's Am. Biography, Ser. H., Vol. VI. pp. 167–376. 16°. *Boston*, 1845

FROTHINGHAM, Richard, Jun. The History of Charlestown, Mass., Part I. 1 plate. pp. 48. *Charlestown* and *Boston*, Nov., 1845

This work, published in Parts (vii.) 1845–49, continues to be the standard history.

OLIVE Branch Lodge, Odd-Fellows, No. 78, Ins'd July 1, 1845; Constitution, By-Laws and Rules. pp. 30.

Printed by Brother Caleb Rand, *Charlestown*, 1845

TRACY, E. C. Life of Jeremiah Evarts. Portrait. pp. 448. (See 1831.) *Boston*, 1845

1846.

AN ACT [Mass. Leg., ch. 98, March 12] to incorporate the C. *Gas Company.*

(Add'l Act) to extend Pipes and Conductors into Somerville, ch. 24, Feb. 23, 1853. Do., in Medford, ch. 66, 1890. Stock increased, ch. 37, 1854, and 51, 1869.

—— [Do., ch. 149, March 25] to authorize Sam¹ Barnard and Jacob Hittinger to extend their Wharf. [Do., ch. 191, April 6] regulating Tolls, Chelsea Bridge.

TOWN DOC's. Receipts and Expenditures (inc. Poor, Schools. Schedule of Property, etc.), year ending Feb. 28, 1846. pp. 26. An. Rep. Trustees of Schools. pp. 16. By-Laws of the Town of C., adopted June 20, 1838, etc. 12°. pp. 60. *Boston*, 1846

CHAPIN, Rev. E. H. Might and Right. Oration to Eurosophian Adelphi, Waterville Col., Aug. 12, 1846. pp. 40. Address on Temperance, Tremont Temple, Nov. 23, 1845. 12°. pp. 20.

Both, *Boston*, 1846

A large number of publications after leaving C.

ELLIS, Rev. G. E. A Lecture on Temperance, Harvard Ch. pp. 22. Artillery Election Sermon, June 1. pp. 32. Both, *Boston*, 1846

FROTHINGHAM, R., Jun. History of C., Part II., pp. 56 (49–104) 3 pl., 1 cut; Part III., pp. 56. (105–60) 2 cuts.

REPORT of the Majority of the Committee appointed by the Town of C. on obtaining a City Charter. pp. 16. Printed and distributed in pursuance of a vote of the Town. *Charlestown*, 1846

CITY PERIOD, 1847–1873.

BRIDGES, *City Period. State Documents :* Senate, 60 (1847). Report, Senate, 50, 1851. See 1854. House, 42, 189 (1855) ; House, agent's report, 16, 52, 57 ; final do. of Commissioners, 176 ; draws, 283 (1856). House, 60, 161, 404, 463 (1867). Report of Legislative Com. 1868. House, widening draws, 338 (1869). House, 361 (1871). Do., 255. (Chelsea and Malden) 354 (1873). *Boston Doc's*, 31 (1871) ; do. Commissioner's Report. 21 (1872).

DIRECTORIES, *City Period.* Fletcher's, pp. 148 + 34 (1848); Adams's (map), pp. 160 + 32 (1852) ; do. pp. 184 + 44 (1854) ; Adams's map, pp. 212 + 68 (1856) ; Adams, Sampson, & Co., pp. 236 + 90 (1858) ; do., pp. 240 + 78 (1860) ; do., pp. 240 + 58 (1862) ; do., pp. 256 + 82 (1864). All 16°. *Charlestown.* Sampson, Davenport & Co. (map), pp. 228 + 56 + 10 (1866) ; do., pp. 294 + 8 (1868) ; do., pp. 352 (1870) ; do. " no. 18 " (1872) ; do., pp. 384 + 14 (1874, and *last*). 5 vols. 8°. A. E. Cutter, *Charlestown.*

1847.

" AN ACT [Mass. Leg., ch. 29, Feb. 22] *to establish the City of Charlestown*," going into operation from and after its passage.

Additional Acts, ch. 258, April 24, 1847 ; ch. 27, Mar h 7, 1849 ; ch. 106, March 21, 1850 ; annexation, ch. 425, 1854 ; water, 217, 1860, and 105, 1861 ; Aldermen to be nine, ch. 135, 1861 ; ceding lands to U. S., ch. 195, 1862 (see also 1880) ; extending Richmond Street, ch. 123, sidewalks, ch. 160, 1864 ; improving streets, 224, 1867 ; no. of School Com., 277, 1847 (accepted Nov. 5) ; filling flats Prison Point Bay, 253, 1868 ; allowances to, Resolves 5 and 44, 1872 ; speed of vessels in Harbor, ch. 16, 1872 ; *annexation to Boston,* etc., see 1873 ; *water supply,* see 1854 (ch. 247, etc.), 1860 and 1861.

———— Do., ch. 54, March 6] to extend Swett's Wharf.
———— Do., ch. 180, April 15] to incorporate the C. Lead Co. (Capital, $75,000.)

TOWN DOC's. Receipts and Expenditures, year ending Feb. 27, 1847, with List of Persons Taxed for 1846, pp. 64. Pub. by Order of the Town, C. 1847. An. Rep. of Trustees of C. Free Schools, pp. 16. *Boston,* 1847

CITY DOC's. Rules and Orders of City Council and List of Officers for 1847, Charter, Special Laws, etc. 12°. pp. 84. Henry S. Warren, City Printer, C. 1847 . The City Charter, pp. 67.

No. 1. The Inaugural Address of the [First] Mayor, Hon. Geo. W. Warren, April 26. pp. 26. Printed at the Freeman Office, *Charlestown,* 1847. *No.* 2. Report of Special Com. on Licenses to sell Liquors. pp. 14. Do., May, 1847. *No.* 3. Communication from the Mayor June 7 (Training Field, etc.). pp. 8. *No.* 4. Rep. Jt. Spec. Com. on Streets, Oct. 18 (200 copies), Opinion of C. P. and B. R. Curtis. pp. 7. *No.* 5. Address of the Mayor, Oct. 7, at Laying Corner-Stone of the High School, Monument Square. pp. 15. Freeman Office, 1847.

ELLIS, Rev. G. E. Life of Wm. Penn in Sparks's Am. Biographies, Ser. II., Vol. XII. pp. 195–408. 16°. *Boston*, 1847

FROTHINGHAM, R. Hist. of C. Part IV., pp. 48, 1 pl., 2 cuts; Part V., pp. 60; Part VI., pp. 41, 2 pl., 1 cut (ends page 312).

URSULINE Convent. See Niles Register.

1848.

AN ACT [Mass. Leg., ch. 325. May 10] in relation to *Railroad Bridges* across Charles and Mystic Rivers.

CITY DOC's. Receipts and Expenses year ending Feb. 29, 1848, Poor, and List of Persons Taxed for 1847. pp. 63. School Report to Feb. 1, 1848. pp. 36. Mayor's Address (G. W. Warren) April 3, 1848 (Doc. No. 1). pp. 36. Municipal Register. pp. 112. Ordinances Burial Grounds, Dogs, etc. 12°. pp. 11.

CHILD, Rev. Wm. C. (First Bap. Ch. 1844–49). Discourse occasioned by the Death of *Mrs. Mary Fosdick*, in First Baptist Ch., April 2, 1848. pp. 20. *Boston*, 1848

HARRINGTON, Ellen T. Valedictory, C. Female Seminary, Aug. 3. pp. 12. *Boston*, 1848

REPORTS, Majority and Minority to School Com., May 24, on petition of Wm. Eager and others for separation of sexes, Harvard School. pp. 36. *Boston*, 1848

——— of Select Com. Common Council on petition of A. R. Decoster, on representation of Ward 2, Feb. 14. pp. 15. Suppressed Rep. of Minority of Com., on same. Feb. 21. pp. 21.

Both, *Boston*, 1848

——— Special Com. Common Council on Lynde and Second Streets. pp. 7.

THOMPSON, J. A Short History of C. for the past 44 years, and other Subjects. pp. 71. *Charlestown*, 1848

——— C. Herald, No. 1, C., Sept. 11, 1848, 8°, pp. 8; No. 2, C., Oct., 1848, pp. 24.

[WHEILDON, W. W.]. Letters from Nahant, historical and descriptive; cuts. 16°. pp. 48. *Charlestown*, 1848

1849.

AN ACT [Mass. Leg., ch. 188, May 1] authorizing Abel Fitz, J. Wesson, and J. Gary, to extend their wharves in C. Do., ch. 203, May 2], Rhodes G. Lockwood and others, to do same.

CITY DOC's. Receipts and Expenses, year to Feb. 28. pp. 34 + 2. School Rep., Oct., 1849. pp. 17. Address of the Mayor, G. W. Warren, April 2 (Doc. I.). pp. 15. Ordinances of Board of Health. pp. 4.

C. FEMALE Seminary, Catalogue, etc. View. pp. 12. Continued.

FROTHINGHAM, R., Jun. The History of Charlestown, Part VII. (and last). pp. 313–68. With a large Map of the Action, June 17, 1775, by Montresor and Page, 1 plate. 2 cuts. This work is continued in the following.

FROTHINGHAM, R., Jun. History of the Siege of Boston, and of the Battles of Lexington, Concord, and Bunker Hill. Also, an Account of the Bunker Hill Monument. With illustrative Documents. Plan of Boston, with Royal Intrenchments, etc., 1775, by Lieut. Page, the Montresor and Page Map, Boston and Environs, 1775–76, 3 plates, 9 cuts. pp. x + 420. *Boston*, 1849

2d ed., 1851; 3d ed., Dec. 2, 1872; 4th ed., 1873. See also Battle of Bunker Hill.

WINTHROP CHURCH, Final Report of Building Committee.

1850.

AN ACT [Mass. Leg., ch. 92, March 19] to incorporate the *Cochituate Lead Co.* (in C.). Capital. $200,000.

—— [Do., ch. 180, April 9] concerning Streets and Private Ways in C.

CITY DOC's. Receipts and Expenses, year to Feb. 28. pp. 34 + 2. School Report. pp. 12. Address of Mayor, G. W. Warren, Feb. 13. pp. 24. Municipal Register. pp. 108.

ELLIS, Rev. G. E. Repentance, etc. Am. Unit. Ass'n Tract, 1 Ser. 275. pp. 24. *Boston*, 1850

" HOBBS, N. T." Humbug, or the Age of Gas : with other Rhymes, and a Poem, Nov. 13, 1849. 16° (?). pp. 45.

Charlestown, 1850 (?)

With local Political Satires relating to 1870–73.

THOMPSON, Hon. Benj. Funeral Oration on the Death of Zachary Taylor, Late President of the U. S., at request of the City Council, July 31, in Winthrop Ch. pp. 28. *Charlestown*, 1850

WAVERLEY MAGAZINE (Weekly) by Moses A. Dow. Vol. I., No. 1, Boston, Thursday, May 30, 1850. Price 6 cents. pp. 8, folio.

This Magazine (16 pp. after Vol. III.) is still continued, — published in C., 1873, and subsequently. It has obtained very wide circulation.

1851.

AN ACT [Mass. Leg., ch. 37, April 5] to authorize John W. Damon to extend his Wharf.

CITY DOC's. Receipts and Expenses, year to Feb. 28, and List of Persons Taxed, 1850. pp. 79. School Rep., Dec., 1851. pp. 16. Mayor's (R. Frothingham, jun.) Address, Jan. 6, and list of City Government. pp. 28. Report on Truancy to the School Committee, April, 1851. pp. 10.

ELLIS, Rev. G. E. Address at Consecration of Woodlawn Cemetery July 2, 1851. Account of Exercises. pp. 32. *Boston*, 1851

FROTHINGHAM, Hon. R. Oration at Newburyport, July 4. pp. 12.
[*Boston*, 1851]

HIGH SCHOOL. Catalogue of Officers, Teachers, and Pupils, with Course of Study. 12°. pp. 23. *Charlestown*, 1851

MALDEN Bridge, widening Draw, Senate Doc. 91.

MINISTRY at Large. Report (6th Semiannual, 1st in pamphlet) by
Rev. O. C. Everett. 12°. pp. 24. *Boston*, 1851

Published in this form, pp. 34, 1852; pp. 22, 1853; pp. 18, 1854; pp. 21, 1855; pp. —,
1856; pp. 23, 1857; pp. 28, 1858; pp. 24, 1859; pp. 34, 1860; pp. 19, 1866; pp. 24,
1867; pp. 31, 1869 (last). Mission closed, 1879. See History Harvard Ch., 1889.

EVERETT, Rev. O. C. R. H. at Ins'n Rev. A. M. Bridge, Bernards-
ton, Feb. 18, 1846, with Sermon by Rev. C. Robbins, etc.
Boston, 1846

MORGAN, John. A Warning against Quackery. 16°. pp. 32.
Boston, 1851

MYSTIC River Improvement, R. H. Dana, jun. Remarks before Jt.
Com. on Mercantile Affairs and Ins. April 17, 1851, on Petition
F. S. Williams, *et als.* pp. 16.

1852.

AN ACT [Mass. Leg., ch. 105, April 15] to authorize the City of C.
and others *to fill* up certain *Flats in Mystic River.* Add'l Act,
ch. 7, Feb. 12, 1853.
———— [Do., ch. 168, April 30] to incorporate the *C. Dock Co.,*
House Doc. 163. Repealed ch. 306, 1855.
———— [Do., ch. 174, May 3] to authorize Geo. W. White and others
to extend their wharf [Water St., by Navy Yard].
CITY Doc's. Receipts and Expenses, year to Feb. 29, and lists of all
Public Officers. pp. 59. School Report, Dec., 1852. pp. 17.
Mayor's (R. Frothingham, jun.) Address, Jan. 5. pp. 19. Muni-
cipal Register. pp. 120.
BELLOWS, Albert F. Sorrows of Boyhood, No. 1, "I'll tell the
Master."

A school-boy struck by a snowball. First eng. published by McKim & Cutter, C.;
first published design (?) by this distinguished painter in water-color, a native of C.; a
tinted lithographic engraving well done (Bufford), 12 × 14½ in., and the first (?) published in C.

BUDINGTON, Rev. W. I. Our Puritan Fathers our Glory. A Ser-
mon in Commemoration of the 220th Anniversary of the Founding
of the First Ch. in C., Nov. 14, 1852. pp. 32. *Charlestown*, 1852
"CHARLESTOWN CITY ADVERTISER. Published semi-weekly by De
Costa and Williams, Proprietors, at No. 1 Chelsea Street, Charlestown Square. Two dollars per annum." No. 1, Prospectus, Sat.,
Oct. 25, 1851, 4°, pp. 4; No. 2, full size, folio, pp. 4. Wed., Jan. 7,
1852. Published until Vol. XXVI., Sat., Dec. 2, 1876. For
Memorial of Mr. De Costa, see 1878.
ELLIS, Rev. G. E. Report on the Relations between the Theological
School and Harvard College (and Memorial of the Corporation).
pp. 30. *Boston*, 1852. The Organ and Church Music, Two Dis-
courses, Harvard Ch., C., Sept. 26. pp. 40. *Boston*, 1852. Re-
marks, Harvard Ch., at the Funeral of *Hon. Benj. Thompson,* Sept.
27. pp. 16. Notes. *Charlestown*, 1852. Discourse at Unitarian
Convention, Baltimore, Oct. 27. pp. 31. *Boston*, 1853
FIRST Baptist Church in C. A Short History of, with Names of the
Present Members. 16°. pp. 88. *Boston*, 1852

Gas Co. Rules and Regulations. pp. 8.   *Charlestown*, 1852

Gorham and Phelps Purchase, etc., History of the Pioneer Settlement of, by O. Turner. 8°.   *Rochester*, 1852

   The history of a large tract of land bought by Hon. Nath. Gorham of C., occupied by his son Nathaniel about 1789-1826. See also Description of the Genesee Country, 4°, *Albany*, 1798; 8°, *New York*, 1799; and [Robert Munro] Description, etc., 8°, *New York*, 1804, (Doc. Hist. of N. Y., Vol. II.).

Mystic River Improvement, House Doc. 163, Senate 48.

Townley, Rev. R. Christianity in the 19th Century. A Sermon in the Universalist Ch., C., Sept. 28. pp. 28.   *Boston*, 1852

   Min. U. Ch. 1849-53. Also by him; Gibbons's Objection to Christianity, pp. 11; Second Advent of Christ; Letter to Rev. Wm. Digby, pp. 24. All *Liverpool*, 1845-46.

Ursuline Convent, Report on Petition for Indemnity, House Doc. 210. pp. 3.

1853.

"An Act [Mass. Leg., ch. 415, May 25] to incorporate the *Mystic River Railroad*."

   (From B. and Maine R. R. to Chelsea Bridge.) Add'l Acts, ch. 31, 1854; ch. 436, 1855; ch. 89, 1857; capital reduced, time extended, ch. 5, 1859; extended ch. 2, 1841; do., and connecting with other roads, ch. 14, 1863; revived, ch. 54, 1854; extended, ch. 56, 1855; see 278, 1856; 21, 1858. Boston and Lowell R. R. to construct branch to, ch. 9, 1870 (or buy or lease), extended time, 101, 1870.

City Doc's. Receipts and Expenses, year to Feb. 28, and City Government. pp. 52. School Report, Dec., 1853. pp. 23. Mayor's (R. Frothingham, jun.) Address, Jan. 3, and City Government. pp. 28. Report of the Joint Standing Committee on Public Instruction concerning a Public Library, April 11, 1853. pp. 7.

Bunker Hill Mutual Loan and Fund Ass'n, Articles of Association. 16°. pp. 16.   *Charlestown*, 1853

Caldicott, Rev. T. F. Hannah Corcoran, An Authentic Narrative of her Conversion, Abduction from C., etc. 12°. pp. 130.   *Boston*, 1853

   Minister of the First Bap. Ch., 1850-53. This case occasioned much disturbance, and almost an anti-Catholic riot. It was, however, soon quietly settled.

Ellis, Rev. G. E. Sermon at Installation of Rev. Rufus Ellis, First Ch., Boston, May 4, etc. pp. 55.   *Boston*, 1853

High St. Baptist Church, History of, with Names of Members. 16°. pp. 36.   *Boston*, 1853

Mishawam Literary Association. By-Laws adopted May 16, 1853, and Catalogue of Books. pp. 24.   *Charlestown*, 1853

Morse, S. F. B. Memoir (and portrait) in Memoirs of Distinguished Americans. New York, April, 1853.

Townley, Rev. R. Lecture on the Deluge, City Hall, C., Jan. 9. pp. 29.   *Boston*, 1853

Ursuline Convent. Report on Indemnification for Losses, House Doc. 75, pp. 9, and Do., 120.

Young Men's Evangelical Union of C., organized June, 1853, Constitution and By-Laws. 12°. pp. 12. Also, pp. 13.   *Charlestown*, 1853

   The members were from the First and Winthrop (Congregational); First, High St., and Neck (Baptist); High St. and Union (Methodist); Bethesda; and St. John's (Episcopal) Churches.

1854.

An Act [Mass. Leg., ch. 28, Feb. 22] to change the Name of the Neck Village Baptist Society of C. (to Perkins St. Bap. Soc. in Somerville).

———— [Do., ch. 146, March 28] to incorporate the *Monument Bank* in C. (Continued 1880.)

———— [Do., ch. 228, April 7] to incorporate the *C. Five Cents Savings Bank.* May hold $40,000 Real Estate in C., ch. 67, 1864.

This has become one of the large banks of the State, and occupies the most substantial and elegant business structure ever in C.

———— Do., ch. 297, April 13] to incorporate the *C. Water-Works.* Add'l Act, ch. 286, 1857.

———— [Do., ch. 353] authorizing B. and Maine, Fitchburg, and Eastern Railroads to tap the Cochituate Water Pipe in C.

———— [Do., ch. 376] to alter Highway and Bridge between C. and Cambridge.

———— [Do., ch. 402, April 28] to incorporate the *Bunker Hill Library Association.*

———— [Do., ch. 433, April 29] for the *Annexation of Charlestown to Boston.* See 1873. This Act was accepted, but was finally defeated.

———— [Do., ch. 434, April 29] to incorporate the *Middlesex Railroad Co.* (the first horse-railroad, extending the whole length of C.).

Tracks extended, ch. 43, 1857; do., in Boston, ch 205, 1859. Affected by ch. 35, 1860; 15, 1861; 118 and 175, 1862; 170, 1863; 75, 1864. A mortgage confirmed, etc., 139, 1867; fares, 317, 1867; obligations on bridges, 322, 1868, and 272, sec. 7, 1869; and 305, sec. 6, 1870; Union with Suburban R. R. Co, ch. 29, 1870.

———— [Do., ch. 445] to incorporate the *Boston and Chelsea Railroad* (horse, through C.).

Extended, ch. 133, 1856, and ch. 62, 1877. See 36, 1863. Fares, ch. 266, 1864. Use other tracks, ch. 75, 1864, affected by ch. 256, 1869, and ch. 324, 1870.

———— [Do., ch. 451] establishing tolls on *C. R. and Warren Bridges.* to raise a fund to rebuild C. R., and repair W., and $100,000 repair fund. Tolls to cease. ch. 96, secs. 11, 12, 1858.

City Doc's. Receipts and Expenses, year to Feb. 28. with Report of Chief Engineer, etc. pp. 72. School Report, Dec. pp. 15. Mayor's (J. Adams) Address, Jan. 2, and City Government. pp. 16. Report on Monument Avenue. pp. 22. *Charlestown*, 1854

Bridges (C. R. and Warren), Report on. with large map, House Doc. 9. Report and Act on, House Doc's 178, 188.

Annexation to Boston, Considerations on the proposed. by Josiah Quincy, Sen. pp. 11. *Boston*, 1854. Brief Review of the same, "by a Native of Boston." pp. 15. *Boston*. 1854. A Candid Review of the project by a Charlestown Man. pp. 12. *Charlestown*, 1854

Budington, Rev. Wm. I. A Farewell Discourse, First Ch., C., Sept. 17, 1854. pp. 24. On leaving this Ch. and C. *Philadelphia*, 1854

See Humphrey, 1856. Memorial to Lieut. G. F. Ward (privately printed). Patriotism and the Ministry. Address to Am. Education Soc., Boston, May 28. pp. 12. *Boston*, 1861. Pastoral Letter, New Year's, 1870. Responsive Worship. A Discourse, with Notes. 12°. pp. 84. *New York*, 1873.

ELLIS, Rev. G. E. The Christian's Dependence on the Great Hope. Ser., Harvard Ch., C., Feb. 19, Sunday after death of Hon. H. P. Fairbanks. pp. 15. Commemorative Discourse on Rev. Alex. Young (also by Rev. E. S. Gannett), and Appendix. pp. 40. Our Good Land, etc. Discourse, Thanksgiving, Nov. 30, pp. 26. Three, *Boston*, 1854. Address to Middlesex Co. Agricultural Soc., Concord, Oct. 4. pp. 17. n. p.

FROTHINGHAM, Chas. W. The Convent's Doom, a Tale of C. in 1834. The Haunted Convent. pp. 32. (40,000 copies sold within ten days, and before the 5th ed.) *Boston*, 1854

MYSTIC River Co., E. H. Derby. The Principal Points in relation to the change of the Line of their Sea-wall. April. pp. 4. n. p.

URSULINE Convent, on Indemnities, etc. House Doc's, 160, pp. 8, and 166, pp. 4.

1855.

AN ACT [Mass. Leg., ch. 11] to regulate *Sidewalks* in C. (Repealed, ch. 165, 1859.)

———— [Do., ch. 253] in relation to *Charles River and Warren Bridges*.

C. to assume control (see 1841); Add'l land or wharf, ch. 389, May 18, 1855. Liabilities to W. Bridge, ch. 419, May 21, 1855. Tenders and Regulations draw, ch. 282, 1856. Leasing wharf, ch. 306, 1856, and 100, 1857.

———— [Do., ch. 259] to authorize *Fitchburg R. R.* to widen and make solid a Bridge between Somerville and C.

———— Do., ch. 306 to incorporate the *C. Dock Co.* See 1852.

———— [Do., ch. 336] to incorporate the *Medford and C. Railroad Co.* (Horse). Amended, etc., ch. 17, 1857.

———— [Do., ch. 481] relating to the *Mystic River Corporation.* Add'l Acts, ch. 19, 1859 : ch. 150, 1867.

CITY Doc's. Receipts and Expenses, year to Feb. 28, and Report Chief Engineer, pp. 55. School Report, Dec., pp. 20. Mayor's (T. T. Sawyer) Address, Jan. 1, pp. 15.

ANNEXATION C. to Boston. Review of the Opinion of the Supreme Court, pp. 24. W. W. Wheildon, C., 1855. Some Fresh Suggestions on the Project, by a Bunker Hill Boy. pp. 18. De Costa and Williams, C., 1855.

BADGER, Catherine N. Life of *Martha Whiting* (Teacher in C., 1823–53). Port. 12°. pp. 284. *Boston*, 1855

BLAGDEN, Rev. G. W. Memorial Discourse on *Mrs. Elizabeth Livingston Budington* (wife of Rev. W. I. Budington), Jan. 14. pp. 26. *Boston*, 1855

CITY MISSION and Tract Society, Report (1st in pamphlet) and History. pp. 16. *Boston*, 1855

A joint work by the First Ch.; First, High St., and Bunker Hill, Baptist; Winthrop, St. John's; First and Union Methodist, Churches.

ELLIS, Rev. G. E. Sermon in Harvard Ch., C., May 6. pp. 29. *Boston*, 1855. Sermon at Ins'n Rev. H. Stebbins, Portland, Me., Jan. 31. pp. 64. *Portland*, 1855

FARNHAM, L.   Glance at Private Libraries; that of R. Frothingham, jun. (p. 32) the only one in C. mentioned.

FROTHINGHAM, C. W.   Six Hours in a Convent, etc., a Tale of C., 1854.   pp. 44.   (Three large editions.)   *Boston*, 1855

HALE, Chas.   A Review of the Proceedings of the Nunnery Committee of the Mass. Leg., and Visit to Catholic School, Roxbury. pp. 62.   *Boston*, 1855

HIGH SCHOOL, Catalogue of Teachers and Pupils of.   With Report by Rev. G. E. Ellis.   16°, pp. 39; also, 12°, pp. 27.   1857.

MYSTIC River Corporation.   Act extending charter.   House Doc. 85.

TAPPAN, Rev. B., Jr.   Our Help in God, when the Godly cease: Discourse on the Death of *Dea. Chester Adams*, June 3, Winthrop Ch., C.   pp. 24.   *Boston*, 1855

1856.

CITY DOC's.   Receipts and Expenses, year to Feb. 29, and Fire Department.   pp. 57.   School Report, Dec., with List of Trustees, 1847–57.   pp. 24.   Mayor's (T. T. Sawyer) Address, Jan. 1. pp. 16.   Rules and Orders of the School Committee.   12°.   pp. 24.

BARNARD, H.   Life of Ezekiel Cheever.   pp. 32.   *Hartford*, 1856

C. FEMALE Seminary.   Catalogue.   12°.   pp. 16.

ELLIS, Rev. G. E.   Address to Convention S. S. Soc., Salem, Oct. 29, 1856.   pp. 40.   *Worcester*, 1857

FEMALE Benevolent Society, formed Nov. 1, 1819; organized as the Devens Ben. Soc., Dec. 26, 1856.   Constitution and Members. 12°.   pp. 19.   *Charlestown*, 1857

HUMPHREY, Rev. John.   A Selection from the Sermons of (15), edited by his father, Rev. Heman (D. D., President of Amherst Col.), with a Memoir by Rev. W. I. Budington.   pp. xcix. (3), 320.   *New York*, 1856

Mr. H. was minister of the Winthrop Ch. 1842–47.   Dr. B., an intimate friend at First Ch., 1840–54, affectionately describes the amiability and refinement of his character.

THOMPSON, Dr. A. R. (and others), Speech, Mass. Med. Soc., May 8. pp. 12.

1857.

ACTS [Mass. Leg.] relating to the State Prison.

On purchases for, ch. 260: discipline, ch. 284; favor families of Warden Tenny and Deputy-warden Walker (murdered Dec., 1856), ch. 7, Resolves; Resolves, 87 and 88. Government, ch. 162, 1858.

(*Continued from* 1811.)   Acts: salaries of officers, 270, 1854: 331, 1855; 122, and 196, 1857; 342, 1867; 301, 1871; visiting, 302, 1854; diet and clothing, 101, 1859; persons sentenced to, 248, 1859; use for convicts from U. S. Courts, 334, 1869; insane convicts, 254, 1859; solitary confinement, 254, 1856; do., cells, etc., 143, 1873; exercise of convicts, 275, 1869; education at, 255, 1869; 336, 1871; Library, Resolve, 35, 1871; 9, 1859; expenditures for discharged convicts, 122, 1869; Chaplain and Physician, 243, 1870; to protect persons employed in, 73, 1873; on Reports, 155, 1859; on Reports, 155, 1859; 303, 1864; 94, 1873; enlargement enclosure, Res. 13, 1859; improvements, 300, 1867, and Resolves, 70, 1866; 8, 1867; 33, 1868; 8, 1869; twelve new houses for officers, Res. 36, 1869; 5, 1870; workshops, Res. 99, 1869; establishing bounds, Act 294, 1871, and Res. 57, 1873; repairs, Res. 5, 61, 1859; 6, 1872; officers, 240, 1859; sub, do., Res. 41, 1866; Inspectors, 84, 1866; 3, 1873; officers' uniforms, 193, 1873; inquiry on expediency of new prison, Res. 39, 1872; authorizing do. and sale C. property, 155, 1873; taking land for do., 339, 1873.

City Doc's. Receipts and Expenses, year to Feb. 28, and Fire Department. pp. 56. School Report, Dec., with Dedication of the Prescott School-House, Addresses by Mayor Sawyer, and Rev. G. E. Ellis, etc. pp. 60. Mayor's (T. T. Sawyer) Address, Jan. 8. pp. 16.
Charlestown Gas Co., organized May 24, 1851. Rules, etc. pp. 30. W. W. Wheildon, C., 1857.
City Mission and Tract Soc., Report (last in pamphlet). pp. 16.
Boston, 1857
Dexter, Hon. Franklin (C., 1793). Oration July 4, 1819. pp. 19. Correspondence with J. Q. Adams, and Appeal to Citizens of U. S. pp. 80. *Boston*, 1829
Ellis, Rev. G. E. Commemoration of Washington, a Discourse, Harvard Ch., Feb. 22. pp. 30. *Charlestown*, 1857. Sermon, Dedication, First Unitarian Ch., Marietta, Ohio, etc., June 4. pp. 14. *Boston*, 1857. Inaugural Address as Prof. at H. U., Cambridge, July 14. pp. 48. *Boston*, 1857. See City Doc's above.
—— Half-Century of the Unitarian Controversy, with Reference to its Origin, etc. With Appendix. pp. xxiv. + 511. *Boston*, 1857
Frothingham, R. Sketch of C. See Hayward's N. E. Gazetteer.
Marshall, J. F. B. Address at the Annual Meeting of the Royal Hawaiian Agricultural Soc., Oct. 22, 1857. Roy. 8°. pp. 8. (See 1840.) *Honolulu*, 1857
Miles, Rev. J. B. (First Ch., 1855-71). The Absence of Christ the Reason for Fasting. A Sermon, First Ch., Fast Day, April 16. pp. 24. *Charlestown*, 1857
Mishawum Literary Association, By-Laws, and Catalogue of Books. pp. 46. *Boston*, 1857
Warren Institution for Savings, Acts, By-Laws, Members, etc. 12°. pp. 47. C., 1857. Also pp. 17. 1854. Specifications for a Bank Building, J. H. Rand, Architect. pp. 25. n. d. (1859?)

1858.

An Act [Mass. Leg., ch. 101] to incorporate the *Mishawum Literary Association*. Additional Act, ch. 155, 1860.
City Doc's. Receipts and Expenses, year to Feb. 28, and Fire Department. pp. 62. School Report, Dec. pp. 26. Mayor's (J. Dana) Address, Jan. 4, and List Government. pp. 16. Contract, City of C., with Woodlawn Cemetery, 1858. Plan, pp. 15.
C. Female Seminary. Catalogue. pp. 11. (Also other years.)
Ellis, Rev. G. E. Sermon before Convention Congregational Ministers of Mass., Brattle Sq. Ch., Boston, May 27. pp. 38. *Boston*, 1858. Address at Installation Rev. G. Reynolds, Concord, July 8, with Ser. by Rev. C. Robbins.
Hunt, Wm. Sabbath Hymns, from various Authors. (16°.) pp. 72. *Boston*, 1858
Pratt, Phinehas. A Declaration of the Affairs of the English People that first inhabited New England. Edited by Richard Frothingham, jun. pp. 20. *Boston*, 1858
Warren, Hon. G. W. Speech at Democratic Meeting, City Hall, C., Nov. 1, 1858. pp. 14. *Charlestown*, 1858

1859.

AN ACT [Mass. Leg., ch. 120] authorizing the City of C. to establish a *Fire Department.*

—— [Do., ch. 165] to regulate *Sidewalks* in the City of C.

ACTS relating to *Charles River and Warren Bridges,* ch. 32 : do. agent abolished, draw-tenders appointed, ch. 186 ; fund applied, ch. 198, sec. 5, 1859.

—— Do., see 1855, 1854, 1841, 1828, 1792, 1785, also 1867.

Lease of W. B. pier, 96, 1862; fund to pay debt, etc., 257, 1864; both to become highways, etc., 237, 1865 (Ho. Doc. 268); superintendence of, 66, 1867; Commissioners appointed, 322, 1868; widening draws, 272, 1869 (amended, 55, 1872, for C. R.) and 401, 1870; maintenance, 303, 1870.

CITY DOC'S. Receipts and Expenses, year to Feb. 28, Fire Department, and List of Persons Taxed, 1858. pp. 135. School Report, Dec. pp. 28. Mayor's (J. Dana) Address, Jan. 3, and List of Government. pp. 18.

DOWSE, Thomas. Proceedings of the Mass. Hist. Soc. on the gift of his Library to it, with a Eulogy by Edward Everett, Music Hall, Boston, Dec. 9, 1858. 3 plates, pp. 80. *Boston,* 1859. Catalogue of the Private Library of, presented to the Mass. Historical Society, July 30, 1856. pp. 214. *Boston,* 1856

Contains 2808 numbers. 25 copies printed for private distribution. T. D., born in C., 1772, formed the above, perhaps best private library of English literature in New England. See Hist. Mag. 1. (1857) 7-14; also Cambridge Chronicle, Nov. 15, 1856.

HARVARD Church, Specifications for Alterations of, J. H. Rand, Architect, pp. 8, and Report of Committee of Parish on altering their meeting-house, pp. 8. (Addition at N. end.) Two plans of pews.

MILES, Rev. J. B. A Discourse, First Ch., Jan. 2, reviewing the history of the Ch. pp. 20. *Boston,* 1859

MYSTIC River Co. Charter, By-Laws, and Report 1858-9. pp. 30. *Charlestown,* 1859

1860.

AN ACT [Mass. Leg., ch. 217] for *supplying* the *City* of C. *with Pure Water.*

(See also 1847, 29, and 1849, 27.) To take water from Boston, see 1861 for a New Act (Mystic).

CITY DOC'S. Receipts and Expenses, year to Feb. 29, and Fire Department. pp. 79. School Report, Dec. pp. 32. Mayor's (J. Dana) Address, Jan. 2. pp. 24. Ordinance establishing Fire Department, passed Dec. 27, 1859. pp. 12. C., 1860. Report by Geo. R. Baldwin and Chas. L. Stevenson on supplying the City of C. with Pure Water, for City Council, etc. Large plan, pp. 77. *Boston,* 1860

ANNEXATION Petition of J. V. C. Smith, House Doc. 109.

ELLIS, Rev. G. E. The Christian Trinity, a Discourse, Harvard Ch. Feb. 5. pp. 94. The Unity of Christ's Church, do. do., March 4. pp. 51. The Preservation of the States United, do., do., Thanksgiving Day, Nov. 29. pp. 29. All *Charlestown,* 1860. Sermon, Harvard Ch., Dec. 9, being the Sunday after the Interment of Mrs. Eliza Bradford. pp. 18. Privately printed.

FIRST CHURCH.   Catalogue Sunday School Library.   pp. 9.

MILES. Rev. J. B.   The Measure of Life, a Sermon, First Ch., Jan. 1. Printed by request of the family of the late Mr. *Samuel Devens.* pp. 20.   *Charlestown,* 1860

1861.

AN ACT [Mass. Leg., ch. 105] for *supplying* the *City* of C. *with pure Water* (Mystic Works).

<small>Amended ch. 9, 1863; ch. 176, 1864; ch. 135, 1865; supplying Chelsea, ch. 144, 1865; see 234, 1864; supply to Malden and Somerville, ch. 212, 1866; do. Medford, ch. 60, 1867; may supply Roxbury, see. 16, ch. 343, 1867; Somerville and C., ch. 202, 1868. Add'l Act, ch. 216, 1870. Issue of bonds authorized, ch. 159, 1871, and 85, 1872. Dam near Horn Pond, ch. 307, sec. 11, 1871.</small>

———— [Do., ch. 15] to incorporate the *C. Freight Railroad Co.*

———— [Do., ch. 185] to incorporate the *Mutual Protection Fire Insurance Co.*   Revived ch. 36, 1864.

CITY DOC'S.   Mayor's (H. G. Hutchins) Address. Jan. 7.   pp. 19. Rules and Orders of the School Committee, etc.   (12°.) pp. 48. First Report of the Trustees of the Public Library (Nov.).   pp. 12.   Report on Tidal Investigations on Mystic River and Pond, by order of City Council. C. L. Stevenson, Engineer.   pp. 16.   *Boston,* 1861. Special Report of Commissioners on Boston Harbor, in relation of Mystic River and Pond to it.   Boston Doc. 12.   11 maps and charts. 1864.

<small>NOTE. — Reports of Receipts and Expenses, of Schools, and of the Public Library continued this year and annually to 1873, which see. List of Persons taxed in Rep. for 1862 ; No. of Polls, 1846-62, in 1863.</small>

LAMBERT. Rev. T. R.   Discourse in St. John's Ch., National Fast, Jan. 4, 1861.   pp. 16.   *Charlestown,* 1861

1862.

AN ACT [Mass. Leg., ch. 107] to establish the Police Court of C. House Doc., 167.

<small>Salaries increased, 108, 1872; provided for after annexation, 286, sec. 4, 1873.</small>

CITY DOC'S.   See 1861. Mayor's (P. J. Stone) Address, Jan. 6. pp. 27.   Prof. Silliman's Report on the Water Supply from upper Mystic Pond for C., July, 1862.   pp. 31.   C., 1862.   Catalogue of the Public Library, with Ordinance establishing it (1860).   Rules, etc.   pp. 200.   Caleb Rand, *Charlestown,* 1862

FATHER MATTHEW Total Abstinence Soc., St. Mary's Ch., etc.   (Instituted Aug. 30, 1849), Constitution and List of Members.   12°. pp. 14.   *Boston,* 1862

GARDNER, Rev. G. W. (First Baptist Ch., 1861-72).   Treason and the Fate of Traitors. A Sermon, First Baptist Ch., April 12. pp. 20.   *Boston,* 1862

MILES, Rev. J. B.   The Safeguard of the Young. A Discourse to Concordia Lodge, C. (No. 8, I. O. of G. T.) on their first anniversary, Nov. 23.   pp. 22.   *Boston,* 1862

———— The Soldier's Trust. A Discourse addressed to The Putnam Blues, in the First Church. C., on Sunday morning, Sept. 21, 1862, by Rev. James B. Miles, Pastor. Published by request of the Company. (With a list of its members.) 4½ × 2½° in.   pp. 64, cl. (For pocket use.) Mass. Sabbath School Soc., *Boston* [1862]

WARREN Ins'n for Savings, Charter, By-Laws, Members, etc. 12°. pp. 35. C. 1862.

WYMAN, T. B., Jr. The Hunt Family (Genealogy). 4°. pp. 414 + 16. *Boston*, 1862–63

1863.

AN ACT 'Mass. Leg., ch. 61] to incorporate the *Bunker Hill Fire Insurance Co.*

———— [Do., ch. 92] to incorporate the *Father Matthew Mutual Benevolent Total Abstinence Society* in C.

CITY DOC's. See 1861, Mayor's (P. J. Stone) Address, Jan. 5, and List City Government. pp. 42. First Supplement to Catalogue of the Public Library, to Aug. 1. pp. 12.

BUNKER HILL Soldiers' Relief Society, Report (first in pamphlet, the earlier in B. H. Aurora) for 1862 and 1863. pp. 26.

ELLIS, Rev. G. E. Life of Luther V. Bell, M. D. pp. 75. See Mass. Hist. Soc. Proc. *Boston*, 1863

———— Sermon Sunday after Interment of Mr. *Thomas Marshall*. (Sept. 20,) pp. 22. Printed for the family [*Boston*, 1863]

———— All Saints and all Souls' Day. Ser. C., Nov. 1. pp. 12.

H. B. G[OODWIN] [Mrs.]. Madge; or, Night and Morning. *New York*, 1863. Published also 12°. pp. 407. N. Y., 1876.

———— Roger Deane's Work. By H. B. G. Author of Madge. Written for the Sanitary Fair. 16°. pp. 48. *Boston*, 1863

HAVEN, Rev. Gilbert. The Mission of America. A Discourse to N. E. M. E. Conference, High St. (Methodist) Ch., Fast Day, April 2. pp. 40. *Boston*. 1863

RAY, I. (M. D.). Discourse on the Life and Character of *Dr. Luther V. Bell*, at Providence, R. I., June 10, 1862. pp. 52. *Boston*, 1863

1864.

CITY DOC's. See 1861. Mayor's (P. J. Stone) Address, Jan. 4, and List of City Government. pp. 36. Municipal Register. pp. 161. Rules and Orders, School Committee. pp. 35. Do. City Council. 12°. pp. 23.

BUNKER HILL Soldiers' Relief Soc. Addresses and Report. pp. 23.

C. GAS. Co. Increase of Capital, House Doc. 42.

ELLIS, Rev. G. E. The Nation's Ballot and its Decision ; a Discourse, Cambridgeport and Harvard Ch., Nov. 13. pp. 18. *Boston*, 1864. Commemorative Discourse, New South (Boston), Dec. 25. pp. 46. *Boston*, 1865

MILES, Rev. J. B. Memorial of *Lieut. P. M. Holmes* (36th Reg.). 12°. pp. 12.

KING, Rev. Thomas Starr, lived several years in C., d. San Fr'o, 1864. MEMORIALS of, by Rev. C. A. Bartol, *Boston* ; Rev. H. W. Bellows, *San Francisco* : * Hon. R. Frothingham, Tribute, 16°. pp. 217. *Boston*. 1865 ; Robert B. Swain, pp. 28, *San Francisco* ; In Memoriam Poems by J. G. Whittier and others, *New York*. All, except*. 1864. Character and Genius of [E. P. Whipple], Unitarian Review, May, 1878 (republished, pp. 12).

Works *after leaving C.* The Railroad Jubilee, two Discourses Sept. 21, 1851. pp. 54.
Death of Mr Webster, Ser. Oct. 31, 1852. pp. 40. Ser. on Death of D. Weld, 1852.
Review of Dr. Beecher's "Conflict of Ages," pp. 42 (from Univ. Quarterly, Jan., 1854).
Ser. Installation Rev. C. D. Bradley, Cambridge, Dec. 11, 1854. pp. 42. S. S. Cate-
chism, 18°, pp. 52, 1856. Lecture on Hildebrand, Young Men's Christian Union, Boston. pp. 34. Endless Punishment, two discourses (and Reply with Rev. N. Adams's
"God is Love," 12°) 1858. The White Hills, etc., 4°, many cuts, pp. 463, 1866 (also 2
vols., 12°, 1871). Trinitarianism, two Discourses, Jan. 7, and 14, pp 48, 1860. All published in *Boston.* Patriotism, and Other Papers, 1865. Many articles in the Universalist Quarterly. Christianity and Humanity, Sermons, with Memoir, 16°, pp. 80 + 389;
and Substance and Show, and other Lectures, with Int'n, 16°, pp. 434; both ed., etc.,
by E. P. Whipple, *Boston,* 1877.

TAPPAN, Rev. B. A Discourse Commemorative of *Dea. E. P.
Mackintire,* Feb. 14, 1864, in the Winthrop Ch., C. pp. 22.
Boston, 1864

1865.

CITY DOC's. See 1861. Mayor's (C. Robinson, Jr.). Address,
Jan. 2. pp. 16. Public Library, second Supplement to Catalogue.
pp. 27. Report (final) of the Commissioners and Chief Engineer
of the C. Water Works, Feb. 28, 1865. Map. pp. 94. Contracts
and Specifications (7 parts, 4°). Iron water pipes and castings (27
pages); Laying pipes (31); Brick conduit (46); Mystic Pond Dam
(34); Walnut Hill Reservoir (42); Engine and boiler-house (23);
Grading at Mystic Pond (15). Claim of city against B. H. Monument Association. pp. 8.

BAPTIST Association (North), 17th Anniversary, in First Bap. Ch.,
C., Sept. 20, 21. pp. 20. *Boston,* 1865

ELLIS, Rev. G. E. A Discourse, Harvard Ch., March 12, 1865, on
the 25th Anniversary of his Ordination, with Historical Note.
pp. 43. *Charlestown,* 1865

EVERETT, Hon. Edward. (See 1826.) *Memorials* after his death,
Jan. 15, 1865. American Antiquarian Soc., Proceedings, No. 42,
Jan. 17. * Boston (City) Memorial (compiled by J. M. Bugbee).
* R. H. Dana, Address, Cambridge, Feb. 22. Rev. R. Ellis, Ser-
mon, do., Rev. Nath'l Hall, do., Rev. F. H. Hedge. Mass. Historical Soc., Tribute Jan. 30, Pro. 1864-65. Rev. S. Osgood, Ser. N. Y.
* N. E. Historical Genealogical Soc., plates. Rev. A. P. Putnam,
Sermon, N. Y. Everett School, Services. George Ticknor, Remarks. Rev. J. E. Todd, Sermon. Thursday Evening Club,
R. C. Winthrop, Tributes. See National Portrait Gallery (Long-
acre) Vol. IV., 1839, J. Savage, Representative Men, 1860, and
other works. * Works, Orations and Speeches. 3 vols. *Boston,*
1850-59. * Also printed on Large Paper.

FROTHINGHAM, Hon. R. See Bunker Hill (Life of Warren) and
King, T. S., 1864.

RANKIN, Rev. J. E. (Winthrop Ch., 1864). Moses and Joshua. A
Discourse on the Death of Abraham Lincoln, Winthrop Ch., April
19. pp. 16. The Duty of Commemorating the Deeds of our
Fathers. Ser. Winthrop Ch., C., June 18. pp. 23. *Boston,* 1865
Discourse, St. Albans, Vt., Fast, Jan. 4. *St. Albans,* 1861. Do. Lowell, March 27.
Lowell, 1864.

WHEILDON, W. W. Life of S. Willard, see Bunker Hill Monument.

1866.

CITY DOC's. See 1861. Mayor's (C. Robinson's, jun.) Address, Jan. 1. pp. 29. Ordinance concerning the C. Water Works, and the Use of Mystic Pond Water. pp. 8. Report of M. W. Board for 1865 (Jan. 15, 1866). pp. 32. (ed. 500.) Second Annual do., year to Dec. 31, 1866. pp. 26. Continued to 1875, which see. Ordinance establishing Fire Department passed March 1. pp. 31.

C. POOR's Fund. Report of a Special Committee to the Board of Trustees, Nov. 22 (History of this old fund). pp. 13. *Boston*, 1866

ELLIS, Rev. G. E. Religious Liberalism. pp. 17. (From Monthly Relig. Mag. for Dec.)

FOSS, Jacob. (Many years a resident in C.) Will of (with public bequests). pp. 16. *Charlestown*, 1866

[GOODWIN, Mrs. H. B.] Sherbrooke by H. B. G. Author of " Madge." 12°. pp. 463. New York, 1866, etc.

HENRY PRICE Lodge, C., constituted June 22, 5859. By-Laws, List of Members, Memoir (port.) of Henry Price. Sm. 8°. pp. 39.
Boston, 5866

LAMBERT, Rev. T. R. Sermon, St. John's Ch., Jan. 7. pp. 16. Published by request. *Boston*, 1866

MILES, Rev. J. B. Sermon. First Ch., Oct. 21, after the Funeral of Mrs. *Roxanna Glidden*. pp. 20. *Boston.* Address at the Funeral Obsequies of Serg. *Henry Todd*. pp. 12. *Charlestown*, 1866

THURSTON, Elizabeth A. The Little Wrinkled Old Man. A Christmas Extravaganza, and other Trifles. pp. 124. *Boston*, 1866. Mosaics of Life. pp. 305. *Philadelphia*, 1867

UNION Sugar Refinery *vs.* Francis O. Matthiesen in Circuit Court U. S.

WINCHESTER Home for Aged Indigent Women, Eden St. Opening and Dedication, Oct. 3. Address by Rev. O. C. Everett. Appendix. pp. 27. *Boston*, 1866

The Managers are from the Protestant Religious Societies of C. *Annual reports* (first, Jan., 1867) in pamphlets, 8°, *still continued* (fourteenth, 1880).

From Mrs. Nancy Winchester of C., who bequeathed for the purpose an estate valued at $10,000. About as much more was received from various sources, and the " Home" was established in the house on Eden St., formerly occupied by Mr. James K. Frothingham, an old and well-known citizen. See 1873, when a large and handsome brick building was opened close by the former.

1867.

AUSTIN, Hon. Arthur W. Argument for Jamaica Pond Aqueduct Corporation, Feb. 12, 1867. pp. 25. Address at Dedication of the Town House, Jamaica Plain. pp. 39. *Boston*, 1868. Speech at C., Nov. 1, 1856. pp. 12. n. t. p.

CITY DOC's. See 1861. Also School Report, 1867, Appendix, for Dedication of the Bunker Hill School House (Historical Address by W. H. Finney), and do. Warren do. (Ad. by Rev. G. E. Ellis), and Course of Study, in all pp. 132. Mayor's (L. Hull) Address, Jan. 7, and Appendix (Sdy. Reports). pp. 39. Specifications Warren School House, J. H. Rand, Architect. 4°. pp. 9.

First [Church and] Parish, Semi-Centennial Celebrations of the First Sabbath-School Society in Mass., and of the, on Sunday, Oct. 14, 1866, at First Ch. Portrait of Rev. J. Morse, D. D. Commemorative Discourse by Rev. J. B. Miles, History, List of Officers, etc. 12°. pp. 97 + 9. *Boston, 1867*

King Solomon's Lodge, C. (see 1783). By-Laws, Extracts from Records, List of Members, etc. Plate. pp. 88. *Boston, 1867*

Morse, Rev. J. (D. D.). Memorabilia in his life, by his son Sidney E. Reprinted, with Introduction, from the above. Port. pp. 24. *Boston, 1867*

Mutual Relief Soc. of St. Mary's, C., instituted Jan., 1854. Constitution, and List of Members. 12°. pp. 24. *Boston, 1867*

Naval Library and Institute, Navy Yard, C., instituted 1842. Statutes, History, List of Members, etc. 12°. pp. 36. *Boston, 1867*

Warren Institution for Savings, Acts, By-Laws, Living Members, etc. Sm. 4°. pp. 31. 1867. A similar publication, pp. 26. *Boston, 1877*

1868.

City Doc's. See 1861. Mayor's (L. Hall) Address, Jan. 6, and Rep's Police, Health, Fire, Valuation and Tax 1858–68. pp. 32. Rules and Orders of School Committee, and Regulations Public Schools. pp. 40. (Also pp. 33, 1871.) Report (pp. 71) has List of Graduates of the High School, 1851–68. Report Joint Committee on new City Hall. pp. 8.

Annexation to Boston, Argument against, Sherburne. Do., J. M. Stone, pp. 11. Brief Reply to the latter, M. A. Dow. pp. 10.

Charlestown Chronicle. Issued every Saturday, Richards & Wason, Publishers, $2.50 per year. No. 1, Saturday, Oct. 3, 1868. pp. 4 Called "Saturday Chronicle," Saturday, Sept. 10, 1870, Vol. II., No. 102. (Last No. in Public Library. V. 51, Saturday, Oct. 4, 1873.)

Ellis, John H. Lord Brougham considered as a Lawyer. Privately rep. from American Law Review. pp. 40. *Boston, 1868*

Goodwin, Mrs. H. B. Dr. Howell's Family. Also N. Y. & Boston, 1873. 16°. pp. 361.

Harris Chime in the Ch. of the First Parish, Dedication of, April 15. Address by Rev. J. B. Miles, Poems, etc. Imp. 8°. pp. 23. 250 copies. *Charlestown, 1868*

This chime (of 16 bells), the first in C. (and in a Trinitarian Congregational Ch. in the U. S. ?), was given to the First Ch. and Parish by Miss Charlotte Harris as a memorial of her ancestors, who were members of both. Her kindred for a hundred years have not ceased to be represented in both.

In Memoriam. Remarks of Rev. R. Ellis at the Funeral of Miss Mary Osgood. Boston, March 30. pp. 15.

Preble, Adl. Geo. H. (U. S. N., stationed C., 1866–73, etc.). Genealogical Sketch of the First Three Generations of Prebles in America, Portraits, *fac-similes*, etc. pp. 336. 125 copies for Family Circulation. *Boston, 1868*

WHEILDON, W. W.   The New Arctic Continent (American Association, Aug., 1868).   pp. 8.
WINTHROP Church, Manual, with List of Members, Jan., 1833, to
date.   12°.   pp. 47.   *Boston*, 1868

1869.

AUSTIN, Hon. J. W. (with Hon. E. H. Allen, and Hon. A. S. Hart-
well).   The Penal Code of the Hawaiian Kingdom, compiled from
the Penal Code of 1850, etc.   Published by Authority.   8°.
pp. xliv, 368, 14.   Government Press, *Honolulu*, *Oahu*, 1869

Mr. Austin, a native of C., was an Associate Justice of the Supreme Court at the
Hawaiian Kingdom.   Also, Decisions in Hawaiian Reports, 8°, *Honolulu*, 1877; Oration,
July 4, 1834, at Honolulu.

BRIDGES (Charles River and Warren), History of, see B. H. Aurora,
Nov. 13, 1869.
CITY Doc's.   See 1861.   Mayor's (E. L. Norton) Address, Jan. 4,
and Special Report on Poor.   pp. 27.   Chief Engineer's do.
ELLIS, Rev. G. E.   A Discourse, Harvard Ch., June 13, at the close
of his Ministry.   pp. 37.   *Charlestown*, 1869.   Two Lectures on
the Founders of Mass., Jan. 8 and 12, Lowell Institute, in Mass.
Hist. Soc. Course.   pp. 100.

For works after leaving C., and many contributions to Periodical literature, see History of the Harvard Ch., 1880.   The number and interest of the author's publications,
the thoroughness of the bibliographer's labor, and the elegance of the printer's workman-
ship, especially in the quarto issue of the History, render this list a remarkable combina-
tion of excellences.   The writer is indebted to Mr. Cutter and Mr. Edes for valuable
help in collecting publications by Dr. Ellis.

GAS Co. (of C.).   Act to increase capital, House Doc. 60.
GRINNELL, Rev. C. E.   Services at his Installation, Harvard Ch.,
Nov. 10, 1869.   Sermons by Rev. A. P. Peabody and by him, etc.
pp. 64.   *Charlestown*, 1869.   See History, 1880, for earlier works.
HAYNES, Gideon.   An Historical Sketch of the Mass. State Prison,
with Incidents, Suggestions, etc.   16°.   pp. 290.   *Boston*, 1869
HUNNEWELL, Jas. F.   Civilization at the Hawaiian Islands, an Introduction to a Bibliography of the Hawaiian Islands.   Woodcuts.
4°.   pp. 75.   100 copies privately printed for him.   *Boston*, 1869

The Bibliography from "Hawaiian Club Papers," 1868, was undertaken at the suggestion of J. F. H., who was prevented by important events from doing all he proposed,
and Wm. T. Brigham, Esq., deserves large credit in the work, the best on its subject.

MILES, Rev. J. B.   Memorial Address at the Funeral of *Wm. H.
Goodwin*, Dec. 12, 1868.   Resolutions.   16°.   pp. 61.   *Boston*, 1869
———— A Discourse commemorative of *James Hunnewell* in the First
Ch., C., May 9, 1869.   pp. 32.   *Privately printed*, 1869
———— The Resurrection of the Body (Bibliotheca Sacra, Oct.).
pp. 16.
ODD FELLOWS' Hall, Dedication.   Address by P. G. Thos. B. Har-
ris.   pp. 12.
STONE, Hon. J. M.   Sixty Falsehoods Exposed (at State House, and
relating to alterations of it).   pp. 60.   *Boston*, 1869
WHEILDON, W. W.   Argument before the U. S. Commissioners at C.
Navy Yard, Sept. 16–Oct. 7, on proposed Maverick Bridge.   pp. 40.
                                                  Charlestown, 1869

1870.

An Act [Mass. Leg., ch. 109], to incorporate the *Jasper Sugar Refinery* (in Boston or C.).

———— [Do., ch. 200], to incorporate the *St. Francis de Sales Society* of C., for charitable and benevolent purposes. (See 1880.)

Resolve Do., ch. 12] authorizing issue of Arms to the High School of C. House Doc. 117.

House Doc's. Amendments Annexation Bill, 284. Report on Travel. Charles River Bridge, 401.

"Charlestown Convent, its Destruction by a Mob," Aug. 11, 1834, and Account of subsequent proceedings. pp. 98. *Boston*, 1870.

City Doc's. See 1861. School Report. Dec. 30, do. Superintendent of Schools, and Dedication of High School House. pp. 75. Mayor's (W. H. Kent) Address, Jan. 3. pp. 19. Municipal Register. pp. 192. Regulations Free Evening Drawing Schools. City Ordinances. pp. 76. Do. Accountability in City Expenditures. pp. 8. Studies, Primary and Grammar Schools. pp. 8.

Childs, N. Poem, Golden Wedding, Jan. 27, 1870. pp. 8. n. p.

Forster, Dr. E. J. Pedigree, etc. Jacob Forster, Sen. pp. 25.

For Diary of John Leach, confined by the British in Boston Gaol, 1775, see N. E. H. Gen. Reg. xix., 255-64.

Frothingham, Hon. R. Municipalities, see Am. Antiq. Soc. Proc. No. 55.

Harvard Church, Report on the Organ. pp. 11.

Hunnewell, J. F. An American Shrine (from N. E. H. G. Reg., July). pp. 13. 50 copies. History and Topography First Ch.

Miles, Rev. J. B. Sleep in Jesus. A Discourse commemorative of *Susan Lamson Hunnewell*, First Ch., Feb. 20, 1870, and account of the Services, etc. pp. 32. 150 copies. Privately printed. 1870

Infant School and Children's Home Association, 36 Austin St. C. Dedicatory Address by Rev. O. C. Everett, and First Annual Report, etc. pp. 34. Continued, 11th in 1880. See 1834.

1871.

Annexation to Boston. Argument of Hon. Ellis W. Morton before Com. of Mass. Leg., Feb. 27, in behalf of. pp. 34. *Boston*, 1871. Judge Warren's Argument on the County Question. pp. 4. Hon. C. Robinson, jun. Do. against, at State House, Feb. 27. pp. 35. See also House Doc. 166.

City Doc's. See 1861. Mayor's (W. H. Kent) Address. Jan. 3. pp. 23. Annual Report of Chief Engineer of Fire Department to March 1. pp. 52. Report of Committee on the Reduction of Bunker Hill, filling Mill Pond. Flats, etc. pp. 31.

Edes, H. H. A Memorial of Josiah Barker of C. pp. 25. Privately printed. *Boston*, 1871

Ed. 100 copies. See N. E. Hist. Gen. Register, July, Vol. XXIV. Do. Vols. XXII.-XXV., a series of important Documents on Connecticut, with Notes, contributed by him.

Forster, Dr. E. J. The Family of Foster of C. pp. 6. (N. E. H. G. Reg. Jan., '71).

GRINNELL, Rev. C. E. Fanaticism. Annual Mass. Election Sermon Jan. 4, 1871. With a List of Preachers 1634-1871, (three new names, 17th century,) and Appendix by H. H. Edes. pp. 61. *Boston*, 1871. Rt. Hand at Ord. F. T. Washburn, Milton, March 2.

HUNNEWELL, James F. The Lands of Scott. Portrait of Sir W. Scott, and four maps. Large 16°. pp. 508. *Boston*, 1871
———— The same, revised with slight change. Do. *Boston*, 1871
———— The same. A. and C. Black, *Edinburgh*, 1871

Also reissued, 1879, in different style, by Houghton, Osgood & Co., uniform with their new edition of Scott. In same style, a new edition, 1883. This book and the Edinburgh Catalogue were the largest works on Scott produced at his "Centennial," 1871. James R. Osgood & Co. published the first edition. In the last two maps (plates lost) are re-engraved, with new railways, etc., and another portrait of Scott (the former burned).

LAMBERT, Rev. T. R. A Sermon in St. John's Ch. Jan. 15, 1871, after the Death of *Peter Hubbell*, Senior Warden of the Ch. pp. 16 + 2. *Boston*, 1871

PREBLE, Adl. G. H. Wm. Pitt Fessenden; a Memoir. pp. 24. (N. E. H. G. Reg., April.) *Boston*, 1871
———— *Henry Oxnard*. In Memoriam. pp. 10. n. p. or d. (Son of above, died in C., 1871.)

MILES, Rev. J. B. (last yr. in C.). Le Tribunal International, etc. pp. 16. *Paris*, 1874. The Association for Reform and Codification of the Law of Nations, pp. 12 (Int. Rev. for Jan., 1875). See 1876.

1872.

CITY DOC's. See 1861. School Report with Description and Dedication of the Harvard School House (3 pl.) pp. 76 + 13. Mayor's (W. H. Kent) Address, Jan. 1. pp. 30. Ordinances of the City of C. in force from and after Jan. 1, 1870. pp. 102. *Charlestown*, 1872. Reports: First Annual of City Physician (separate) to Feb. 29. pp. 6. Do. Fire Department. March 1. pp. 50. Supplementary Catalogue of the Public Library, Oct. 1, 1862, to July 1, 1872 (consolidating all Supplements, and last before Annexation). pp. 166. (See Boston Pub. Lib. Cat., Jan., 1874 and after.)

THE *Charlestown Times*, Weekly, Saturdays, by Publishers of the Boston Times, No. 1, Oct. 19, 1872. pp. 4. Became *The Bunker Hill Times*, Vol. II., No. 1, Sat., Oct. 18, 1873, published 18 City Square, Charles R. Byram, Editor. Now (1880) 28 Main St. E. Gerry Brown, Proprietor (since March 20).

C. FIRE Department, Constitution of the Charitable Association of, organized April 23, 1867. (18°.) pp. 12.

CŒUR DE LION Commandery. By-Laws, Feb. 20, 1872. 12°. pp. 36. List of Members. Caleb Rand, *Charlestown*, 1872

FROTHINGHAM, Hon. R. The Rise of the Republic of the United States. pp. xxii + 640. *Boston*, 1872

HUNNEWELL, J. F. Relation of Virginia by Henry Spelman, 1609. First printed from the original MS. with an Introduction. Sm. 4°. pp. 59. Chiswick Press, *London*, 1872

100 copies, also 50 with double columns for Libraries. Privately printed for J. F. H.

MIDDLESEX Horse R. R. Co., Argument for.   Map.   pp. 67.   1872.

PREBLE. Adl. G. H. (U. S. N.).   Our Flag.   Origin and Progress of the Flag of the U. S., etc.   12 col. plates, 64 woodcuts.   pp. 535. *Albany*, 1872.   Do. 2d revised ed., 240 ills., pp. 837.   *Boston*, 1880.

The Chesapeake and Shannon, June 1, 1813, 25 copies from "The United Service." Philadelphia, 1879. Memorial of, to 43d Congress, etc. pp. 50. Boston, 1874. The Chase of the Rebel Steamer Oreto into the Bay of Mobile by the U. S. Steam-ship Oneida, Sept. 4, 1862. *Cambridge*, 1862.

STOWE, Rev. Wm. T. (Univ. Ch. 1871–78).   In Memoriam, *Barnabas Edmunds*.   C., 1778–1872   Sermon, Universalist Ch., C., Jan. 21. Appendix. pp. 19.   *Charlestown*, 1872

SOLDIERS' and Sailors' Monument.   Proceedings at its Dedication, June 17, by the City Council of C.   Address by Hon. R. Frothingham.   pp. 29.   (Separate ed. of the Add.   pp. 15.)   C., 1872

TRAFTON, Adeline.   An American Girl Abroad.   Woodcuts.   pp. 245. 1872.   Katherine Earle.   Illustrated.   pp. 325.   1874.   His Inheritance.   pp. 428.   1878.   All 16°.   *Boston* and *New York*

TWOMBLY. Rev. A. S. (Winthrop Ch., 1872, now there).   The Apocryphal Period of Hebrew History in its relation to Christ.   "New Englander," April, 1877.   8°.   Reprinted.   pp. 24.

Previously, Oration, July 4, Cherry Valley, N. Y. 8°. pp. 11. C. V. 1859. Discourse, Albany, N. Y., July 7, 1863, in memory of Adjutant R. M. Strong. Address, N. Y. Teachers' Association, July 29, 1863. Troy, 1863. Thanksgiving Discourse, Nov. 26, at Albany. 8°. pp. 30. Discourse at do., April 16, 1865, on Assassination of President Lincoln. Peace Discourse, do., Dec. 7, 1865. Articles in "Scribner's" and "New Englander."

1873.

AN ACT [Mass. Leg., ch. 23] to incorporate the *C. Free Dispensary and Hospital*.

———— [Do., ch. 286, approved May 14, 1873] *to unite the City of Charlestown with the City of Boston*.   See 1854.   The mutual acceptance of this Act closed the separate municipal history of C.

———— [Do., ch. 357] Steam R. R.'s in C. may discontinue grade crossings.   [360] To authorize the Eastern R. R. to construct a Freight Track and take lands for freight purposes in C., and for other purposes.   (Great changes made on the Mill-pond and Front St.)

CITY DOC's.   See 1861, Note, and 1866.   See Report of School Committee for Account of Trust Fund, List of Trustees, 1793 to 1874.   pp. 62.   Annual Reports of the Trustees of the C. Free Schools, 1801 to 1838, inc., printed by order of the School Committee of 1873.   pp. 90.   C., 1874.   Mayor's (J. Stone) Address, Jan. 6.   pp. 16.   Also, pp. 21.   Report of Public Library for 1873 (13th).   pp. 12.   Report of Mystic Water Board (9th) to City Council of Boston to Dec. 31, 1873.   Boston Doc. 35.   pp. 27. 10th, do. 86, 1875.   *The last separate municipal reports of Charlestown were issued in 1875.*

ANNEXATION to Boston.   Report of the Commission appointed by Order of the City Council of C.   pp. 17.   *Boston*, 1873.   Acts relating to (also of Brighton, Brookline, and W. Roxbury).   pp. 54. Boston City Doc. 89.   1873.

C. Free Dispensary and Hospital. Act of Incorporation, By-Laws, and First Annual Report, Officers, etc. pp. 21. (Continued, 8th in 1880.) *Charlestown*, 1873

Faith Lodge. (June 10, 5868.) By-Laws, etc., adopted March 12, 1869. 12°. pp. 26. *Charlestown*, 1873

First Baptist Church. History, Covenant, and Catalogue of the Members. 12°. pp. 24. *Boston*, 1873

O'Reilly, John Boyle. Songs from the Southern Seas. pp. 250. *Boston*, 1873. "Songs, Legends, and Ballads." pp. 350, 1878; and "Moondyne: A Story from the Under World." pp. 350, 1879, both *Boston*.

Mr. O'Reilly, a resident of Charlestown for several years, is editor of the Boston Pilot.

The Symmes Memorial. A Biographical Sketch of Rev. Z. Symmes, minister of C., 1634–71, with a Genealogy, etc., of his descendants, by J. A. Vinton. pp. 184. *Boston*, 1873

Winchester Home. Opening of the New Edifice, Eden St. Address by Rev. O. C. Everett, Poem by Rev. Mark Trafton, Order of Services, etc. pp. 32. (See 1866.) *Cambridge*, 1873

1874-1880.

City Doc's. Valedictory Address of Jonathan Stone, last Mayor, Jan. 2, 1874. pp. 12.

Drake, S. A. Historic Fields and Mansions of Middlesex. Illustrated. *Boston*, 1874

Contains a large amount of interesting matter on C.

Frothingham, Hon. R. Oration at Boston, July 4, 1874. With Notes. pp. 55. *Boston*, 1874

Grinnell, Rev. C. E. Farewell Sermon at Harvard Ch., Dec. 28, 1873. pp. 16. *Charlestown*, 1874

Mystic River Corporation. Charter and By-Laws. *Cambridge*, 1874

Sprague, Wm. B. (D. D.). Life of Jedidiah Morse, D. D. pp. viii + 333. *New York*, 1874

Wheildon, W. W. Contributions to Thought. 16°. pp. 236. Author's Private Printing Press, *Concord*, Mass., 1874.

His other works (besides all above): Address, Dedication of New Hall for Corinthian Lodge, Concord. Atmospheric Theory of the Open Polar Sea. Consolidation and Competition. Falling Snow. Genius of Freemasonry. Hoosac Tunnel Consolidation. Masonic Odes. Miscellanies. Papers read to American Association for Advancement of Science. Pilgrim Fathers. Report on Mechanic Apprentices' Library Association. Scientific Excursion, Iowa, and Strictures on Article in N. A. Review, "Architecture in the United States."

Charles River Bridge, Specifications for repairs, etc. *Boston*, 1875

Charlestown. Something of its History. pp. 12. *Charlestown*, 1875

Early Days, Forgotten Centennial, and Revolutionary Period, by E. N. Coburn. Historic Points, by H. H. Edes. Centennial Reminiscences, by A. E. Cutter. Ministerial Lots, etc., by T. B. Wyman.

Foote, Rev. H. W. The Wisdom from above. Sermon at King's Chapel, Jan. 3, 1875, occasioned by the Death of Rev. Jas. Walker, D. D., LL. D. pp. 48. *Boston*, 1875

Howard Lodge, No. 22, I. O. O. F. (ins. Oct. 10, 1843). By-Laws, History, etc. 12°. pp. 136. *Boston*, 1875

Morse, Samuel Finley Breese, Memorial of, including appropriate
ceremonies of respect at the National Capitol and elsewhere. Portrait. 4°. pp. 359. Published by order of Congress. (See 1819,
pp. 49.) *Washington*, 1875. Life of ———, Inventor of the Magnetic Telegraph. 10 plates, many cuts. pp. xiv. + 776.
New York, 1875

McKenzie, Rev. A. *James Browning Miles.* A Memorial Discourse,
First Ch., Dec. 5, 1875, on its late pastor. pp. 32.
Riverside Press, 1876

First Church. Manual. List of Members, etc. 16°. pp. 23. 1876

Boston Water Board, Doc. 69, with 11th Rep. Mystic, May 1, 1875
to May 1, 1876. Continued annually in same connection.

De Costa, Rev. B. F. In Memoriam. Sister Sainte Claire, Order
of St. Ursula. 12°. pp. 25. With an account of the Sisters after
the destruction of the Convent, and a sheet with Genealogy of the
De Costa family. *Charlestown*, 1876

Odd Fellows' Mutual Benefit Ass'n, B. H. Dist. Organized Nov.
29, 1870. pp. 13. *Boston*, 1876

Devens, Gen. Charles (Jr.). See B. H. Celebrations, 1875, p. 27.
Oration at C., June 17, 1875. Author's ed., 303 copies, 8°, 3 do.,
4°. pp. 56. *Boston*, 1876. Address to the Graduating Class of the
U. S. Military Academy, West Point, N. Y., June 14. Small 4°.
pp. 40. *New York*, 1876. Gen. Meade and the Battle of Gettys-
burg. An Oration at New Haven, Conn., May 14. pp. 30. *Morrisania*, 1873. (See Hist. Mag., July, 1873.) Oration, Boston, Sept.
17, 1877, at the dedication of the Soldiers' and Sailors' Monument
on Boston Common. In vol. by City of B.; also privately printed,
178 copies. pp. 16. *Boston*, 1877

Forster, Dr E. J. A Manual for Medical Officers of the Militia of
the U. S. 16°. pp. 102. *New York* and *Boston*, 1877

Whitney, Louisa. The Burning of the Convent. 16°. pp. 198.
Boston, 1877

Charlestown Book of Possessions (C. Archives 31, 1638–1802),
Records of Lands, Surveys, etc., to 1803, being the "Third Report
of the Record Commissioners of the City of Boston, 1878." 8°.
pp. vii + 273. *Boston*, 1878

De Costa, Wm. Hickling. In Memoriam. *Charlestown*, 1878.
Elizabeth De Costa. In Memoriam. *New York*, 1880. Both
sm. 4°. pp. 8. Privately printed.
See 1852. Mr. De C. printed in C. during more than quarter of a century.

Charlestown Trade and Improvement Association. Organized
1879. Constitution and Officers, 1879–80. pp. 11. *Boston*, 1879

The Trinity Bazaar, Trinity (M. E.) Church, Dec. 17, 18. 3 nos.
each. 8°. pp. 8. 1879.
Contains a List of Pastors 1829–80, and a Brief History of the S. School.

Fitchburg R. R. Relief Ass'n. By-Laws and Members. 1878–79.

Catalogue of Books in the C. Branch Library of the Boston Public
Library, with an Appendix, 2d ed., May, 1880. Imp. 8°. pp. 4, 395
(printed covers). Printed by Order of the Trustees, *Boston*, 1880

WYMAN, T. B. The Genealogies and Estates of C., 1629–1818. With an Introductory Note by Henry H. Edes (editor of the work). Portrait. Map of C., 1818. pp. xiv + 1178, 2 title-pages. pp. 1060ᵃ. 1060ᵇ, Schedule of the Ancient Colored Inhabitants on record prior to 1800 (a valuable separate sheet printed at the expense of the editor). 2 vols. *Boston,* 1879

REPORT of St. Francis de Sales Church Debt Society from June 1, 1879, to Jan. 1, 1880, with a long list of Subscribers. pp. 32.
[*Boston,* 1880]

Describes a successful effort to reduce a debt incurred in building the very large, substantial, and handsome church of St. Francis de Sales, on Bunker Hill.

RECORDS of the *First Church* in Charlestown, Mass., 1632–1789. Prepared by Jas. F. Hunnewell, and printed under his care and for him, by David Clapp & Son. Royal quarto. 6 plates. pp. (8) + 168 + xii + (2 + 2) to xxvii. *Boston,* 1880

With a description of the five volumes containing the Records, — the contents of that kept by the ministers entirely reproduced; an Appendix on the topography and early history of the church: and six pages in *facsimile,* showing the styles of writing in the original MS About two thirds of the above matter appeared in the N. E. Hist. Gen. Register, 1869–79, Vols. XXIII. to XXXIII. This complete edition, 62 copies, all of one size.

HISTORY of the *Harvard Church* in Charlestown, 1815–1879 [by Henry H. Edes] with Services at the Ordination of Mr. Pitt Dillingham, Oct. 4, 1876, etc. 8°. pp. 294. Three plates, 2 plans of pews (with names of occupants). Privately Printed, *Boston,* 1879

Issued in 1880. Also 50 copies, 4° (with a map of C., 1818, and 1 pl. add'l.). List of Publications of Rev. Jas. Walker, D. D., pp. 9, and do. of Rev. G E. Ellis, D.D., pp. 11, each 50 copies, 8° ; the three for Mr. Edes, author and editor of this elaborate, interesting, and elegantly printed work. See Ellis, 1869.

GUNNISON, E. Norman. C. 1837, died 1880. Author of poems in Scribner's Monthly, Christian at Work, and other publications.

OSGOOD, Rev. Samuel, D.D. C., 1812, died N. Y., 1880. This distinguished clergyman, settled in Nashua, Providence, and New York City, made very large contributions to literature, for which see Allibone, 1465.

BUDINGTON, William Ives, D. D. In Memoriam. Services and Addresses at his funeral, Clinton Av. Church, Brooklyn, N. Y., Dec. 2, 1879, resolutions, etc. pp. 40. *New York,* 1880

Minister of the First Ch., 1840–54. None among the many honored men who have ministered in C. could have been more beloved. Charitable towards all, learned, eloquent, chivalrous, and courteous, devoted to the highest requirements of his sacred office, this true Christian gentleman and minister died while these pages were being prepared, and the writer sadly records the last title that tells of his intimate and nearly life-long friend.

HUNNEWELL, James. Journal of the Voyage of the "Missionary Packet," Boston to Honolulu, 1826. With (2) Maps, and (6) plates, and a Memoir (by J. F. H.). Royal quarto. pp. xxvii + (1) + 77. James F. Hunnewell's Privately Printed Work, No. VIII. 100 copies. John Wilson & Son, University Press. *Charlestown,* 1880

The daily record of a remarkable voyage of nine months, in a vessel that measured 39 92/100 tons. The North Atlantic, the seas near Cape Horn, and the Straits of Magellan, were traversed during wintry weather. The Memoir tells its own story of courage, enterprise, and integrity.

ARTICLES OMITTED.

RUSSELL, John Miller. Poem July 4. 1798. Pastoral Songs of
Virgil; added (other) poems by R. 12°. 1799. Funeral Oration on Washington, 1800. All. *Boston*. See p. 36.

DEVENS, Richard. The Witness of the Spirit, discourse to the Students of N. J. College, 1773. pp. 16. C., 1799. See p. 36.

PARKER, Daniel. An Oration at C., July 4, 1806, to the "Republican Citizens." pp. 20. *Boston*, 1806

TURNER, Rev. Ed. The Substance of a Discourse, Universalist Meeting-house, C., Sept. 14, 1815, at the Funeral of *Mr. Samuel Thompson*. (C., 1779–Sept. 12, 1815.) pp. 12. *Boston* [1815]

WARREN PHALANX (see p. 46). Rules and Regulations. 16°. pp. 16. *Charlestown*, 1819

UNIVERSALIST Soc. A Sermon June 22, 1825, at Ordination of Rev Calvin Gardner, by T. Jones, of Gloucester. pp. 31. *Boston*, 1825

COVENANT of above Church. List of Members at Organization, Dec. 1811, to Feb. 16, 1844, etc. 16°. pp. 16. *Charlestown*, 1844

C. LIGHT INFANTRY. Rules and Regulations, May 1, 1829.
First Code adopted July 4, 1804; amended and rep., 1812; do. March, 1821.

GLEASON, B. Oration July 4. Lechmere Point. pp. 35. *Boston*, 1826

HARRIS (family of C.) and Others *vs.* Jesse D. Elliot. Case of Trespass on Real Estate, with many historical items. pp. 24. n. p. [Oct. 1834.]

MEMORIAL of Citizens of C. for compensation for losses June 17, 1775. pp. 13. House Doc. 55, 1834 Mass. Leg.

WINTHROP Juvenile Ass'n. Catalogue of Books. 16°. pp. 12. 1839

REPORT (House Doc. 71) on Petition of Chas. Forster and others of C. pp. 36. 1843.

MONUMENT Square Baptist Church. Declaration of Faith and Covenant adopted June 7; ch. constituted April 22, 1844. 12°. pp. 20.
Boston, 1844

HAZEL, HARRY. A Romance of Mt Benedict. *Do.* 1845.

GREENLEAF, Rev. P. H. The New Year, a Sermon, Jan. 9. *Do.* 1848

C. FEMALE SEMINARY. Annual Report of the Writing Association. pp. 27. *Boston*, 1849. [*Boston*, 1852

BALFOUR, Rev. W. Memoir by Thos. Whittemore, 16°. pp. 224.

PETITION of Boston and Chelsea R. R. Co., etc. *Charlestown*, 1854

DAMON, Rev. S. C. Puritan Missions in the Pacific. Honolulu, 1866. Edition printed for James Hunnewell. Rev. H. Bingham, Editor. 12°. pp. 48 + 3. *New Haven*, 1869

EZEKIEL CHEEVER, and some of his descendants. By John T. Hassam. pp. 64. *Boston*, 1879
From N. E. H. G. Reg., April, 1879, with poems by E. C. added.

STATE PRISON, Remarks on; Rules, etc. pp. 62. *Boston*, 1823. Report, Senate Doc. 6, 1826. Laws, Rules, Discipline, etc. pp. 88. *Do.*, 1839. Annual Reports since. *Do.*, with description of the New Prison completed Oct., 1829, view and plan. pp. 112. C. 1830.

BUNKER HILL.

BIXBY, Samuel. Diary. See Frothingham's Illustrations of Siege (27–40), p. 15.

BROADSIDE (large). Address to the Selectmen for a Day of Thanksgiving. 1824.

B. H. ILLUSTRATED Almanac. List of Societies with Officers, etc., in C. 12°. Unpaged. Office of the B. H. Times, 1876

CERTIFICATE of Membership of the B. H. M. Association. A sheet 2 ft. 10 in. ✕ 1 ft. 11 in., engraved. View of the battle; another of the Monument. (1833?)

CRESSY, Noah. The Battle and Monument of B. H. compared with the Agonies and Triumphs of the Cross. A Poem. 12°. pp. 24. *Portland*, n. d.

REPORT, Address, and heading of a Subscription. folio, pp. 3. 1829.

" MR. WEBSTER'S Address at Bunker Hill, June 17, 1775 from the Original Manuscript. Boston : J. N. Bradlee & Co., Daily Mail Office," pp. 15, with an Account of the Celebration, 1843.

MUNICIPAL DOCUMENTS.

TOWN BY-LAWS, approved May 9, 1820. 12°. pp. 10. 1820. Rules and Regulations of Engineers of Fire Department, adopted Sept. 7, 1840. 18°? pp. 8. 1840 Both *Charlestown*.

CITY. Rules and Orders of City Council. 12° (23 pages). Report on reducing City Debt Dec. (8). Ordinance on accountability City Expenditures (8). All, 1848. Ordinance on Assessment and Collection of Taxes (4).

WORKS PRINTED IN CHARLESTOWN, 1786–1836.

Author's names without titles refer to descriptions given above ; the number of pages is within brackets ; all works are octavo unless the size is expressed.

1785. The American Recorder, *the first newspaper*.

1786. Bartlett (12). 12°. By *Allen and Cushing*. First *pamphlet* (?).

1798. Franklin (300). 12°. *First book* (?). 1797. Bartlett (12). Cary (24). Devens (16), Russell (16). All by *John Lamson*, " at his office near the bridge."

1799. * Morse (50) also * (16). Devens (16). By *Samuel Etheridge* (in May ?). *Harris, Rev. T. M., Discourse to Young Men at Dorchester.

Mr. Etheridge was the chief printer of books in C., and printed there 1799 to 1820. He was at "22 Marlborough Street, Boston," in the summer of 1798. From 1799 to 1805, both inclusive, he appears to have been the only printer in C. His first address was " next door to Warren Tavern," on Main St., by Pleasant St. Later (1836 ?) he was on Main St., nearly opposite Wood St. *Works from his press are marked by a star.*

1800. * Bartlett (15). * Proceedings on Washington (16 + 36 + 24). Also, the following Eulogies on Washington : * Oliver Everett, Dorchester, Feb. 22 (22) ; * Rev. T. M. Harris, do. Jan. 7. Masonic (13) ; * Do. do. Dec. 29. 1799 (16); * Rev. Rosewell Messinger, Old York, Me. (16) ; * Rev. Phillips Payson, Chelsea, Jan. 14 (15) ; * D. Tappan (in English) and J. Willard (Pres. Harvard Col.) in Latin, Feb. 21 (44) and also in 4°; * Rev. N. Emmons, Sermon. Mass. Missionary Soc., Boston, May 27, and Add. to the Public, etc. (44) ;

* Rev. T. M. Harris, Beauties of Nature Delineated, etc. ; * Geo. Washington, Farewell Address to the People of the U. S. (24) ; * Do. Selections from his Correspondence with Jas. Anderson (80).
1801. * Austin (29). * Harris (320), *first* 8° *volume in C.* (?), * also (20). * C. R. Aikin, Concise View, Facts concerning Cow Pox, 3d ed. 12° (143). * Rev. Robert Hall, Modern Infidelity, etc., a Sermon (55). * Progress of the Pilgrim Good Intent in Jacobinical Times, 12° (119). * Rev. Phineas Whitney, Ser. at Lunenburg, March 4, at Interment of Rev. Zabdiel Adams (24).
1802. * Morse (thick 8°). * Capt. Jon. Carver, Travels in the Interior Parts of N. America, 1766–68, 4th Am. ed., 12° (312). * Rev. Seth Payson, Proofs of the Existence of Illuminism, 12° (292).
1803. * Morse (32), also * (32). * Constitution of Mass. Soc. for Promoting Christian Knowledge (16).
1804. * Morse, 12° (388). * Austin (312). * Rev. Levi Frisbie, Discourse before Soc. for Propagating the Gospel among the Indians of N. A., Nov. 1 (38). * Mass. Medical Soc., Constitution, By-Laws Members (32). * Rev. D. Osgood, Two Discourses, Malden, at "setting up of a Baptist Society in that place," 12° (83).
1805. * ? Morse (28). * Putnam (18). * J. Milton, Poetical Works; text of Dr. Newton; Essay by J. Aikin. 2 vols. Pocket ed. by *S. Etheridge* and *C. Stebbins.* * Rev. Job Orton, Short Exposition of the Old Testament, etc. First American from 2d London ed., 6 vols., thick 8°, 1805-6. * Plain Advice for Religious Tradesmen, etc. * Watts's Psalm and Hymns, "in miniature, printed on writing paper."
1806. * State Prison (48). Morse, on Miss Russell (18), by *J. Howe*, n. p. * Rev. Thos. Barnard, Discourse before Soc. for Propagating the Gospel among the Indians and others in N. A. (47). * Rev. R. Fleming, The Fulfilling of the Scripture delineated. * Mrs. Eliz. Rowe, Devout Exercises, ed. by Dr. I. Watts. Sm. 18° (189).
1807. Bonar, Archibald, Genuine Religion, etc., (48), *J. Howe.* * A Correct Statement of the Controversy between T. O. Selfridge and B. Austin (52). * Rev. P. Doddridge, Family Expositor. 6 vols. 8°.
1808. Malden Bridge, 16° (9). * Rev. Mr. Corbet, Self-Employment in secret. * Rev. J. Allein, An Alarm to Unconverted Sinners, etc. * Rollin's Ancient History, 12th ed. (2 vols. issued by Feb.). The Great Question answered, etc., with the sentiments of Fenelon. *J. Howe.* * Rev. J. Scott, Discourse, March 9, at Funeral of Rev. S. Foxcroft, Gloucester (44).
1809. † Gleason. † Collier, 4 vols., 12° (1810-11), by *S. T. Armstrong.*

His printing-office was in the second story of the brick building on Main St., nearly opposite Union St. He removed to Boston about 1812. *His work marked* †.

Chickering, Rev. J., Dedication Sermon, Woburn, Jan. 28 (28). Printed by *Hastings, Etheridge,* and *Bliss, Boston.* (Several works bear this imprint.) † Rev. Noah Webster, Solemn Reasons for declining to adopt the Baptist Theory and Practice. † Child's Memorial — the Early Piety and Happy Death of Miss D. Dowdney, Portsea, Eng., with Account of Miss Sarah Barrow.

1810. Balfour (72) by *Jonathan Howe.* Brown, Trial (131).
† Morse (72), "price 37½ cts." ** Mosheim, J. L., Ecclesiastical
History, Ancient and Modern, from Latin by A. Maclaine, D. D.,
6 vols. 8°. **Wm. Newcome, Our Lord's Conduct as a Divine
Instructor (12 + 516). **These two works by *S. Etheridge,
jun.,* who appears, 1810, continuing his father's business. *Works
by him are marked* **. N. H. General Ass'n, Extracts from Min-
utes of. † Universalist Collection of Hymns, 2d ed. 12° (360).
† Poetical Works of T. Smollet, M. D., with Life of the Author.
Ashael Brown (pub'r ?).

1811. † Collier, 12°. Edward Young, Works, 3 vols. 12°. † Rev.
E. Smith (Hopkinton, N. H.), A Dissertation on the Prophecies.
† Richard Baxter, The Saint's Everlasting Rest, 12°, pp. 319.

1812. ** Evarts (32). ** Morse (32). J. G. Bevan, Refutation of
Aspersions of Soc. of Friends in Mosheim's History. ** Aug. Calmet, Great Dictionary of the Holy Bible, Taylor's ed., 4 vols.
4°. S. E. Jr., 1812–14.

Vol. I., 1 plate; II., 1 do., both unpaged; III., 105 pl., 3 maps (538 + 12); IV., 69
pl., 6 maps (6 — 536 – 20). Published at $9 per vol., boards, and a few superior copies
at $12. It is the largest and finest work from the C. Press, and compares favorably
with large publications at that time in other places, even London. See 1817. See Fi-
notti (J. M.) Bibliographia Cath. Amer. N. Y. 1872, p. 63.

* D. Ramsay, Life of Martha Laurens Ramsay. Price, 75 cts. 16°
(270). Gen. Geo. Washington, Farewell Address to the Citizens
of the U.S. of A. (8). Printed and sold by *Hans Lund,* C. 1812.

1813. Balfour (96), by *J. Howe.* ** Bartlett (15). ** New Testament (4½ × 2¾ in.). **Thos. Reid, Works, With his Life and
Writings by Dugald Stuart, 4 vols. ** Rules and Regulations for
the Army of the U. S., 12° (18).

1814. Morse (192). ** Tufts (16). Turner (24) by *J. Howe.*

1815. Turner. Rev. Cotton Mather, The Christian Philosopher, etc.,
published at the Middlesex Bookstore. *F. McKown,* Printer. 16°
(324). 1816. ** Bradford (38).

1817. Ware (16). ** Sacred Geography, etc., by Edward Wells,
D. D., revised, corrected, and augmented ; pub'd under direction of
the Editor of Calmet's Dictionary, intended as a fifth vol. to that
work. 4° (496). 31 plates, 12 maps.

1818. Turner (12), by *J. Howe.*

1819. Gleason (16) by *T. Green.* Morse, 2 vols. (see 1792, p. 33).
Turner (25) and (13); also School Report, Broadside, *Bellamy
and Green,* Printers, C. * The Christian Orator, 3d ed. 18° (298).

1820. First Church (11), and Town Reports, by *David Wilson,* printer, C. Walker (8). The Hieroglyphick Bible, etc., 3d ed., pub'd
by Joseph Avery. Plymouth, printed at *Geo. Clark & Co.'s* Office,
C. Woodcuts. 12°. pp. 144. Morse, 12° (324), see p. 40.

1821. State Prison (small pamphlet). 1822. Turner (15), by *J. Howe.*
1824. Balfour (456), by *Geo. Davidson,* C. Thos. Paine, Political
writings, etc. 2 vols. (*G. D.* continued printing in C., 1835.)

1825–27. Town Reports by same. B. H. Aurora, *W. W. Wheildon.*

1828. Balfour (72), and 12° (360), by *G. Davidson.* Everett (13),
by *Wheildon and Raymond.*

1829. Balfour, 12° (360) Warren Ins., 12° (12), by *Geo. Davidson*. Town Documents, this year, and afterwards.

1830. Everett (51) and E. Phinney, Address Middlesex Soc. Husbandmen, Oct. 7 (28), by *Wm. W. Wheildon*.

1831. Directory, 16° (125). Fessenden (16), Sumner, by *W. W. W.*

1832. Proceedings against Mrs. Emily Richardson, 2d Cong. Ch., Reading, 2d ed. (38). *W. W. W.*

1834. School Report, *W. W. W.* Directory.

1835. Hon. E. Everett. Address, Lexington. April 19th (66).

1836. Directory, 16° (93). By-Laws, 16° (8). C. Wharf Co., 12° (29), by *W. W. W.* State Prison Laws. Paul et Virginie. Histoire par J. H. B. de St. Pierre. Avec des notes en Anglois de l'usage des écoles. 16° (165). Simon Rodenburgh. Beginning a series of works by eminent French authors.

The productions of the C. Press after this date, like those during several years before it, were occasional pamphlets and the one news-paper of the town. The printing of books had passed to other places. In later years Mr. Caleb Rand has printed several handsome volumes.

GENERAL INDEX.

Articles classed with *Bunker Hill* are alphabetically arranged on pages 13 to 29, and are not included here.

Acts Massachusetts Legislature, *public*, see 1781 to 1873, *private*, see 1827, 1837, 1840, 1841, 1846, 1847, 1849, 1851, 1852.

Annexation. Sundry to Cambridge, Act, 1802; Tufts to C., 1811; to W. Cambridge, 1842; to Somerville, 1842.

—— **to Boston.** Acts 1854, 1873. Publications on, 1854 (3), 1855 (2), 1868 (5), 1871 (4), 1873 (2). Petition, 1860.

Banks. Bunker - Hill, Act, 1825. Charlestown, 1832. Monument, 1854. Phœnix, 1832. Savings Banks, C. Five Cent, Act, 1854; Warren, Act and By-Laws, 1829; By-Laws, etc., 1837, 1857, 1862, 1867.

Bridges. *Charles River*, Acts, 1785, 1792, 1841. Reports on, 1827. Against Warren B., 1828, 1830, 1837. See 1839; page 66 (sds 1847-73); 1854, 1855, 1859, 1869, history 1869, 1871, 1875. *Chelsea*, Acts, 1802, 1846. *Malden*, Acts, 1787, Rules, 1808. Address of, 1829. See 1851. *Maverick*, see Wheildon. 1869. *Prison Point*, Acts, 1838, 1854. *Railroad*, Acts, 1848, 1855. *Warren*, Reasons, 1825, 1827; Acts, etc., 1828, 1841; History, 1869. See 1830, 1855, 1857,

1839, 1840, page 66 (1847-73), 1854, 1855, 1859 (items to 1870), 1871-73.

Bunker Hill. Battle, etc., pages 13-29. Monument Association, Act 1823, Sale 1833. Whig Declaration, 1840. See p. 88.

Charities. *C. Charity Fund*, Act 1806. *C. Fire Department*, 1872. *C. Fire Dispensary*, Act and Reports, 1873. *C. Infant School*, Act, 1834; Reports, 1870. *C. Mechanic*, 1839. *C. Poors' Fund*, 1825, 1868, (history) 1806. *City Mission*, 1855, 1857. *Female Benevolent (Devens) Soc.*, 1856. *Ministry at Large*, 1854. *Mutual Relief* (St. Mary's), 1867. *Winchester Home*, Openings, 1865, 1873; Reports, 1866. See *Societies*.

Charlestown Affairs (Town). Assessors, 1826. *Board of Health*, Acts 1818, 1832; Rules, 1819, 1855. *Building Acts*, 1810, 1824. *By-Laws*, (Town) 1828, 1846. *Engine Men*, Acts 1800, 1826. *Expenses*, 1810 (for 1810-23), 1824 and after. *Do. of Schools*, 1842. *Documents*, 1825 and after. *Finance*, 1841. *Fire*, Act 1810, (1824), 1822. *Fire Department*, Act 1829, 1840; Rules, etc., 1840. *Gunpowder*, keeping of, Acts 1814, 1825. *Sidewalks*, Act 1824 (see

PERSONAL INDEX.

Bunker Hill, and references pp. 11–13, alphabetically arranged, which see.
Dates only, indicate works by persons named.
Biographical Notices are indicated by *abbreviations*, viz. : —

A.   Allen, W., American Biographical Dictionary, Boston, 1857.
B.   Budington, W. 1., History First Church, 1845.
D.   Drake, F. S., Dictionary of American Biography, Boston, 1872.
F.   Frothingham, R., History of Charlestown.
M. Coll. or M. Pro.   Massachusetts Historical Society Collections or Proceedings, in volumes given.
Mem.   Memorial of the person mentioned.
Reg.   New England Historic-Genealogical Society Register.

The above Personal Index contains references to about a dozen "Lives," in volumes, eighty memorial pamphlets, and three hundred and sixty notices of various lengths, or about four hundred and fifty articles describing about two hundred and forty persons, natives or residents of Charlestown. This large amount of material already printed seems to render unnecessary a biographical dictionary of the town, that the writer, several years ago, designed. For the present, at least, he prints only one memoir described under the date 1880. Although the above list is large, it can probably be increased. Many obituary notices, not included, are to be found in newspapers, especially in the Bunker-Hill Aurora. Articles of this sort are often hurriedly written, and more careful performances are desirable, but the former are, in many cases, the only accounts that exist. No complete collection has, probably, ever been made of the memorial pamphlets. That which is the least incomplete has only been formed by much research. Even explorations among the greater antiquities of various nations created within the past thousand years hardly impress one more with a sense of the perishable nature of human things, than do these monuments of some of the persons most notable in their time among their fellow townspeople. They belong to a valuable class of local literature that deserves better preservation than it has been apt to obtain, and that is wanted and welcomed in not a few libraries.

The Antiquities of a Town, that are its historical monuments, are interesting subjects for description, and it would be pleasant, when writing this list of literary works, to add a chapter about Charlestown, such as might be written about some other places. But neither the modes nor the means of the earlier people created any considerable object that could survive the great fire of 1775. Many stones or tombs in the Burial Ground, indeed, escaped destruction, and the inscriptions they bear may be published, the writer has been informed. An article on the public or private structures of more recent times would be, if correct, of some value in showing how American ways have grown to expression in one of the most prominent of the arts, — that of building, — but it is not necessary to make it so personal or limited as to apply it to any one town.

ADDITIONAL ITEMS. 1702, Hale, Rev. J., "Modest Inquiry," reprinted, *Boston*, 1768. 1842, Service Book for (Unitarian) Sunday Schools. 5th ed. 12°. pp. 28. *Boston*, 1842. Pamphlets, page 92. 1830, Phinney, and 1832, Richardson, should have appeared with the town matter.